Table For Two

A Bethany Beach Summer Romance

Robin Paul

These Three
PUBLISHING

Lakewood Ranch, Florida

tuesday, may 27

"THEY CALL IT MEDIATION FOR A REASON."

The speaker was a blunt, sixty-something woman whose enormity caused her chair to groan when she moved. She arrived ten minutes late and immediately shooed Javier Rocha from the seat at the head of his own conference table. Then she told Javier's attorney to put a sock in it when he tried to treat the session like a court hearing.

"Now, somebody tell me why y'all want to spend lots of hard-earned money taking this little misunderstanding to court." She looked to her right, where Javier and his business partner, Lance, flanked their balding, buttoned-down lawyer. Then she looked to her left. Damon Palmer, Regina Cole's attorney, rose to speak but stopped when the mediator raised her index finger.

"Don't go lawyering on me, boy." Her eyes softened when they shifted to Regina. "Miss Cole, why are we here?"

"I want my job back at Gasconade."

The mediator blinked several times. Empathy, perhaps?

Kindness? One woman watching out for another? She looked back at Javier and his crew. "Why can't she have her job back, gentlemen?"

Their lawyer was itching to speak, but Javier placed his hand on the guy's arm and took the lead.

"When Regina returned from her leave of absence, she had changed. She was obstinate and moody. We tried to work with her, but she was unwilling to accept correction."

Regina did her best to keep her voice level. "You would not let me do my job."

"Nonsense." Javier shifted in his seat and addressed the mediator as if Regina wasn't there. "She had the same title. She kept her office. Her pay was the same. But none of that was acceptable." Javier shrugged. "Like I said, she changed."

Regina took a deep breath to steady herself, but the words still rushed out. "You took away my duties as executive chef. I spoke to you and Lance. I even tried speaking to Blossom, but she—"

"Blossom?" The mediator raised an eyebrow. "Is that a person or a pet?"

Damon snorted, but the mediator's icy glare stopped him from laughing out loud.

Regina continued. "Blossom is Lance's girlfriend. She—"

"Blossom is our liaison at the restaurant," Javier said quickly. "Her being in a relationship with my business partner is irrelevant. She filled in while Regina took her leave of absence and proved herself quite capable of overseeing the day-to-day operation of Gasconade."

"Blossom was Lance's massage therapist," Regina snapped. "The closest she ever got to managing the kitchen

2

of a five-star restaurant was working at Burger King in high school."

"See what I mean," Javier said to the mediator. "Obstinate. And after we were so patient with her during her leave of absence."

"So this…Blossom is still employed?"

Regina leaned in. "She's doing my job. And frankly, she's terrible at it."

"That's a lie," Javier said testily.

Lance and the attorney flinched at his tone of voice. The mediator's eyes bored into Javier's, but he didn't blink. He was a Brooklyn boy who knew his way around a fight. He held the mediator's gaze until she looked away. A small victory for their side? Maybe, but having Damon beside her gave Regina confidence. He was more than a pretty good lawyer. He was her boyfriend, too.

But, at the moment, he wasn't pulling his weight. *Say something, baby. Win this thing. Get my job back.* Regina considered nudging him but didn't get the chance.

"If I may…" the lawyer for the other side said. The mediator motioned for him to continue.

"The fact of the matter is," he intoned in his New England brogue, "we wouldn't be here had Miss Cole not threatened to quit. It was a ploy to get her way, and when Mr. Rocha called her on it, she tried to walk it back."

"Is that true, Miss Cole? Did you threaten to quit?"

Damon started to interject something—*finally*—but one glance from the mediator shut him down. Regina took a deep breath and waded in.

"It was a frustrating day," she said slowly. "I spent two hours putting together the evening's dinner specials, only to have Blossom change everything. Later, I—"

Javier cut her off. "She *suggested* the changes. You flew into a rage and wouldn't discuss it with her."

"You weren't even there!"

Javier took a deep breath. "Regina, I understand the past few months have been hard, but you're forgetting how difficult it was for us as well. We had to keep Gasconade operating during your leave of absence. Had it not been for Blossom, we might have lost the restaurant."

He was doing a good job of posturing himself as the benevolent rich guy who took care of his employees. He was a big phony.

"You keep referring to it as a leave of absence like I *asked* to be gone."

"Well," Javier replied, "you were gone a month longer than expected."

Regina had concealed her left hand in her lap since the session began. She did that much of the time. It had become a habit. She placed it on the table in plain sight so everyone could see the jagged scars where her pinky and ring finger used to be. The mediator stared for a couple of beats before realizing her gaffe and raising her gaze to meet Regina's. The other side's lawyer gawked openly. So did Lance. It didn't faze Javier in the least.

"I wouldn't have needed a leave of absence if you had replaced that walk-in cooler like I asked."

The tension in the room ratcheted up. Their attorney's bald head turned pink. His eyes narrowed. He was ready to do battle. Javier remained unaffected.

The attorney stabbed his index finger on the table as he said, "We covered Miss Cole's medical expenses. She was given time for recovery. And there is no record that she told anyone about an issue with the cooler."

The mediator turned to Regina. "Tell me more about that cooler."

"It's irrelevant to the situation at hand," the attorney snapped.

"I'll be the judge of that. Miss Cole?"

"The walk-in cooler was installed by the building's previous tenant, a French bistro. It was a problem from the beginning. The door didn't seal properly, and it was close to the dishwasher, which meant there was condensation. I brought a repairman in who said it would cost $1500 to fix the door seal and make some other modifications. I emailed the price quote to Javier, along with my recommendation that we take care of it immediately. Several weeks passed, but nothing happened, so I brought it up to Lance one night when he was in for dinner."

"That did not happen," Lance said quickly.

"It was a Tuesday night in November. You had crab imperial, then complained that it was undercooked. You got into an argument with Blossom about her brother coming to town." She turned to the mediator. "Blossom had started working as a shift leader after she got laid off at the spa. Lance also drank three Rob Roys and left without paying. Again."

"That's a load of crap." Lance glanced at the mediator, saw the reproachful look she gave him, and mumbled an apology.

The mediator motioned for Regina to continue.

"It got to where I never let my line staff go into the cooler. I was concerned that someone might slip on the damp floor. If they needed something, I got it for them. That went on for two months. I mentioned the problem to Blossom at least once a week, but she said it was out of her hands."

The next part of the story brought Regina's emotions to the surface. She hated herself for that. She was a strong, successful woman who didn't use feelings to make her point. Damon knew that, too. He patted her hand and took over.

"Miss Cole went into the cooler for coleslaw. She was on her tiptoes, retrieving it from a top shelf when one of her assistants opened the door to ask her something. She turned to see who it was and lost her footing on the damp floor."

The room was silent. The men on the other side of the table knew the rest of the story and realized there was little they could do to minimize the tragedy. Their attorney still gave it the old college try.

"She slipped because she didn't follow safety protocols. She tried to retrieve something from a shelf that was too high for her. It was an unfortunate decision but also an unwise one."

"You're an idiot," Damon snapped. He was slipping from lawyer mode to boyfriend mode.

Regina needed lawyer Damon, though, so she shot him a look that said chill out. The attorney for the other side looked pleased at being the provocateur. The mediator ignored the exchange. Regina picked up the story.

"I slipped and fell against the side of the cooler. I reached out to catch myself, but my hand caught on a jagged spot on the wall." She took a deep breath and choked back a sob. "I didn't know what had happened until I tried to use my left hand to pull myself up. She shook her head and stared at a spot on the table.

Damon continued for her. "Regina's fingers were severed. The employee who came in yelled for help. An ambulance was there in ten minutes."

"They couldn't reattach your fingers?"

"They couldn't *find* her damn fingers," Damon said, shooting daggers across the table. "They fell into a space inside the wall of the cooler."

The mediator gasped. Lance's eyes were closed. His attorney was busy taking notes. Javier looked on with quiet detachment.

"By the time someone could get there and tear into the wall," Damon said, "it was too late."

"A safety violation on her part," their lawyer repeated. "Unfortunate but completely avoidable."

"Are you capable of working now, Miss Cole?" the mediator asked.

"Yes, ma'am. I've learned to adapt. I had occupational therapy—"

"Paid for by my clients," the attorney interjected.

"Paid for by worker's compensation. They helped me learn to make adjustments in how I perform certain tasks and cleared me to return to work."

"And she did return to work," Javier said. "Until she threatened to quit."

Regina was preparing her response when the mediator beat her to the chase. "I don't think mediation will help here." When she looked at Regina again, there was compassion in her eyes. "Miss Cole, I'm sorry for what happened to you, but there are no guarantees that job duties will remain the same after an extended absence. As much as I hate to admit it, Mr. Rocha and his partner gave you back your title and salary."

"But they wouldn't let me do my job."

"I understand how you might feel that way." The mediator cast a look of utter contempt at the three men on the other side of the table. "And while I believe to my very core that these...men are of questionable character—"

Their lawyer beat his fist on the table. "You can't disparage my clients!"

"I wasn't just referring to your clients, counselor." Then, she turned back to Regina. "But you threatened to quit."

"But—"

"Sweetheart," the mediator said, "you don't need to work for them. You're young and smart. I read about you in the *New York Times*. You're one of the brightest executive chefs in the city. Show them they can't keep you down." She pointed at Javier and the others, then used her thumb to motion to the door. "This session is over. You three, out of here." Then to Damon. "You too."

When it was just the two of them, the mediator took Regina's hand in hers. "Honey, you should sue those arrogant rich boys from here to New Jersey and back."

"Yes, ma'am. I guess that's our next step, but I don't know if it will do any good." Regina's voice broke as she spoke. She pulled a tissue from her purse and daubed at her eyes. "I'm a chef. It's all I've ever wanted to be. And I've been applying for jobs all over town, but inevitably they call for references."

The tears came more freely. The mediator sat patiently while Regina pulled herself together. "Those calls go to Javier, and he feeds them the same lies he used here. I'm difficult. I'm reckless." She looked into the mediator's sympathetic eyes. "He's blackballing me in New York. One restaurant at a time, he's killing my reputation."

The mediator squeezed her hand like a kindly aunt. "You get that lawsuit filed. And then you go out and find yourself a restaurant to run. If you can't find anything here in New York, look someplace else. Wherever it is, you'll make it a success. And when you come back for your day in court, those rich boys are going to know they messed with the wrong woman."

thursday, may 29

REGINA RECOGNIZED the number of the incoming call. The previous week, she had met with two women fronting a group that owned nine upscale restaurants in Queens. They were desperate for an executive chef at a little spot tucked into the middle of a busy residential street that was on the verge of going under. The interview was supposed to be forty-five minutes but stretched to two hours. Regina knew she had wowed them with her plans for breathing new life into their tired little eatery.

Even so, she couldn't bring herself to answer the call. In the two days since the remediation session, she'd not been able to do much of anything. Her moods were as gray as the New York sky. Spring was two months old, but someone had forgotten to tell the weather forecasters. Cold, drizzly weather persisted day after gloomy day. Regina had never been one to let the weather affect her, but that was what getting knocked on your ass did to a girl. She *knew* she could turn that place around, and the women who interviewed her knew it, too.

But she also knew they weren't going to offer her the job.

A year earlier she wouldn't have considered the position. If the culinary world was professional baseball, the job was high minor leagues. Gasconade was the big leagues, or at least, it was when she ran the kitchen. And not just any big league. It was the best.

She had made it that way.

Gasconade was Gasconade because of her.

And she could do it again: start with a little and make it into a lot. But would she get the chance?

Seventeen restaurants. Seventeen interviews. Seventeen *awesome* interviews.

No offers. Zilch.

At first, she'd grabbed the phone, anticipating offers too good to turn down. By the fifth rejection, she was more tentative. By the twelfth, she was letting them go to voicemail. Eighteen could go to voicemail, too. She went to the living room window and gazed over the sliver of Bronx skyline visible from Damon's apartment. The place wasn't much bigger than hers, but his view was nicer. He had been after her to move in, but she'd been warned about recently divorced men being on the rebound and all that. He'd obviously gotten the message because it had been three weeks since he'd brought it up. That was unfortunate because she might be ready to take him up on it.

Ding.

Voicemail.

Screw it. Damon was due back any moment, and they had reservations at a Japanese fusion place on Third Avenue that she'd been dying to try before the accident. Damon was always game for going out, but Regina criticized every little detail of whatever place they went to. If it wasn't overcooked veggies, it was an inattentive waitstaff or watered-down drinks. It had to get tiresome for Damon, who barely noticed those kinds of things.

It was time for her to stop that crap. *Enjoy the evening, girl. Have fun being with your man. Let him know how much you appreciate his support.*

Try to be more like the old you.

And check that voicemail.

Damon's boisterous arrival put her thoughts on hold. He swept into the apartment, tossed his sports coat onto the couch, and pulled Regina into an enthusiastic embrace.

"I've got something you need to see!"

Regina's reply was muffled by his muscular shoulder. "Wuffisit?"

He pulled away to grab his laptop from the coffee table. "Your next restaurant."

Regina's heart sped up. Had he found her the job she couldn't find for herself? What if he had? And what if it wasn't that great a job after all? She hated to burst his bubble after everything he had done for her over the past year. Handling her case. Being a friend. Being more than a friend. She didn't know how he kept the plates spinning. Busy lawyer with his own fledgling practice. Hustling clients. Court appearances. And all the meetings. Especially in recent weeks. The meetings were taking more and more time. *It's all good, baby*, he'd said when she mentioned his hectic schedule. *The more meetings I have, the more money I make.*

She couldn't argue with that.

He pulled up a web page and stepped aside so she could see it. Her eyes were drawn to the headline.

RESTAURANT FOR SALE OR LEASE.

"I can't afford to buy a place. Especially with how crazy real estate prices are right now."

"That's the point," Damon said excitedly. "What was it that mediator told you after she kicked us out?"

Regina remembered well. "If I can't find something in the city, look someplace else, but I don't want to—"

"At least take a look. You owe it to yourself. You need to get out of this funk and get back to being the girl I know."

He was right but didn't have to be so blunt about it. Then again, maybe blunt was what she needed.

She bent over to scan the ad. "Isn't there a picture?"

Damon leaned in so their cheeks were touching. "No, but look where it is."

Regina scrolled down. "Bethany Beach?"

"Delaware Shore. Between Rehoboth Beach and Ocean City, Maryland."

"I don't want to go all the way to Delaware, Damon. That's like...hours away."

"Nah, hon." He pulled his phone out, opened a map, and pointed to a spot in the center of the screen. "Here's where we are." He slid his index finger down and to the right until the Atlantic Ocean came into view. "You go through Jersey, past Philly, and you're there. Four hours, tops."

"Three hours? No way am I considering that."

"Listen to this description." Damon kissed her cheek, picked up the laptop, and took it to the sofa. She scrunched up next to him and drew her legs under her.

"'Longtime popular beach restaurant located near the ocean. A blank slate for the right person with an eye for what it takes to operate a successful business.'" Damon looked at her and smiled. "They're talking about you, babe. Just think of it. A blank slate. Make it anything you want."

Regina shook her head. "I'm not so sure about that. Every new restaurant has to deal with leftover sentiment for the place that came before it. Remember how hard it was for that creperie next to the YMCA? Their food was to die for, but people expected them to sling hash like the pancake house that used to be there."

Damon tilted his head and gave her his best lawyerly look. The one he used when he was being all logical and stuff. "Gasconade was known for small portions of bland food before a certain executive chef turned it around."

He had a point. And he was darn cute making it.

He turned back to the laptop. "'Help return this wonderful Bethany Beach landmark to its former glory.'"

"It's probably rundown or has termites or something."

Damon raised his hand. "Don't be so quick to judge. And when did you ever shy away from hard work?" He continued reading. "'Some equipment and fixtures remain from the previous tenant. Keep what you want. What could be better than living and working where others vacation?'" Damon looked up and grinned. "I like that. Live where others vacation."

"Is that what you want? Are you thinking of closing shop and hanging your shingle at the beach?"

"It's tempting, but nah. I'm hitting my stride here. It would be giving up too much." He took her hands in his and kissed her fingers. "But with the way you're getting black-balled around town, it's something to think about."

"But..." Regina paused, unsure where her thoughts were heading. Yeah, a place of her own was intriguing. And if Bethany Beach was anything like the coastal towns along the Jersey shore, there was plenty of opportunity.

And she had to admit, she liked the idea of a blank slate. Not just for the restaurant, but for herself. People in

Bethany Beach wouldn't know her as the damaged executive chef nobody would hire. She could take the best of what she had set into motion at Gasconade and build upon it. No Javier looking over her shoulder. No Lance freeloading food and drinks. And no Blossom getting up in her business and being a general pain in the ass.

A blank slate.

Except...

"I can't do it."

"Why not?"

"Money. It takes it, and I don't have it."

He set the laptop aside and turned so they were face-to-face. "Borrow it."

"Who's going to make a loan to an unemployed executive chef with eleven hundred bucks in the bank and a rent payment coming up that will take all of it and them some?"

"I'll front you a little. There ain't much, but I can go in about fifteen large."

"I can't take your— What? Where did you get fifteen thousand dollars? Last time I saw your bank statement it was worse than mine."

"I wasn't going to say anything," Damon said, thrusting out his chest. "But I scored a new client last week. Nice lady whose old man kicked the bucket. The kids and grandkids are circling like buzzards, and she wants me to hold them off."

"Damon, darling, congratulations!" Regina hugged him hard.

He had been looking for that first big break, something more substantial than bankruptcies or divorces. Why hadn't he said anything sooner, though? Probably because he had to listen to her whiny laments about how crappy the job market was treating her. And about how she hoped

Javier got hit by a bus as payback for the way he was dissing her around town.

She needed to do better.

And maybe Damon was onto something. It didn't hurt to look, did it? It was only Delaware. She could zip back to the city anytime she wanted. Of course, if she was busy getting a new restaurant up and running, there might not be time to zip anywhere.

Which led to her other concern.

"What about us?" she murmured as she nuzzled the side of his neck. "I'm growing pretty fond of you."

She liked how he moaned when she did that. "Same here, baby, but it's the beach, remember? You'll see more of me than ever. I can drive down Saturday, spend the day." He waggled his eyes lasciviously. "Spend the night. Then head back Sunday afternoon. It'll be great."

Regina sat back and stared at the ceiling. "Yeah, but it seems so...permanent. New York is the only place I've ever lived. And now we're talking about... I don't think it's a good plan." She brightened. "And besides, I got a voicemail from those girls I interviewed with in Queens. Maybe it's serendipity." She pointed at the laptop. "Perhaps you finding this was a teaser before the real show starts."

"You mean like at a strip club?"

"I wouldn't know anything about that." She playfully slapped his head, then reached for her phone. "And neither should you."

"All in the past, baby. All in the past."

Regina hit the voicemail button and put the phone on speaker.

"Hi Miss Cole, this is Penelope Corrales. We spoke last week about the executive chef position..."

Get on with it already.

"Belinda and I enjoyed visiting with you...but we've decided to go in a different direction..."

Those all-too-familiar feelings returned. The heaviness that starts deep inside and creeps outward. The aching in the gut. The thoughts of worthlessness and defeat. Things Regina had experienced seventeen times over the past couple months.

"I don't understand," Damon said, shaking his head. "You thought it went great."

It did. Better than any of the previous interviews that also resulted in her being passed over.

"Maybe I'm a terrible judge of my own abilities," she said, trying to make a joke but feeling it fall flat. Then her eyes returned to the laptop where the listing in Bethany Beach was still on the screen. "I guess I'm going to Delaware this weekend."

Damon pulled her close and rubbed her shoulders. "Correction, sweetheart. *We're* going to Delaware. We'll stay at the best hotel in town, eat at the best restaurants, and take a look at the place that might be your next big success."

Regina found strength in his strength. Damon's career was on the rise, and she was lucky to have him alongside her as she struggled through the funk. But still, it was time to fight back. And that mediator was right. A court battle with Javier and Lance could take months. Months she could be doing what she loved instead of sitting around her tiny apartment stewing about the way she was being screwed over.

It was time to take a step forward. And if that step had to be taken in Delaware, then so be it.

She barely moved when her phone buzzed again. The number wasn't one she recognized, and she wasn't expecting any return calls, so she let it go.

"We'll leave early Saturday morning," Damon said. "We can be there by noon, have some lunch, and go see the place. Do you want me to set up a meeting with the owner, or do you want to do it?"

"I'll do it," Regina said after a deep breath. "This is my show. I need to make this happen."

She picked up her phone and saw she actually had two messages. She hit the play button and put it back on speaker.

"Hey, Miss Cole...Regina. It's Penelope Corrales again..."

Regina grabbed Damon's hand. *Had they changed their mind?*

"I'm calling on my personal phone, and I hope you'll listen to what I have to say, then erase this message because I could get fired if my bosses find out..."

What?

"The truth is, Regina, our people won't let us pull the trigger on hiring you because of some stuff they've heard. I must ask, who exactly did you piss off? Because whoever it is wants to make sure you never work in New York again."

There was a pause as the caller, Penelope, gathered her thoughts.

"That damned Javier," Damon said, as he scrambled to his feet. "I'm going to call that dimwit attorney of theirs and tell him we're going to sue their asses for—"

"Damon, hold on."

Penelope had started speaking again. Regina missed the first few words, but it wasn't hard to figure them out.

"—that you probably know who it is, and if you need someone down the road to help when you take them on in court, give me a call, okay? Because you were head and shoulders above everyone else we interviewed... I'll do what

I can because I hate to see someone as good as you be blackballed. Good wishes, Regina. I know you're going to come out on top."

Regina sat back and tried to absorb the message. Not the part about someone being out to sabotage her career. She already knew that. Javier and Lance were behind that. Mostly Javier, because Lance wasn't that smart, and most of his brains were in his shorts.

Nope, it was mostly Javier. He had expected to steamroll the mediator, but when she proved too strong, he stepped up his effort to make sure Regina's name was mud.

She looked up at Damon. He was clenching his fists as if preparing to go into battle.

"Let's not do anything yet," she whispered. Then she remembered the second message.

"Hello, Miss Cole, I'm Art Geller from the *City Beat Investigator*. We're a small newspaper that covers the legal scene. Maybe you've heard of us. Anyway, I received a tip that you were injured on the job at Gasconade and have had difficulty finding employment. I'm going to dig deeper into this story but wanted to speak to you first. You can call me back anytime."

"Do it," Damon said. "Go on the record. Some negative press will get Javier's attention. That and a lawsuit for slander."

It was tempting. Javier was a street brawler. He was using his influence to screw her out of her right to work at a job she loved. A court fight highlighted by an investigative report might be just the thing to shut him up and shut him down.

But at the moment, she wasn't feeling it.

For the first time in weeks, her thoughts weren't consumed by Javier or her job at Gasconade. She wasn't thinking about court fights or investigative reports. Or even revenge.

Her thoughts were on a little restaurant in a little beach town in Delaware.

Could she make it into something special?

Was there potential there?

Because if there was. And if she did.

That would be the greatest revenge of all.

saturday, may 31

BROOKLYN TO BETHANY Beach. 221 miles.

Four hours and one minute, according to GPS.

That didn't account for thunderstorms and torrential rain. It started as a light drizzle when they'd exited the Bronx parking garage but became a steady downpour by Newark. Even worse by Trenton. Damon clenched the wheel, and despite his bravado, Regina felt his stress. She suggested they turn back, but the condo had a no-refund policy.

"It will let up by the time we get to Philly."

Except it hadn't. I-295 was reduced to a crawl. Visibility was about twenty car lengths. Fortunately, most people had remained at home. Regina was starving, but Damon was intent on getting through the worst of it before stopping. Breakfast time became lunchtime as they crossed the Delaware Memorial Bridge. Five hours after leaving the city, they still had two hours to go.

"We need gas," Damon said in the same grave tone he had used two months earlier to inform her it was time for his first colonoscopy. Regina checked the map and felt a ray of hope when she located a Wawa two miles ahead.

And then, miracle of miracles, the rain stopped. Damon bumped the speed up to forty, then forty-five. Everything felt better when they wheeled into a gas bay. Regina made a beeline for the restroom while Damon filled the tank.

"You won't believe it," she exclaimed when she returned to the car. "They make sandwiches and salads to order. There are even tables where we can sit and eat."

Damon hung up the gas nozzle and surveyed the surroundings. "We're already behind schedule. How about we get something to go?"

"Eat in *your car*?"

That was a serious no-no. Damon never allowed food in his Caddy. He barely even drove it. It was two years old and had nine thousand miles on the odometer.

He grinned. "I know, but it's a special occasion." He narrowed his eyes and pointed his finger at her. "But if you drop even one crumb on the seat..."

Regina giggled, then led the way inside, where they stepped up to a self-service kiosk. Two chicken quesadillas for him, a cheesy Italian panini for her. Ten minutes later, they were enjoying their lunch while cruising along a mostly clear Route 1. It was three-thirty when they reached the Bethany Beach city limits.

"Not much going on," Damon observed as he checked the address of their condo. Bethany was different than Regina had imagined—quieter. But it was still spring. The mid-Atlantic beaches were summer destinations with peak season between July Fourth and Labor Day. Bethany was no exception. Many storefronts were closed, and traffic was light. She had hoped they might get a peek at the restaurant before the next morning's meeting with the owner, but the sky was growing darker by the minute. Damon was intent on getting to the condo. They turned off the main road, known along the Delaware shore as Coastal Highway, onto a narrow street lined with a mishmash of vintage cottages and elevated homes with sharp corners and large windows.

And then, straight ahead, the Atlantic Ocean appeared over the dunes. Gray and foreboding but breathtakingly beautiful. Waves lashed the sandy shore while gulls circled in search of their next meal.

"Look at the size of those waves," Damon said as he drove along a tree-lined street that paralleled the surf. "I wonder where a guy can rent a surfboard."

"I read that the water temperature is only sixty degrees," Regina replied. "But if you want to try it, I'll find you a board."

He laughed. The man was New York City through and through. Like her, his beach excursions were limited to occasional day trips to Jones Beach or Coney Island. He had spent time in Florida with his ex-wife, and there had been a trip to Jamaica with a former girlfriend—but she didn't ask many questions and frankly didn't want to know. The whole married-before thing was a stumbling block she still struggled with occasionally. Damon was a wonderful guy, though, and she had to face the fact that, at thirty-seven, her options were limited. Divorce often came with the territory, unless you took the married-man route. And that was a route she had no interest in.

A left turn, followed by a couple of rights, brought them to a row of modern-looking white buildings. Damon pulled into the first, consulted an email he'd received from the property manager, and continued into a parking garage.

They found their assigned space, grabbed their luggage, and headed up the elevator to the top floor. Regina had watched Damon a few nights earlier as he mulled over the options. Calculating, recalculating, and finally deciding that the unit at the end of the hall was the best value. He punched in a code that opened the door, then stepped aside to let her enter first.

"Oh, Damon, it's lovely."

The first thing to get her attention was the view. The angry Atlantic was majestic in the dimming light, and it felt as if the ocean encircled them. Regina rushed in and pulled open a slider leading to a balcony. The sound of waves crashing against the shore was immediate and close. She wrapped her arms around Damon and kissed him.

"You're so good to me. Thank you for setting up everything."

He kissed her again. Longer. More lingering. His lips were salty. And needy. Regina went with it. He was a good man. Her man. And he'd worked hard to make the trip a reality. He seemed as excited about the restaurant's potential as she did. Maybe more. She pressed against him and moaned. It was time to make him happy. She pushed him toward the bedroom. He turned and led her by the hand. It was a good-sized space with a king bed and a second balcony. They paused to gaze out.

When his phone buzzed, she expected him to ignore it. The ring was different than usual. Some classical piece Regina vaguely recognized.

"I need to get this." He pulled away and answered. "Damon Palmer... Oh, hello Alice!"

Alice? It wasn't a name Regina recognized, but the way Damon said it—*Alice!*—made it clear it was someone he knew well. How well?

"Yes, Alice— We took care of that— That too— There's no chance of that..."

Took care of what?

No chance of what?

And why was he so darn happy?

Regina eased close to catch the other side of the conversation but tried to do it in a way that didn't look so obvious.

Alice?

Client? She'd never heard of anyone named Alice. And Damon never gave his personal number to clients. Most were divorces or bankruptcies. The kinds of cases that made people want to cry on their attorneys' shoulders. Not Damon's shoulder, though. He kept that stuff at work.

Relative? Again, no Alice that Regina could recall. There was an Alberta. Aunt Alberta actually. But she'd died five or six years ago.

Ex-girlfriend? If so, he sounded pretty damned happy to hear from her. It wasn't the ex-wife. Her name was Kimberly. She lived in Connecticut with her new husband. She had taken Damon for half of everything, which was fair, but still, she was living the good life while poor Damon chased clients and worked seventy-hour weeks.

"Yes, Alice. I'm available Monday night..."

"That's Presidents' Day," Regina whispered.

Damon held up his finger. "I'm out of town, but I can be back. It might be late, though. Is nine okay?"

Something about the exchange made Regina's stomach hurt. This was their weekend. Time for the two of them, away from the city. And here was *Alice* inserting herself into the middle of everything.

"Okay, I'll see you at your place. Have a good weekend."

Damon didn't have time to set the phone aside before Regina closed in.

"Who is Alice and why is she horning in on my man time?"

Damon spread his arms in front of him. "C'mon, baby. I told you about Alice."

"I don't know anyone named Alice."

"The new client? Husband died suddenly. Kids and grandkids are trying to jump line and get their share of the estate. Ring a bell?"

It rang a bell.

"One grandkid is in law school. He's claiming that dear old Grandpa promised some cash to help him along. Alice knows better, but she needs me to make that clear to the kid." Damon considered the ocean. "The grandkids are worse than their parents. They're coming at Alice from every direction." When he reached for Regina's hand, she moved closer. "Sorry it cut into our long weekend. We can still stay until three or four, though."

"It's okay," Regina said as she laid her head on his shoulder. "That poor woman. What would possess those people to act that way toward her?"

"Money," Damon said simply. "I suspect Grandpa was slipping a little lettuce in their pockets now and then. They got used to it. Then when Alice took over the bank accounts it stopped, and they're angry."

"But it's family."

"Family means nothing when the cheddar stops."

Regina laughed. "What does that even mean?"

"Don't you listen to Jay-Z? *Public Service Announcement*?"

"I know the song but always assumed he was referring to cheese."

Damon shook his head. "How can I be with a woman who doesn't get Jay-Z?"

Regina kissed him and led him toward the bed, intent on reminding him how good it was to be with a woman who didn't understand Jay-Z but had plenty of other talents.

sunday, june 1

REGINA AWOKE TO A PITCH-BLACK STRANGENESS. It took a moment to recall where she was. Bethany Beach. The condo. She yawned and backed her booty up to Damon's warmth.

But there was nothing there. No warmth. No Damon.

She lay there for a moment as the cobwebs cleared, then reached for her phone. Eight-twenty. She considered pulling back the fluffy down comforter and going to find him, but she knew the bedroom would be frigid. That was Damon's way. Sixty-five. Maybe lower. She took wool jammies when she stayed over. She'd brought them to Bethany Beach, too, but never got the chance to crawl into them after they'd gotten busy the night before. She raised her head and could barely make out her open suitcase six feet away. Too far. She pulled the comforter over her head and felt sleep's approach when Damon barged in, phone in hand, mouth going a mile a minute.

"You worry too much. There's nothing they can do this weekend. The courts are closed, and they aren't going to find a judge willing to sign— *What?* She's friends with a judge? Which one?" He leaned over, pulled back the comforter, and kissed Regina's forehead, then grabbed his briefcase from the dresser and headed out, not bothering to close the bedroom door behind him. Regina threw back the covers and made a naked dash for the bathroom. The lights nearly blinded her. She felt around until she found the shower faucet, turned it on hot, and jumped in.

Paradise.

Bliss!

Nothing like that ancient low-pressure monstrosity in her apartment. She luxuriated in the mist until she felt alive again, then adjusted the shower head until the water shot pinpricks against her skin. It felt so good she started to sing. An old Macy Gray song from back when she was in high school. She even tried to sing it like Macy. She wasn't sure how much time passed, but her skin was wrinkling. She had hoped that Damon might join her. Showering together wasn't something they'd done much of. His shower was a little better than hers, but still, the pressure was almost nothing. This could be fun.

But after a few more minutes of waiting, she gave up and turned off the water. The towels were the thick, fancy kind that caressed your skin. She took her time and enjoyed the luxury. One towel for her body, another for her hair. She was hanging up the body towel when Damon barged in.

"Um-umm, that booty looks good enough to—"

"Too late, Romeo. That booty is cleaned up and ready to get on with its day. You need to do the same."

He fake-sulked for a moment, dropped his shorts and fraternity t-shirt in the middle of the floor, and sauntered to the shower.

"This thing any good?"

"Oh, hell to the yes."

"Sure you won't join me?"

"There's always tonight. I want to get out and see the sights. Who was on the phone?"

"Alice."

Regina rolled her eyes. "Again?"

Damon turned on the water. "One of the grandkids is threatening to get a signed order giving her access to some of Grandpa's savings accounts. I headed it off, though."

"That old lady's going to make you earn your pay."

"She'll figure out the ground rules soon enough. You hungry?"

"My stomach's been growling since I woke up. Want to find something?"

"Yeah. We have a couple of hours before we meet the restaurant owner. Let's see what's good in Bethany Beach... unless you want to reconsider and hop in here with me."

"I'm good. Next time, tell old Alice that your woman is waiting on you."

Damon saluted, then stepped under the stream of water.

THE MORNING SKY was bright and sunny in complete contrast to the rainy weather they'd left behind. Many of the parking spaces along Garfield Parkway were open, but most of the businesses weren't. Damon pulled into a spot near the end of the street closest to the beach.

"GPS says there's a boardwalk right up there," he said, pointing toward the surf.

They strolled past a bandstand as a brisk breeze whipped off the ocean, turned left, and passed several souvenir shops before coming to a small diner with an open sign in the window. Regina leaned close and cupped her hands around her eyes to peer in, then recoiled when she saw another set of eyes looking back at her.

The door opened, and a grizzled man in a white apron stepped outside. "Come in or don't but stop staring through the window."

Regina stood up straight and prepared to give the guy what for. The pin on his apron said his name was Harvey. And the sign over the door proclaimed the place as Milo's. He eyed Regina defiantly, having decided it was her and not Damon who would have something to say. And he was right.

"Look here... Harvey, you—"

"Don't worry about him," a woman about Regina's age said as she approached the front door. "He does that to scare off tourists. You need to be kinder to your guests, Harvey."

"Suzanne, you mind your own business. It's my place, and I'll be—"

He didn't finish. The woman, Suzanne, had already gone inside and closed the door behind her. He returned his attention to Regina. "C'mon in. I got twofers today."

"Twofers?" Damon said, speaking for the first time.

"Yeah. Twofers. Two for the price of one. Waffles and pancakes. Eggs too." When his eyes met Regina's, there was a hint of remorse. Was it because of the way he'd spoken to her or because he needed the business?

"I'm down for twofers," Damon said.

"Not me," Regina replied quickly, her eyes not leaving Harvey's. "Your customer was correct. You need to be kinder to your guests." She grabbed Damon's hand. "Let's go."

"But I want twofers," he protested.

"Not today. Not here."

REGINA TOOK a bite of the gas station bagel and chewed with everything she had to get it to go down. She turned to look across the car seat at Damon, gnawing on a sticky bun with a look of dejection.

"If all the restaurants are run like that one on the boardwalk, I'll have no trouble making a go of it."

"Did you get a whiff of the smells coming out of there?" he asked as he reached for his foam coffee cup. "Bacon. Hash browns." He tossed the last few bites of his bun into a plastic sack. "I'm still hungry."

"There's more to it than the food," Regina said. "You know that, Damon. Anybody can sling hash. Dining out should be a total experience. A treat to the eyes, ears, and palate. That's what Bethany Beach needs."

"Sometimes, it just has to taste good, though," he countered. "Seriously. Like that rib joint on One Hundred and Sixty-Fifth in the Bronx. You've been there, right?"

"I've seen it, but that's not my thing."

"The place is nothing to look at. The walls need a good cleaning. Those girls need new uniforms." Damon paused and shook his head. "But, baby, when I bite into their baby backs, my mouth gets so *happy*."

His facial expression made Regina giggle. "Happy meals for grownups."

"Something like that."

"But you can't compare it to dinner at Gasconade...back when I was in charge."

"I can't compare playground basketball to the New York Knicks, either, but I like both."

"I want to be the Knicks," she replied as she reached over and stroked his cheek. "I want to create an experience that leaves people speechless." She checked the time on the dashboard clock. "Now, let's head out to see the restaurant."

THEY TURNED off Coastal Highway and headed west. The road narrowed as they moved away from the beach. Damon's eyes shifted back and forth from the road to the GPS app on his phone. As they passed a miniature golf and ice cream stand, he handed the phone to Regina.

"Something's not right. Check the address I entered."

He pulled a slip of paper from his shirt pocket.

Regina examined both. "It's the same."

"Well, something's off for sure because there's the city limit sign for Bethany Beach."

He was right. They were officially outside the city. Beach cottages gave way to the same kinds of businesses one might see in any American town. A laundromat, then a liquor store. A vet's office next to a propane company.

"Maybe we should call the owner," Regina suggested.

"We would if we could, but all we have is his email."

The road wound to the south, past an auto parts store and one of those big pharmacy chains, before coming to a housing development. No hint of beachiness there. Basic ranch-style homes interspersed with vacant lots.

"I say we turn around and go back to the condo," Regina said as she laid the phone aside. "We can email the owner and figure out what road we missed."

Damon picked up the phone and took another look at

GPS. "It says the address is a mile ahead. Let's at least go that far."

"It's not even in Bethany Beach, Damon. I vote we go back and start over after we hear from him."

Damon continued until they came to a wide spot in the road as GPS announced, *You have arrived.* As Damon pulled over, Regina gazed out her side at one of those storage places people rented by the month. It had seen better days. She turned back to Damon and was about to suggest they turn around in the storage place's drive when she saw him gaping out the window. She looked past him and felt anger rising from deep inside.

It was a gas station. Or it used to be. There weren't pumps out front, but the overhang was still there where they used to be. Four cars were parked in the stalls, older ones from the fifties or sixties. Two were freshly painted and polished. The others were in rough shape. A sign over the door of the gas station identified it as *Walt's Restorations.*

But it was the other half of the building that held their attention.

"Do you believe this shit?" Damon said, barely above a whisper.

Regina didn't. And if it was a joke, they had driven way too far to find it funny. The dirty red and white awnings over the two front windows flapped in the breeze. A red sign over the front entrance, a double wooden door that had seen better days, appeared to be intact with the word *CAFÉ* printed in white. And above that, looming over the entire forlorn operation, was the gaudiest neon sign Regina had ever seen. And while it wasn't lighted, it was easy to make out the words.

Three Mile Millie's.

Damon was the first to find his voice. "What the...is Three Mile Millie's?"

Regina was speechless.

Damon wasn't. "It's like in one of those slasher flicks. You know, when the kids go to camp or stay in an old house that's haunted."

Regina knew. Even in the middle of the day, under a bright sun, the place was scary as hell.

"Let's go," she whispered.

"Hell, no," Damon said. "Not until I tell that crooked liar what I think of him dragging us out here to the middle of nowhere to see this rundown place. And if he gives me any crap, I might kick his ass."

The words weren't out of Damon's mouth before the gas station door opened and a slender man stepped out. He eyed them for a moment before coming to the car. Regina's age, maybe a few years older, with windswept brown hair and a neatly trimmed gray beard. He wore dark blue coveralls with *Walt* stitched over the heart. He was wiping his hands with a shop cloth when Damon rolled down his window. "We're looking for Mickens."

"I'm Walt Mickens. You must be Mr. Palmer and Miss Cole."

The accent was European, but his English wasn't the fractured type that came from being a second language. Quite the contrary, his diction was measured and precise. And his smile was genuine and disarming.

At least to Regina. Damon, not so much.

"I don't know what you're trying to pull, Mickens, but you flat-out lied about this place. You're lucky if I don't sue you for damages."

If Damon was going for intimidation, he wasn't succeeding. Mickens looked at him curiously, like one might an exotic animal. "I beg your pardon, Mr. Palmer. Damages for what?"

"For representing this place as something it ain't."

Mickens glanced over his shoulder at the building, then back at Damon. "It's definitely a restaurant. Or at least it was until a few years ago. Now, I could understand you being agitated if I had claimed it to be a flower shop or a boutique, but I'm certain I said it was a restaurant."

If it was his accent or his logic, Regina couldn't be sure. What she was sure of, though, was that Walt Mickens wasn't a scammer. His eyes communicated that much. Maybe he hadn't done the best job describing the place, but they hadn't asked a lot of questions, either. And when she giggled, Damon looked at her as if she was nuts.

"It's obviously a restaurant, Damon," she said. "It's seen better days, though, Mr. Mickens. Wouldn't you say?"

That earned her a lopsided grin. Mickens took another look at the property. "I used to think that, Miss Cole. But two things have changed my mind." He pointed to the road. "When I opened my shop fifteen years ago, I could count on one hand the number of cars passing by."

Regina followed Mickens's gaze as three cars sped by, heading west, away from the beach.

"I'm told that more people than ever are working from home." Looking at Damon, he added, "Telecommuting, I believe it's called."

Damon shrugged. He was still miffed about the condition of the place. Mickens turned to Regina. "Personally, I don't understand the allure. There's something incredibly satisfying about heading off to work each day, doing something you love, then returning home tired and happy."

Regina didn't personally know any auto mechanics. That was what Mr. Mickens appeared to be, judging by the coveralls and the dirty fingernails. And if she was right, he had to be the first mechanic she'd ever heard use the word *allure*. And to hear him say it with that accent? Walt Mickens was turning out to be one interesting person. She waited for him to continue.

"So, with more people telecommuting, they're also purchasing homes in the area. For years, it was too far to drive to Dover or Salisbury, but that's not a big thing anymore, so..." He motioned to the road as several more cars streaked by.

"Any idea how many?" Damon said, emerging a little from his sullenness.

"I do some restoration work for a gentleman who works for DelDot—that's what they call the Department of Transportation. He claims the daily traffic count is close to fifteen thousand during the cold weather months. And during beach season? Easily four times that."

Regina had no idea if the numbers were good, but she was intrigued by Mr. Mickens's ability to toss them out so easily. "You said two things caused you to change your mind. Increased traffic is the first."

"Oh, yes." He chuckled. "The second came to me in Boston a couple months ago. As you can tell, the place does look a bit tired."

"You think?" Damon said sarcastically.

Regina punched his arm.

"Yes, I think. And frankly, I've done nothing to help its condition. If you were to venture inside, you would find that I've been using it for storage. But back to my story, I was in Boston visiting a customer. He suggested going out for dinner. The place he chose started its life as a nineteenth century horse stable. The food was sumptuous. I had to remind myself a few times I was enjoying one of the best meals of my life in a converted stable. I was eating lobster in the same space where some prized steed had munched on straw and oats a century before."

"The Guernsey," Regina said.

"That's it!" Mr. Mickens exclaimed. "You've been there?"

"No, but I've attended conventions with their executive chef. A delightful man."

"It caused me to wonder if this place could be brought back to life. It's structurally sound. The roof doesn't leak and the walls are good and thick. So I put the announcement together that you saw."

"Maybe you left a few things out," Damon said. "It was a pleasure meeting you, Mickens, but Regina is looking for something nicer than a roadside diner."

Regina saw the pain in Mr. Mickens's eyes. He nodded and took a step back from the car. Then he bowed slightly with his hands clasped in front of him.

"I'm sorry the location doesn't meet your expectations, Miss Cole. I won't waste any more of your time. I know you have a long trip back to—"

"Can we look around?"

Damon gave her the stink eye. "Regina, what are you—"

"We came this far. Let's at least look."

"If your goal is to show Javier how big a mistake he made—and sway a jury to see your side of things—you'll never accomplish it in this rundown place."

Instead of getting into it with Damon, Regina leaned past him and spoke through the window to Mr. Mickens. "May we take a look?"

"Certainly," he said with a smile. "I'll retrieve the keys from my office and meet you in front."

Damon barely had the window raised before exclaiming, "Why are you wasting our time, Regina? We're miles from the beach, at a dilapidated old joint that will come crashing down with the next stiff wind."

"Take a chill pill, boo. We're staying the night. What's it hurt to look around?" She paused and took a breath. "He's been to The Guernsey, Damon. A meal there is at least three hundred dollars. I'm guessing Mr. Mickens isn't some run-of-the-mill auto mechanic."

"What does that have to do with us?"

"Maybe he's worth taking a chance on."

MR. MICKENS UNLOCKED the front door and put his shoulder against it. It stuck for a second before squeaking open.

"Needs a new door," Damon said as he pulled out his phone. "I'm starting a list."

"WD-40," Mr. Mickens good-naturedly countered as he flipped on the lights and started their voyage down a time tunnel to two decades before. Dust-covered wooden tables were pushed to the center of the room with matching chairs turned upside down on top of them. It was as if the place had closed for the night and no one came back. There were booths along the side and front walls, also wood and quite uncomfortable looking.

"New tables and chairs," Damon mumbled as he continued his list. "And lighting."

He was right. The overhead lights were fluorescent, more suitable for a hospital hallway than a place where people came to enjoy a good meal.

The smell was a mixture of must, dust, and rubber.

Regina spotted a stack of tires next to what was probably the kitchen entrance.

"Those don't go with the restaurant," Mr. Mickens said, flashing his lopsided grin.

"They're worth more than everything else in the place," Damon said. He was becoming obnoxious, and Regina was tiring of it. There was no need to be mean.

Undeterred, Mickens led them past the tires and through a swinging door into the kitchen. Another time skip, but not as pronounced as out front. Most of the previous tenant's equipment had been left behind. Regina recognized some of it as being of decent quality. A Hobart dishwasher newer than the one at Gasconade. A darn good Garland range and two matching convection ovens. Filthy from years of disuse, but not unlike what was still used in many restaurants. Regina's heart raced when she spotted the door to a walk-in cooler. Same brand and make as the one at Gasconade—the cooler that had led to her accident. She took a deep breath, strode across the room with as much confidence as she could muster, and pulled open the door.

Spotlessly clean.

"I did little with the other equipment, but I knew if I left the cooler dirty it would cause problems," Mr. Mickens said as he peered over her shoulder into the emptiness.

"Very nice job," Regina said, her heart slowing. The shelves shined in a way that Gasconade's never did, even after repeated cleanings. That alone created a soft spot in her heart for the old place. "Mr. Mickens, why—"

"Walt," he replied. "Call me Walt, please."

"Why...Walt, did the previous tenant leave behind such good equipment?"

"Ahh, Armand. Such a gentleman. Such grandiose plans. He barely got started before everything went awry."

Even Damon was tuned in now. There was a story behind dear old Armand, and they wanted to hear it.

"Four months after opening, poor Armand was hit with a divorce he never saw coming. It devastated the dear man. He kept things going for a few more weeks, but it soon became apparent that he had to liquidate. I was helping him clean up one morning when a couple came in from Ocean City. Big names in the restaurant business down there. They wanted to buy the kitchen fixtures, and when I heard what they were offering, I nearly fell over. So low. So unfair."

"There are vultures in this business."

Walt nodded. "As there are in any enterprise. Armand told me after they left that their insulting offer was better than two others he'd received. I felt it might be easier to attract new tenants if there was equipment in place, so I made an offer of my own that included forgiveness of the last few months of his lease. It far exceeded the others and allowed Armand to divest himself of the place." Walt smiled softly. "That was four years ago. Armand stops by now and then, and we keep in touch by email."

"But no offers since then?" Damon asked.

"None, but admittedly, I've been lackadaisical about it. Work takes most of my time, and the months got away from me."

Regina took a final look around before returning to the dining room. For as much potential as there was in the back, the front was depressing. She tried to envision it in many forms, including stripping everything to the walls and going with the industrial look that was popular in cities where empty warehouses was abundant and chefs were constructing menus that fit the space.

But that vibe wasn't happening there in... "Walt, tell me about the name on the building."

"Three Mile Millie's," he said with a chuckle. "The sign is a remnant from the sixties when it was a diner operated by a woman named Millie Darby. The 'three-mile' part is a reference to the distance to town."

Damon snorted. "It's at least five miles to the beach. Maybe more."

"But only three to the city limits. That's the best I could come up with. The sign was in storage for years before Armand had it cleaned up and rehung. Sadly, he never got it to work."

"I hope someone can bring the old girl back to life," Regina said. "Unfortunately, Walt, it won't be me. The vision I have can't be accomplished in this space."

"I understand," he said, sounding as if he really did. "But it was a pleasure to meet you both, and I wish you well with your endeavors."

He held out his hand. Regina was surprised at how soft it was. And how the nails were neatly manicured underneath the grease.

"Do you have a restroom I could use before we leave?"

"The restroom in back is operational. Please, use it."

Damon took a quick look around before heading for the door. "Regina, I'll pull up the car."

Regina was washing her hands when her phone buzzed with a text.

Miss Cole, this is Howard Glass of Whittaker and Glass. We spoke several weeks ago about an opening in one of our restaurants. I have something you'll be interested in. If you would like to discuss it, I'll be available tomorrow.

She recalled the meeting. Glass and his people owned a half-dozen restaurants on Manhattan's Upper East Side, including three in upscale hotels. Their executive chef opening was at a nice little American place formerly called Tapscott. The location was in a tough part of the city, but the potential was there. The interview went well enough, then crickets. Not even a rejection.

But at least they remembered me!

Walt was turning off the lights when she stepped out of the restroom. "I'll make sure you get out of here without tripping over anything," he said. There was something different in his demeanor now that Damon was outside. More whimsical. Less guarded. He was a good man, she could tell.

"It would have been good getting to know you," he said as he pulled open the front door. "But I understand your reasons for taking a pass. Bethany isn't New York City, but you know something, Miss Cole? It's a delightful spot none-theless."

"I'm sure it is, Walt. And perhaps Damon and I will come back sometime." She took one final look around. "And perhaps we'll even stop by for dinner."

He laughed. "Yes, perhaps. And please look me up if you do."

REGINA COULD BARELY CONTAIN her excitement about the text from New York, but Damon was still fuming about the wasted time. She let him get it out of his system before telling him. His mood immediately brightened.

"Maybe it's the one, babe."

"Maybe," Regina replied. "I'll text them back and tell them I can be there late in the afternoon. What time is your appointment with your new client?"

"Alice? Oh, I can meet her anytime. I was thinking, though, that maybe we should chuck our plans for the night and head back." He checked his watch. "We can be there by ten. We'll get a good night's sleep, and you can meet with people at Whittaker and Glass anytime they want."

It was a plan.

monday, june 2

REGINA'S WORRIES about the location were confirmed when she emerged from the subway and saw the blight and decay. The Lower East Side was home to some of the trendiest clubs and boutiques in the city. Regina appreciated the area as a melting pot of races and cultures. Sadly, it was also home to poverty and strife, and the location of Whittaker and Glass's new restaurant was on the fringe of some of the worst. She respected what they were trying to do—and would love to be a part of it—but she questioned if they had the commitment to pull it off. They had recently closed two restaurants she'd considered potential goldmines had there been more commitment.

The restaurant was set to open in four weeks. Not a lot of time but enough for a good executive chef to plan a menu, train staff, and set up a kitchen. She already had some people in mind. Jacob Klein was her last hire at Gasconade before the accident. When she had returned in what turned out to be a diminished role, Jacob still accorded her the respect she'd earned. He was relentlessly positive and funny in that cutting way she'd always liked. He'd called a few weeks earlier to let her know that things weren't going well at Gasconade and he would be amenable to following her when she found something new. Despite his youth and having less than a year's experience under his belt, she wanted him as her head chef.

The desire to poach a few others from Gasconade was tempting, but she didn't want to give people any reason to believe the lies Javier was peddling about being difficult. Jacob would be her lone recruit.

She approached the front of the restaurant and tapped on the door. The exterior signage was in place with *Schulyer's* in bold blue script over the door. A curious name, but one she had learned was the middle name of one of the Whittaker and Glass partners. So, if they asked her opinion, she would be effusive in her praise. A restaurant's name didn't mean as much as what happened inside. She giggled as she recalled the sign over the Bethany Beach diner.

Three Mile Millie's.

Now there was a name that needed help.

An older man with close-cropped gray hair came out of the back and opened the door for her.

"Miss Cole?"

"Are you Mr. Keller?"

"I sure am. Please, come back and meet my associate, Mr. Lucchesi."

Lucchesi was at least as old as Keller, both were in their seventies. Neither was a Whittaker or Glass, and Regina was curious about how they fit into the mix. They seemed intent on regaling her with anecdotes from their decades as restaurant owners.

"So, what do you think of the place?" Lucchesi said when they finally came up for air.

Regina took in the surroundings. The kitchen was a

quarter finished. The only furnishings in the dining room were sawhorses. "The space is a surprise," she noted. "It looks smaller from outside."

They nodded enthusiastically. Then, following an awkward pause, Keller asked what she thought of the name. He prefaced his question with his opinion that, "Schuyler's is too convoluted, don't you think? But it's what the guys in charge want, so it's what they get. I'm concerned that people will never be able to find it in the phone book, given how hard it is to spell."

Regina was not about to remind them that people didn't use phone books anymore. She instead shared her conviction that the name took a backseat to quality and experience.

"Perhaps," Keller said skeptically. "We never expected them to be so forceful in their demands, though."

What did that even mean? Who was being forceful? And who, exactly, were Keller and Lucchesi? Her previous interview had been with the partners, Whittaker and Glass. Where did these guys fit in? She needed to find out, so she asked.

They chuckled at her forthrightness. "Avril and I have owned and operated this restaurant for forty years," Lucchesi explained. "We're leasing the location to the men you spoke to before, but we retain a one-third stake for the next five years."

What? How many bosses were there, exactly?

"We're only involved peripherally," Keller said. "We've chosen to sit in on interviews and make recommendations, but sadly, I'm not sure our voices are being heard."

Concerns swirled in Regina's mind. If they weren't making the decisions, why were they there? And why was she there? As she considered her next move, she heard someone enter through the front.

"That will be Lydia," Lucchesi said.

The woman seemed familiar. Windblown auburn hair, long aquiline nose, and brown lipstick that made it look like she'd eaten a chocolate bar. She barely acknowledged the men as she shrugged off her jacket and tossed it over a file cabinet.

"It's good to see you again, Regina. You might not remember me, but I'm—"

Regina didn't need for her to finish. She had put the pieces of the puzzle together. And she didn't much care for the finished product.

"Lydia Morgenstern. We interviewed you for a position at Gasconade."

"You *do* remember! As you can see, I've done okay since you turned me down."

Regina bit her tongue. She vividly recalled the interview. Lydia showed up in that same poop-brown lipstick, then dropped two f-bombs during the interview.

"Yes," Lydia continued. "Mr. Whittaker and Mr. Glass saw my potential when you didn't. They hired me as a sous chef, and here I am two years later. Executive chef."

Wait a minute. Roll back the tape. Instant replay. Did she say *executive chef?*

Executive chef of what?

Regina received no help from the men. Their eyes were blank. Lucchesi might have nodded off. Two old warriors of the restaurant wars who were being put out to pasture. She felt a twinge of sadness for them, but not as much as she felt for herself.

What position was she interviewing for? It was a question that needed asking, but with all the disappointment over the past few months, Regina could barely bring herself to ask.

Brown-lipped Lydia made it easy for her.

"We think you would make a serviceable sous chef."

———

REGINA KNEW BETTER than to cry on the subway. She'd seen it happen before, and it brought out the good Samaritans who wanted to help or the perverts who wanted to cop a feel while telling you things would be okay.

But it was hard to stay strong after Lydia Morgenstern's stinging rebuke. Though she hadn't actually spoken the words, Lydia's demeanor spoke for her.

You used to be somebody but not anymore.

You thought you were high and mighty, but you got knocked down.

And look at me! You didn't offer me a job, but here I am, being magnanimous about everything. Allowing you to be my sous chef despite your messed-up hand and messed-up mental state.

"Screw you."

The words flew from her mouth before she could stop them. The woman seated next to her glanced over before returning to her phone. Just another day in New York City. Regina put her head back and closed her eyes. What happened next? Should she lower her career expectations? Reconsider Lydia Morgenstern's offer? Was it time to step back, get her head on straight, and begin anew the climb to the top?

No.

No, no, no.

It wasn't time because she'd done nothing to deserve

where she was. She had been injured. Badly injured. In a work-related accident that was completely avoidable had those above her only listened.

She didn't deserve that.

And she would not take that.

The lady beside her gave her a nudge. "I think you have a call."

Was that actual concern in her eyes? A stranger who cared? Regina pulled out her phone. Damon.

"Hey," she said softly.

"A good interview?" he asked.

"Nope."

He was silent for a few moments before pushing ahead. "Boo, I have some information to share with you. It's about Gasconade and Javier."

"Do I need to hear this now, Damon? I'm exhausted and kind of beat up."

He must have thought that she did because he charged ahead. "They offered ten thousand to make this go away."

"What does that even mean?"

"You sign an agreement absolving them of liability, and they hand over a check. And I think I can convince Javier to lay off the negative references."

The idea of signing something that made it all go away was tempting, especially after what she'd been through with brown-lipped Lydia. And ten grand would provide a bit of a cushion.

But Damon's assertion that he *thought* he could get Javier to stop saying bad things about her?

That hurt. That hurt bad.

She had done nothing to deserve those negative comments. All she had ever done was her job.

"Well?" Damon was waiting.

"What do you think?" she asked.

"I have to separate the legal stuff from the personal stuff. I care about you, Regina. I see how this is taking a toll on you."

"But?"

"But these people need to pay for their treatment of you. And ten large is nothing. If we stay the course, I believe we can get more."

Regina suddenly felt completely and utterly exhausted. "Let me think about it. I'll see you later."

She disconnected before Damon could reply. She closed her eyes again. The next thing she knew was when the woman seated next to her said, "I'm sorry, but I need to get off here."

Regina was woozy when she stood. She gripped the back of the seat as she moved out of the woman's way. She handed Regina a business card.

"I don't usually do this on a subway, but maybe I can help sometime."

Regina looked at the card.

Sandra Del Greco, Professional Counselor.

She allowed the card to drop onto the seat next to her, then reconsidered. She picked it up and shoved it in her pocket as she remembered the kindness.

tuesday, june 3

REGINA KISSED Damon then straightened his tie because that was what they did in the movies when the guy was leaving for a business trip.

"You sure you don't want to stay here, babe? I'll be back tomorrow night." He moved in for another kiss and grabbed her butt for good measure. "It would be nice to have my lady greet me at the door with a martini and a negligee."

"Your lady hasn't left any negligees here, and you hate martinis. Besides, I have stuff to do."

The two days since the job offer from Lydia Morgernstern had taken some of the edge off the humiliation, but not enough to make it go away. There was unfinished business to attend to, but nothing Damon needed to know about yet.

They embraced once more before he headed out. Boston was four hours by train. An hour more by car, and as much as Damon enjoyed driving his Caddy, the train was a nobrainer. She gave him a ten-minute head start, then hurriedly showered and dressed in a comfy pair of jeans and a soft and roomy NYU sweatshirt she'd appropriated from Damon's closet after they started dating. She grabbed the overnight bag she'd secretly filled with the necessities the night before and caught an Uber to Penn Station. Once there, she checked the schedule to make sure Damon's train had departed, then purchased a ticket of her own.

Wilmington, Delaware.

The logistics were tricky. The train to Wilmington was easy. They left every half hour, arriving in under two hours. Next was a bus to the tiny community of Georgetown, Delaware. The ticket was cheap, but the schedule was impossible to figure out. She might arrive that afternoon at one or three. Or, gasp, seven-thirty. From there it was Uber. That was the priciest part of the excursion: forty-five to seventy dollars depending on the time of day. A rental car would have cost much less. Regina got mad at herself all over again for allowing her driver's license to expire. Stupid tax was what that investment guy on the radio called it. And while she had never owned a car and rarely rented one, she was paying stupid tax for not having that license.

But darn it, she wanted one more look at that little restaurant.

The train departed on time, and she reached Wilmington Station ten minutes early. Things went downhill from there. She arrived at the bus depot only to find it was the wrong one. The regional depot was two miles away. The Uber was eleven dollars—another dose of stupid tax for not double-checking the details. The first bus was pulling out as her Uber pulled in. Regina considered trying to chase it down, but it was big and fast and an overnight rain shower had left the road slippery in spots, so she went inside and purchased a ticket for the next bus in two hours. When she saw that the only food options were from vending machines, she stepped back outside and looked around for a place to eat.

Nothing.

The warehouse district was busy, but there was not a restaurant in sight. Not even a burger place. She considered another Uber but settled for a vending machine ham sandwich and a bag of chips.

Then the bus was late.

What was there to do but wait? And waiting became increasingly interesting as passengers complained about the late bus. One woman, a grandmotherly type traveling with a preschool-aged boy, let loose on the ticket agent with a string of profanities. The little boy appeared nonplussed, and even tossed out a few expletives of his own.

Riding the bus was going to be very interesting.

"YOU GO HOME to Cassie and the girls, Felix. I'll close up."

Walt Mickens walked his best and only employee to the door and locked up behind him, then turned off the *OPEN* sign before heading to his office. Two months of invoices were stacked on the credenza behind his desk, taunting him for ignoring them. He picked up a pile, considered them, and then put them back. It was nearly six, and he had only eaten a turkey sandwich and an apple for lunch. He needed sustenance. But first, he needed to call a prospective client, a well-known author from someplace up north. Walt had read some of his books and found him too reliant on sex and profanity. But hey, if the guy's checks cashed, they could do business.

He placed the call and was put on hold by a personal assistant. Five minutes passed before something caught his eye on one of the TV screens mounted over his desk. Someone was walking along the perimeter of the building, on the restaurant end. Break-ins were uncommon. There were three in his early years operating the shop. One was especially disastrous. The intruders got away with a 1965 Rolls Royce Silver Cloud worth a quarter-million dollars. Fortunately, they were detained while attempting to cross the Chesapeake Bay Bridge, and the car was recovered intact. It had spurred Walt to spend a couple month's profits on a beefed-up security system. All had been quiet since.

So why was someone snooping around now? And why the restaurant? Didn't they know that the real value was in the shop? There was a million dollars' worth of classic automobiles out there. He disconnected his call and leaned in close to the screen. The wind picked up suddenly and blew the intruder's hood down. He smiled when he recognized her. He made plenty of noise as he stepped outside so as not to startle her, but her eyes still grew large when she picked up on his approach.

"Miss Cole?"

"Mr. Mickens? Is that you?"

"Yes, it's me. Would you like to come inside?"

"Um...okay. I didn't think anyone was here."

"I was about to leave for the evening, but I'll be happy to stay."

She looked over her shoulder toward the road. Walt noticed there was no vehicle in the parking lot.

"Miss Cole, how did you arrive?"

"Long story," she said, flashing an embarrassed smile. "I took the train...and the bus...and an Uber..." She looked as if she might start crying. "I hoped to be here this afternoon, but the bus was late and the Uber driver didn't want to come this far, and..." Her shoulders slumped.

"Come inside. I turned the coffee pot off, but it's still warm."

He led the way to his office where he poured two mugs of coffee. She cradled the mug in her hands for a few moments before taking a sip. How had she lost the pinky and ring finger of her left hand? From the look of the scarring, it had happened recently. Automobile accident? Was that why she didn't drive? He motioned to the worn leather chair on the visitor's side of his desk. She sat. He did too. He tried to imagine the route she had taken to get to Bethany Beach. It was basically impossible. The train was easy enough to figure out, but the rest?

"Where did you find a bus?"

Her story moved him more than he expected. He had never considered life without a vehicle. It was one thing to depend on public transportation in the city, but unfathomable at a Delaware beach resort.

"You probably think I'm nuts," she said.

Walt grinned. "I wouldn't say that. People have been coming to Bethany for years. Most drive. A few come on bicycles. Some hitchhike." He chuckled. "Four or five years ago, a delightful Amish gentleman stopped in requesting water for his horse. He'd ridden all the way from Pennsylvania, searching for a son who'd run off during his Rumspringa."

"Did he find him?"

"He certainly did. The boy was attempting surfing for the first time when we found him on the south end of the boardwalk. I think he was as delighted to see his papa as papa was to see him."

Her laugh was a happy one. The cares of the day were retreating.

"What about you, Miss Cole? Is this your Rumspringa?"

"No, Mr. Mickens. Though I might have had a better trip on horseback." She downed the last of her coffee and placed the mug on a coaster before tucking her left hand into her right. "I wanted another look at the restaurant."

"Shall I assume that Mr. Palmer was unavailable?"

"He's in Boston. New client."

"Are you spending the night in town?"

She was.

"Then please join me for dinner. Then we'll get you to your hotel for a good night's sleep. Tomorrow, we can start fresh. I'll give you the keys to the restaurant, and you can spend as much time as you wish."

"I didn't make a reservation. I figured I would stay someplace close by."

He wiped his hands on a towel as he considered offering her his guest room. Probably too forward a gesture. She was still feeling the situation out. She didn't know him well, and for that matter, he didn't know her. Not that there was anything frightening or intimidating about her. He could tell she was strong, yet vulnerable. Something in her vulnerability was related to her left hand, he suspected. That was unfortunate because she was quite beautiful. Mocha skin, expressive brown eyes, a dimpled smile. But it was her hair that was her most intriguing feature. Long, brown, and naturally curly, flowing in every direction. Her lawyer boyfriend was quite the lucky man.

Did he know it?

"I have a friend who owns a little place along the beach.

It's not one of the big chain hotels, but it's nice and clean. He'll give you a good rate."

Was that a look of hesitation in her eyes? It would make sense, Walt supposed.

"Or I could call you an Uber. Or find you a horse."

That did it. She giggled. "I hate to put you out, Mr. Mickens. But as you know, I'm without transportation, so I happily accept your offer."

"Shall we be on our way, then? And, as I said when you were here last time, it's Walt. Everyone calls me Walt."

HE APPEARED SAFE ENOUGH. She hadn't caught him ogling her chest or butt. He might have glanced a second time at her hand, or he could have been checking to see if her coffee cup needed refilling.

A cool breeze made her shiver as they stepped outside his shop . He locked up and led her to a light-colored pickup truck in the rear. After hurriedly moving some things from the seat, he held open the passenger door for her.

"My apologies for the untidiness."

"It's better than the horse," she joked. The dashboard lights provided ample illumination to see the laugh lines around his eyes and mouth when he smiled.

He turned down the radio, fiddled with the climate controls, then put the truck into gear and headed toward Bethany Beach.

"Unfortunately, there aren't a lot of restaurants that remain open this late before the start of tourist season. Fast food and a few local places, but that's about it."

"Can we try something local?"

"Of course. What sounds good?"

"I'm famished. And underdressed for anything fancy."

"Fancy isn't an option, and since you're hungry, I know just the place. Provided you don't mind bar food."

It sounded perfect. Ten minutes later, they turned onto Coastal Highway and made another turn a few blocks later. The place was small, run down, and shared a parking lot with a bank.

"I'll come around and get the door," he said. "It's difficult to open sometimes."

It didn't appear to be hard to open at all, but she liked that he did that. Damon opened her door sometimes too, usually when they were headed someplace nice for dinner. For Walt, though, it was second nature, and Regina wondered how a proper gentleman with such an alluring accent had remained single.

Or had he?

Was someone waiting for him at home? A wife? Husband? Kids?

"I hope I'm not pulling you away from your family." She detected a flash of pain in his eyes.

"Not at all. The only family is my mother, and she lives in Detroit." He pushed open the thick wood door of the tavern and heat emanated from inside.

The air smelled of burgers and beer, making Regina's stomach growl. Two men and a woman seated at the bar smiled and waved. They called Walt by name. Two attractive women at a pool table also called out. Walt returned greetings all around as he led her to a table in the corner closest to the kitchen.

"Do you know everyone?"

He chuckled. "Don't be fooled by this being a beach resort. There might be fifteen thousand people here in the summer, but only about a thousand live here year-round.

Bethany is a small town that gives off big-town vibes until you get to know it better.

A server dropped off laminated plastic menus and took drink orders. Walt had a beer. Regina requested water and then added a beer to her order as well. They were served in large, cold mugs. Walt raised his and waited for her to do the same.

"To Rumspringa," he said.

She tapped her mug against his. "And bus trips from hell."

She ordered a double cheeseburger with everything. He ordered a salad.

"Seriously? You spent most of the drive talking about how great the food is, then you order a salad?"

He shrugged and flashed that easy smile. "What can I say? I'm at the age when too many cheeseburgers add too many inches to my waist."

If that was the case, he was avoiding cheeseburgers every day, because there weren't any extra inches around his waist. He was in remarkable shape. Not the kind that came from a gym membership. He wasn't tall or especially muscular, no more than five-nine. His stomach was flat. His shoulders were solid. And even in a long-sleeve shirt, Regina could tell his arms were muscular, particularly his forearms. That probably came from pulling out engine parts or whatever other stuff mechanics did.

He looked at her as he took a sip of his beer. "It's certainly a surprise to see you again. I was left with the distinct impression that you had no interest in the restaurant."

"It intrigues me, Walt. And there's nothing happening for me career-wise in New York."

He started to speak but held off. Probably wanted to ask

what she meant. It passed, though, and she was glad because that wasn't a story she was ready to share. She turned the conversation to him.

"How did you come to own both the restaurant and the garage?"

"It was a package deal. As you can see, they're connected. When I first moved into the garage, it was as a tenant. The family who ran the restaurant owned the entire building. They got out of the business and sold it to another family. When they ran into trouble, they decided to sell. I had been in business for a few years by then, so I made an offer. The next thing I knew, I owned a restaurant."

"And you never considered running it yourself?" She looked at the food on his side of the table and grinned. "Perhaps a nice salad place? They're quite trendy, you know."

That made him smile. "There might be some who would say I'm better suited for salad making than my chosen occupation."

Regina was about to comment that he needn't be self-deprecating, but their food arrived. The burger was smaller than expected, the edges thin and crispy. She pulled off a small piece and popped it into her mouth.

"Quite tasty, aren't they?"

Rather than answer, she picked up the burger and took a big bite. Juice from a tomato dribbled onto her chin. She grabbed a napkin and wiped at it, then took another bite while she tried to figure out what they were using to get that delicious crispy texture.

"Secret recipe," Walt said, reading her thoughts. "Some say they special source the meat. Others say it's twenty years of seasoning that has built up on the grill."

"Do you know the owner well enough to find out? I would pay for that recipe."

"She's a good friend. But I suspect she would disown me if she knew I was asking for the recipe on behalf of someone who might be her competitor one day."

Good friend? Not just a friend? What was going on behind that handsome face? Did Walt Mickens have a few secrets? Regina certainly did, and she had done what she needed to do to avoid bringing them up. He was entitled to do the same.

"How many people have attempted to make a go of it in your restaurant?"

He thought about it. "Hmm, let's see... Millie, of course, but she was before my time. There were the people I leased from, then the couple who followed them. After I bought the place, there was Abby and Bill. Paul and Eliseo did Mexican. The Larussa sisters. And Armand of course."

"What's the longest someone kept it open?"

He cast his eyes toward the ceiling as he considered the question. It was an endearing trait that gave him a studious look.

"Paul and Eliseo were in business for three years before Paul was deported. They were doing well. Eliseo was a wonderful cook, but his bookkeeping skills left something to be desired. Armand would still be there had he not gone through the divorce."

"Maybe the location is snakebit," Regina said between bites of her burger. "I've seen it before. Four locations on the same block. Three thrive and one constantly turns over. New name, new owners. Six months later, it all happens again."

Walt flagged down the server and asked for a glass of water. "I must respectfully disagree. My experience has been that there is always an underlying cause for the failure of one business in an otherwise good location."

"Maybe with a garage, but for restaurants, I'm not so sure."

"I think it's the same with any business. When there's a lack of success, there's inevitably something that causes it. The wrong product. A lack of good customer service."

"If that's the case," Regina countered, "then Three Mile Millie's should be thriving."

"Wrong people. Or the right people in the wrong circumstances. Paul's deportation. Armand's divorce."

"But you said there were others. What about them?"

"Abby and Bill served terrible food. The Larussa sisters were sinister toward their customers." He closed his eyes for a second before saying, "I practically needed a whip and chair when I collected the rent."

Regina laughed despite the seriousness on his face.

Her laughter made him laugh, too. "So tell me, Regina. Are you the kind of person who will attempt to tear me limb from limb to avoid paying rent?"

"Wouldn't you like to find out?" she teased. She polished off the burger, washed it down with the final sip of beer, and sighed deeply. "That was wonderful. Thank you for a delightful dinner, Walt. Now please allow me to pick up the check."

He didn't refuse her request. She paid the modest bill and followed him to his truck. It was a short drive to the beach. Regina heard the foamy crash of the waves against the shore. Streetlamps lit the boardwalk a couple of blocks to their right. And on their left was a two-story motel called the SaltAire. It looked a bit tired in the evening light, but Walt hadn't steered her wrong so far.

"I called ahead while you were in the restroom," he said

as he pulled up in front. "Michael is working the front desk. He's also the owner. He will take care of you."

Regina turned to look at him.

"Thank you for everything, Walt."

"And thank you for dinner. What time shall I pick you up in the morning?"

"That's not necessary. I'll call a cab."

"Cabs can be hard to come by. How about seven-forty-five? The motel serves a complimentary breakfast that you can enjoy before we drive out to the restaurant. I'll get my day started while you look around."

After they said their goodbyes, Regina grabbed her bag and walked into the SaltAire's lobby. A happy-looking man was waiting for her behind the counter.

"Miss Cole?"

"Yes, and you must be Michael."

He beamed. "I am, indeed. Walt said you might open the old restaurant next to his place. Phyllis and I enjoyed many meals there over the years. We especially liked it when Millie ran the place, but it's been so long ago."

"That's good to hear, Michael. I assume you have an available room?"

"Quite a few," he replied. "Off-season, you know. Everything will change in a week or two. I've put you in one of our best."

"Oh, that's not necessary. I would prefer to keep the cost down and just—"

"But we insist. Walt Mickens is a special person. And if you're a friend of his, you're a friend of ours." He slid an old-fashioned register across the counter. "Now, if you'll sign here, I'll get your key and send you on your way."

Regina blanched when she saw the price of the room.

"Are you sure this is right, Michael? I mean...this is well below what I expected to pay."

"Perhaps you'll become part of our community some-day, Miss Cole. If so, I want you to recall our first meeting as a positive one." He handed her a key. An actual key. Not a plastic card like every other hotel had used for the last twenty-five years. "Second floor, end of the hall. It was a pleasure meeting you, Miss Cole. And don't forget breakfast in the morning."

wednesday, june 4

A MAN APPROACHED Regina's table as she finished breakfast in the hotel's modest lobby restaurant. Middle-aged, thinning brown hair going to gray. Jeans and a blue flannel shirt.

"Miss Cole?"

"Yes?"

"I'm Felix Whitlow. I work with Walt Mickens. He received an important phone call and was unable to break away."

"Oh, my. I hope everything is okay."

Felix nodded. "Oh, yes. A work thing. He asked me to pick you up. Michael is at the front desk. He'll vouch for me."

Regina pushed back her chair and got to her feet. "Does poor Michael work all the time? He checked me in last night."

"His wife Patsy takes the midday shift. This place is their life. They raised three kids here. One is a veterinarian in Salisbury. The other two are schoolteachers. Wonderful family."

Felix grabbed Regina's rolling suitcase and headed for the door. Michael greeted him by name and wished Regina a good day. Felix drove a late-model sedan with a hint of new car smell inside. Regina took a few moments to gaze at the ocean as they pulled from the SaltAire parking lot.

"I never get tired of it," Felix said, nodding toward the beach. "The summer crowds are a pain in the neck, so I rarely come down then. But I enjoy long walks along the shoreline during the offseason. I consider it one of God's greatest gifts."

He tinkered with the radio for a few moments before giving up and turning it off.

"Have you and Walt worked together a long time?" Regina asked.

"Ten years this spring, and so you don't get the wrong impression, I work *for* Walt. The operation is his." He offered a slight smile. "But nobody works *for* Walt as much as *with* him. He respects my skills. He treats me as an equal. I can't say that for some of my former employers."

It seemed everyone had something good to say about Walt Mickens. Michael at the hotel. Now Felix. Everyone except Damon, who felt the guy was a snake oil salesman, and the fancy cars parked around his place were part of the act. *Just another shyster mechanic trying to impress customers so he can take their money.*

Regina wasn't so sure.

And that was why she was back.

"I take it you and Walt stay busy?"

"Busy enough," Felix said. "It's not like it used to be, though. Five or six years ago, I was raking in more from overtime than from my regular check."

"Oh, that's too bad. Are not as many people needing car repairs?"

Felix laughed. "Miss Cole, I'm not sure you understand what we do."

Oh, my goodness. What exactly was going on in that shop? Regina's breath caught. *Was it a front for something sinister? Oh, God. Damon was right. Walt was some kind of con man.*

"Perhaps I don't, Felix, because it looks like every repair shop I see in Brooklyn."

Felix turned off Coastal Highway and headed out of town. Regina planned her exit strategy.

I've changed my mind.

I prefer to stay in New York.

Even if it's as a sous chef at a restaurant that won't last six months.

Anything to avoid being part of some diabolical operation Walt Mickens is running out of his garage.

I don't want to be arrested as an accessory to...whatever.

I don't want to go to jail.

I just want to go home.

"Miss Cole, Walt Mickens is one of the leading restoration experts in America."

What the heck does that even mean? Is it code for cocaine dealer? Or hit man?

"His customers include show business stars, professional athletes, even billionaires."

Yeah, but some of them do cocaine, right? Or need a friend or relative knocked off?

Regina flinched when Felix reached across her lap and opened the glove box. But he only pulled out a small scrapbook and placed it on the seat between them.

"These are some of my favorite projects."

The first picture was of a much-younger Walt standing with that lantern-jawed guy who used to host the Tonight

Show. There was a bright red hotrod behind them. The next picture was Walt with Jerry Seinfeld and another sporty car. The book was full of stars and cars. Some, Regina recognized. Many, she didn't.

"I had no idea."

"And you wouldn't," Felix said as he signaled his intention to pull into the parking lot of the restaurant. "Walt doesn't keep mementos or pictures. And he's completely unaffected by his famous friends." He replaced the scrapbook in the glove compartment. "In fact, if he knew I showed you those pictures, he would say he wished I hadn't."

He pulled to a stop in front of the restaurant and handed Regina a set of keys. "Walt said to look around as long as you like. He'll be tied up for a couple hours but will be available later to run you to the train station in Wilmington."

Regina wanted to protest. To insist she didn't need a ride. But the tedium of the previous day's odyssey was too fresh. She took the keys, thanked Felix, and headed for the front door, happy that there was one less thing to worry about.

ONE PHONE CALL BECAME FOUR, followed by an exhaustive internet search for a replacement quarter panel for a 1977 Aston Martin. Then another call. And an unannounced visit from a United States Senator wishing to have his vintage Mustang restored. The senator was unhappy that Walt's schedule had no immediate openings. Still smarting from the failed internet search, Walt wasn't happy with the senator either but kept it to himself. The Mustang would never see the inside of his shop. Some jobs weren't worth the headaches. It was lunchtime when he peered out his office window and saw Regina standing in front of the restaurant, eyeing it from a customer's perspective. Her presence lifted his spirits. How nice it would be to have the restaurant operating again. And it would be even nicer if the operator were Regina.

He left his desk and passed through the shop to let Felix know he might be gone for a while. When he stepped outside, Regina was gone, but the restaurant door was ajar. He called her name as he went in.

"Back here."

He found her sitting on a table in the center of the kitchen. She had her legs drawn up underneath her, yoga style, and was contemplating the space.

"Shall I run and get the sales contract?" he joked as he sat down on the table a few feet away.

She smiled as she said, "ABS."

"I'm afraid I don't know what that means."

"ABS. Always be selling."

"Ahh, I see. The bigger question is, are you ready to buy?"

"No, Walt. I can't see that happening."

A piece of his insides did a jiggly thing. "I understand. Would you consider a lease?"

It was a few moments before she replied, "What if it's a colossal failure?"

"What if it's a stunning success?"

"Touche." Then another pause. "Owning a restaurant has been my dream since I was a little girl. When the neighbor kids and I would play grown-up in my backyard, I always had a restaurant. I would even bake cookies or make pizzas." As she looked around, she ran her hand through her hair, which was already cascading in every direction. "But this is not how it's supposed to be."

"You can sell pizza and cookies. I'll be a regular customer."

She smiled at him. "I would have salads, too. Because I know you like them."

Walt wiped at the corner of the table and noticed that it didn't need wiping. It had been dusty when he was last inside. Everything was dusty. As he looked around, he realized she had cleaned up much of the kitchen. Metal surfaces gleamed. Even the floors had been swept.

"How much do I owe you for cleaning up the kitchen?"

"No charge. I hate seeing such nice equipment being neglected. There's still a lot more that needs to be done."

"But not by you?"

"No, Walt. Unfortunately, not. Like I said, it's not where I envisioned myself."

"You envisioned yourself in New York?"

"Yeah, but that dream has..." She didn't finish, and Walt didn't push. And after a few more moments, she uncrossed her legs and stood up. Each move was more graceful than the previous. She tucked her left hand into the pocket of her jeans, concealing it as she had the day before. Something had hurt her physically, and Walt was starting to believe it might have injured her emotionally, too.

But it wasn't his place to pry.

And when she said she was ready to head home, he said he would get his car and meet her out front. She protested. Mildly. Her backside probably still smarted from the previous day's bus ride.

She gave him time to walk out of the restaurant before taking one last look around. The kitchen space was more than ample. She had done plenty with much less. The dining room might seat sixty. Maybe a few more. But it needed work. More work than she wanted to put in. Or was it?

Damn it, where was her self-assurance? Her swagger? When had she lost them?

Easy question. She'd lost them when she allowed Javier and the others at Gasconade to treat her so shabbily. It wasn't an overnight thing. She hadn't been strong, determined Regina one day and…whatever she was now the next. They had taken the first piece from her, though. They'd nudged the domino that tumbled the rest.

What would the old Regina have said about the surrounding space?

Same as the present Regina. Then she would also point out that redesigning the dining room would not only be doable, but exciting as hell.

She needed that Regina. Because this one didn't have it in her anymore.

"Regina?"

Walt was back.

"Are you ready?"

She took a deep breath, threw back her shoulders in a display of bravado she wasn't feeling inside, and tossed him the keys.

"I sure am."

IT WAS two hours from Bethany Beach to the Wilmington train station. Walt had considered taking his daily driver, a two-year-old Ford SUV. A plain-Jane base model with no bells and whistles because he didn't need that stuff after spending his days around some of the finest cars in the world.

But something made him change his mind, and when Regina stepped out and saw his second choice, he was glad he had.

"Oh, my goodness!" she exclaimed as she eyed the wood-paneled station wagon. "My Uncle Clarence had one of these."

"They made a lot of them, and most were owned by nice folks like your uncle. Let me guess. He had four kids?"

"Seven. Three in the back seat and three in the..." She approached the rear of the 1970 Buick station wagon and peered through the window. "Yep, you have the way-back seat. Three of my cousins sat back there."

"And the seventh?" Walt asked as he opened the front door for her.

"That was my cousin Everett. He was in the front seat between Uncle Clarence and Aunt Shirley. A booster seat at first, then he just stood up on the seat."

"Oh, goodness. Did Everett make it to adulthood?"

"Funny you should ask," Regina said with a laugh. "He's a defense attorney who specializes in auto injuries."

Walt pulled from the restaurant lot, and they were on their way. The car met Walt's intended use of breaking the ice. A way to ease into conversation about life and memories and dreams for the future. Regina was interested in hearing the story behind the wagon. He explained it was a nearly finished restoration project for a Baltimore-area police chief who had also ridden in the reverse-facing way-back seat when he was a boy.

"Aren't you worried about damaging it?"

He shook his head. "I don't worry about things like that. Not anymore."

If his cryptic reply intrigued her, she didn't ask. Like the car, he had planted it there to spur the conversation. He wanted to get to know her. To find out what had happened. Not just to her hand, but to her psyche. Because he sensed that something was amiss. And it involved more than whether to open a restaurant at the Delaware shore.

But he didn't go there.

Yet.

IT DIDN'T FEEL like they'd been on the road for an hour, but Regina's watch said otherwise. Walt was an engaging conversationalist and an excellent listener. He wasn't concerned with things like stature or who he impressed. And that made him even more impressive. Still, there was something lurking under the surface. A melancholy.

And what was that throwaway line he'd used? Something about not worrying about things *anymore*? That had heartache written all over it, but it was someone else's heartache because, in about four hours, Regina would be back in the city with her own man.

And speaking of which, why hadn't Damon called or texted? Sure, he got busy sometimes, especially when he was chasing new business like Grandma Alice in Boston. And she hadn't exactly burned up the airwaves calling and texting him either. There was the text the evening before, telling him she loved him and hoping things were good in Boston. And that was it. She pulled out her phone and double-checked, but there was nothing new. She hadn't mentioned the quick trip to Delaware because she wanted to see things without Damon's preconceptions getting in the way. She would tell him, though, because that was what couples did.

Walt pulled off Route 1 into a convenience store gas station. "Would you like anything?"

"I'll run in and use the restroom. Can I get you something?"

He requested coffee with two sugars. As she was getting out of the car a couple about her age came over to let them know their families had also driven massive wagons. Regina left them to Walt and headed inside. When she returned, he was waiting in front of the car.

"Why don't you take the wheel?" he asked.

She raised her hands, a coffee in each, in protest. "I don't have a license."

"Yes, but if you move to Bethany Beach, you'll need one. Consider me your driving instructor. And this..." He motioned toward the wagon with the same flourish the TV game show models used. "... is your training vehicle."

She smiled at how he worked Bethany Beach into his reasoning. "Well, as a matter of fact, I used to be an awesome driver. I could whip through the city streets as well as any cabbie."

He moved to the driver's side, pulled open the door, and motioned for her to get in. "It's a straight and easy route to Wilmington, so please refrain from driving like a cabbie."

"Maybe I will and maybe I won't," she teased as she handed him his coffee. She looked around to familiarize herself with the layout. She'd never driven a car from that era, nor one that large, but everything was pretty much where she expected it to be.

Except for the cupholder. She held up her still-steaming coffee. "What do I do with this?"

"I'll hold it for you."

"Just be ready," Regina said as she turned the key. "New Yorkers drive fast and brake hard." She checked both ways and pulled onto Route 1. The wagon was huge, but the engine was up to the task. Regina was surprised at how easily it drove. She got up to speed and fell in with the other northbound traffic. It felt good to be behind the wheel again.

And Walt? He leisurely sipped his coffee as if he didn't have a care in the world. He watched the surroundings pass for a few miles. Regina stole glances at him as she drove. He had a strong profile. Unlike some guys with facial hair, his wasn't hiding a weak chin. His jaw was chiseled, and the graying beard added sophistication. She wondered if that was the look he was going for, or if he'd grown tired of shaving. His hairline was starting to recede, but his hair was cut to allow some of what was left to fall forward. A few strands reached his eyebrows. His look communicated a feeling of graceful maturity that didn't jibe with his profession. But then again, as Felix had said, Walt Mickens wasn't just some small-town auto mechanic.

"What led you to work on cars?"

He turned from the window and seemed to remember he was still holding her coffee. He offered. She accepted and took a sip, then handed it back.

"I grew up around it."

"Let me guess. You and your father spent hours in the garage tinkering with engines."

"Actually, it was my mums and me, but close enough."

She took her eyes off the road long enough to see if he was kidding. His smile was still there, but he was serious.

"Mums learned from her father, Papa as my sister and I called him. He always had a few cars in various states of restoration. When I started showing an interest, Mums took me to some car shows. I was always drawn to the older ones, which chagrined her no small amount."

"Your mother likes new cars? I don't blame her."

"Well, she designed many of them, so there's that."

"Your mother designs cars?"

"She used to. She's retired now, but yes. In Europe at first, then here in the States for a time. She has degrees in design and engineering. She's quite successful."

Regina could see the immense pride he had for his mother. His eyes lit up as he named the manufacturers she had worked with. Big ones that made some of the nicest and most expensive cars in the world. He stopped short of saying how involved she was, but Regina could tell she was someone important. And that made the eloquent yet simple man sitting next to her even more of an enigma.

"You're probably wondering how someone like my mums can have a son who tinkers with old cars and lives at the beach."

"Actually...yes. Though Felix told me about the work you do. And he name-dropped a few of your customers."

Walt rolled his eyes. "Felix shouldn't have done that."

"Don't be too hard on him. He's proud to work for you."

"He is a valued employee. And a friend. I could never have gotten to this point without him."

"I know the truth about you, Mr. Mickens, so stop selling yourself short. And as far as Bethany Beach, yeah, I wondered how you wound up there instead of someplace closer to the city."

He pointed out an exit coming up. "My grandparents summered in Bethany. Back when we still lived in the UK,

77

our parents sent my sister and me to stay with them each July, so it's the place I associated with America. We lived in Detroit when we moved here, but I spent more and more time in Bethany. Especially after Papa and Grandmother retired and made it their full-time home."

There was undoubtedly much more to the story of how a boy from the UK wound up in Bethany Beach restoring classic cars for famous people, but they were entering the outskirts of Wilmington and traffic was heavier. Walt had to pause his story to give her directions several times, so they moved on to idle chatter as Regina navigated narrow streets in the jumbo station wagon. At one point, she asked if he would prefer to take the wheel.

He smiled and demurred. "You're proving quite capable."

Plenty was said of his mums and grandparents. And she learned that his sister Leah had graduated from Brown University and returned to Europe for a career in finance. But there was no mention of his father.

It was approaching four when they pulled into the train station parking lot. Walt directed her to a ten-minute parking area. "How long until your train?"

"Twenty minutes."

He turned serious. "I know you said you've decided against the restaurant, Regina, but please know that if things change, the offer stands."

She smiled at him. "I appreciate that, Walt, but you need to find someone else."

He shrugged. "I've decided not to do anything with it. Even if I find an interested party, they won't be someone who cares for it like you would." He gazed out the window as he said, "I would rather use it for storage than have someone try and fail."

Regina didn't know what to say. The possibilities were intriguing, but the location and timing were all wrong. And besides, even with Damon's help, she couldn't afford to purchase or even lease the space long-term.

"I'll make my final pitch and allow you to be on your way," he said, turning so he was facing her full-on. He reached into his coat pocket and pulled out a folded sheet of paper. "Here's a lease for one year. You reserve the right to pull out at any time, but I believe when you see what I'm proposing, you'll agree that it might make it easier for you to take a chance."

Regina took the sheet and started to unfold it, but then noticed her departure time was getting close. She put it in her purse instead. "I'll look at it, Walt, but I don't see it being in the cards for me."

"And I will respect that, but may I say one more thing?"

"Of course."

"Forgive me if this is too personal. It's not like me to make such a statement, but I sense something...or someone has hurt you. And—"

Regina started to cut him off but reconsidered. It would likely be the last time they crossed paths, so let him say what he needed to say.

"I barely know you, but I sense greatness in you, Regina. And whatever is getting in the way of you realizing that greatness is..."

There was a hint of emotion as he searched for what he wanted to say. In that quiet moment, Regina felt as if she was sitting next to a friend. He somehow perceived her hurt and was reaching out.

He took a deep breath. "You asked why I never considered starting my business in the city. Many people believe that you can't find true success unless it's on the largest stage."

She nodded and hoped he kept going. He did. "I disagree. I feel success is more in here." He patted his heart. "It's a feeling that comes with doing something better than anyone else. I suspect you've known that feeling."

Again, she nodded. With anyone else, it might have felt that her agreement was self-serving. Not with Walt.

"Find that again, Regina."

And with that, he got out of the car and came around to the driver's side. She was already getting out. When she extended her hand, he clasped it. Was there a trace of disappointment in his expression? If so, it was probably because of a missed opportunity to fill the space next to his garage.

She rushed off toward the entrance. Once inside, she glanced back through the large glass doors to where she had left him. He was still there. He caught her eye and waved. She waved back. He grinned and stepped away. Regina hurriedly purchased her ticket and hustled onto her train with moments to spare. The car was about half-full, and she had a row to herself.

What was it about that guy? He had such a way of discerning things. And he was spot on. Success for Regina had always been more a gut feeling than anything overt. Glowing reviews of Gasconade or requests for sit-down interviews with New York's leading food journalists were heady stuff, but they had never been her aim. She'd seen more than a few executive chefs lauded one moment and cast aside the next.

She was now one of them. The castoffs.

And if it took moving a few hours away to rebuild what she had before, was that so bad?

Her fingers brushed against the envelope in her coat pocket. What kind of proposal was he making? It didn't matter because she couldn't afford it.

But it didn't hurt to look.

As she pulled it from her pocket, something else fell out and onto the floor below her feet. She reached for it and held it up for a closer look.

Sandra Del Greco, Professional Counselor.

Who the— Ah, the woman from the subway two days earlier.

I don't usually do this on a subway, but maybe I can help sometime.

No way. A counselor? Ha!

She could imagine Sandra Del Greco's reply if she went to her and poured out her heart.

Don't throw away everything you've worked for in New York.

Stay and fight. Make them pay.

This is your town, too.

And she would be right. There was a job out there someplace. Someplace closer than Delaware. A place where the owners could tell that Javier was trying to poison everyone against her, but happily hired her nonetheless.

She just needed to try a little harder.

And maybe a little harder than that.

She jammed the business card back into her pocket and was about to do the same with Walt's envelope. But curiosity got the best of her, so she tore it open. There was only one sheet inside. Not a contract or proposal at all. More like a stream-of-consciousness note. She read through it and wasn't certain she understood, so she read it again.

What in the world?

Was he nuts?

But what if he wasn't?

What if Walt Mickens was dead serious?

Regina reached back into her pocket and pulled out Sandra Del Greco's card again. She dialed the number, expecting a receptionist or voicemail. It was, after all, a quarter to five.

"This is Sandra."

What kind of counselor answers her own phone? Regina nearly disconnected, but knew if she did, she would not have the courage to call back.

"Hi. This is Regina Cole. We met on the subway two nights ago. I was the—"

"Of course, Regina. I remember. Do you want to come see me at six-thirty?"

Come see you? Like, in person? Will I have to lie on a couch?

"Well, I wasn't planning on... I've never..." Regina felt a tightening in her chest. So much was pressing in on her. From so many directions. If she was going to cry, she might as well do it in person. She checked the office address and saw it was a couple of blocks from the train station. She could just make it.

"I'll be there. And thank you."

HOLY GUACAMOLE!

Either Sandra Del Greco was the best counselor in the entire freaking world, or Regina had needed to let it all out real bad.

After ten minutes of pleasantries, Sandra had started probing. It didn't take long before the floodgates swung open. In minutes, Regina went from apprehensive to practically rolling on the floor in tears. Sandra probably thought she was a basket case.

But then, wasn't that what professional counselors lived for? It was like Sandra had a hidden button that magically got Regina to open up. Her questions would press that button, and Regina would take off.

Her love for food and restaurants.

Her career trajectory.

The challenges at Gasconade.

The accident.

Learning to cope with the long-term nature of her injuries.

Her physical recovery.

Javier.

Her fruitless job search.

Her self-doubts.

They also delved into her relationship with Damon.

And her visit with Walt Mickens.

"He sounds quite intuitive," Sandra remarked after Regina shared their parting conversation.

I sense so much greatness in you, Regina.

"Yeah," Regina said, trying to inject humor into what had been a mostly humorless session. "Maybe he just wants to get in my pants."

"Do you really think that?" Sandra countered.

Regina shook her head. She didn't think that at all. Quite the contrary. Walt's eyes had never strayed like some guys did. They locked on hers while they talked.

"Nope," she said, regretting she'd made the joke. "He was so kind. And his offer is intriguing."

Sandra leaned forward and placed her elbows on her knees. "That I can't help you with, Regina. I suck at business."

"I doubt that."

"No, really. If it weren't for my partner, I would forget to charge my clients."

Fortunately, Regina had just the person for a second opinion. Unfortunately, he wouldn't be returning to the city as planned. Damon had texted before she went into her session with Sandra.

He would be staying another night in Boston.

thursday, june 5

THE SELF-DOUBTS JUMPED into Regina's dreams a little after 3 a.m. It was stupid to think she could pull up stakes and move to Delaware. Despite what Sandra Del Greco might say, that was messed-up thinking. She was a New York girl, and New York was where she belonged. She gave up going back to sleep, pulled out her laptop, and went to work.

After a morning poring through a half-dozen job search websites, Regina had clicked the *APPLY* button for four positions. They included two sous chefs and a purchasing manager spot with a chain of New York pubs. The fourth position was the first job she had ever applied for that wasn't food-related.

Teaching assistant at a school for special needs children.

She had no idea what a teaching assistant did and had never known any special needs children, but it sounded good and noble. Perhaps it would help her feel good about herself again.

Damon texted a little after ten to let her know he would

be catching the train back to New York that afternoon. Regina punched out a long text about her trip to Delaware and her decision to stay in the city and make a go of it. She even mentioned her visit with the counselor, but in the end, she deleted everything.

Love you! See you tonight! she texted instead.

For sure! I'll bring Chinese, Damon texted back.

Things were already looking up.

Until her phone buzzed twenty minutes later. She flinched when she saw the name on caller ID.

Javier Rocha

She wanted to toss the phone onto the floor and run from it, much like she had run from the mice that took up residence in her family's Brooklyn flat every fall when the weather turned cool.

But Javier wasn't a mouse. A rat, perhaps. But not a mouse.

Still, she didn't have to answer his call.

Unless...had there been a change of heart? Had Javier finally realized how cruel he had been? And if he had, was it sincere, or was he hoping to get her back because Blossom was making a mess of things?

And if he was going to ask her to return, could she? Would she?

After everything he had done?

No way. Not a chance.

Unless... People could change, couldn't they? And Javier had been okay to work for before.

Before the accident.

Before her rehabilitation leave.

Of course, back then, everything was great at Gasconade. Profits were at their highest point ever. The staff was happy. Even later, after Regina returned and

Blossom was usurping many of her duties, Gasconade continued to prosper.

Had Javier finally realized that she was the vital cog in Gasconade's success?

Yeah, Regina decided as she reached for the phone. She would return. Provided Javier was contrite. Sincerely remorseful.

And Blossom wouldn't be around anymore.

She could do it.

She could be the better person.

And then, as she reached for her phone, a second call came through. This one was from a number she didn't recognize. She hit the decline button, swallowed, and accepted Javier's call.

"Hello?" Did she sound nervous? God, she hoped not. She wanted to sound busy like everything was good and her life was full of rainbows and unicorns.

But she sounded nervous.

And Javier? He wasn't nervous. He was seriously pissed off.

"Regina, if you think siccing that second-rate newspaper on me is going to help your cause, you are seriously mistaken."

Regina recoiled and wanted to run, but it was too late. What was he even talking about?

"What... I don't know—"

"Don't play me for a fool. You cried to that hack writer from the *City Beat Investigator*."

"Javier, I didn't—"

"I knew you would deny it. I told Lance as much."

Things were spinning out of control. And Javier's voice sounded like it was a thousand miles away. Regina's head pounded with white pain. Was this what a panic attack felt like? And why was this even happening? She hadn't given the reporter another thought since he'd contacted her the previous Friday. She tried to spit out a reply, but it took two tries and sounded defensive even to her.

"He had already heard that you—"

Javier cut her off again. "Don't lie to me, Regina."

And then everything became as clear as a bell. The spinning sensation was gone. The headache, too.

He was calling her a liar.

After everything he'd done to keep her down, he had the *audacity* to call her a liar. When she spoke again it was complete clarity.

"Javier, you need to know that I didn't contact Art Geller."

Even Regina couldn't believe how calm she sounded.

Javier must have picked up on it because when he replied, his tone was softer. "Well, if you didn't, then I wonder—"

"He called me last week, and I hadn't considered returning his call." Still understated. Still strong.

"I guess I was mistaken, Regina, because—"

"But I want you to know that as soon as I end this call I plan to call Mr. Geller and offer my complete cooperation with his investigation."

That did the trick. Javier exploded. And every word of his expletive-filled tirade was recorded by the app Regina had installed on her phone back when the trouble first started. It was Damon's idea. And she would be sure to thank him for it. But for the moment, she allowed Javier to continue at full throttle until he ran out of steam. And then, she calmly asked, "Is there anything else?"

There wasn't. Javier was gone.

And Regina felt better than she had in weeks.

And more resolute than ever that she needed to go after the owners of Gasconade with everything she—and Damon—had. Every weapon in their arsenal. Depositions of employees, medical records, and emails between Javier and Lance.

And of course, the recording. The cherry on top of the sundae.

She opened the one window in her apartment that wasn't painted shut and allowed the brisk winter air to fill her lungs. She wanted to call Damon and play the recording for him, but he would still be tied up with Alice the widow.

That was when she remembered the other call.

She checked her phone, expecting spam. There was a message. She played it.

Art Geller.

"Miss Cole, I wanted to give you a heads-up that I started my investigation this weekend. I've spoken to a few employees at Gasconade. They love you, by the way. I just got off the phone with Javier Rocha, and I believe it's safe to say that he isn't exactly a fan of yours." Geller laughed. "Or a fan of mine. At least after that call. But anyway, I again extend my offer to include your side in this story. I hope you'll consider taking me up on it and give me a call. Take care."

Regina pressed the button to return Geller's call, then thought better of it. She would get Damon's opinion first. But darn it, he wouldn't be back for a few more hours. She picked up her laptop and returned to the job search for a few minutes before growing bored and turning to some of the internet's lighter fare. Her surfing eventually took her back to the website where Walt Mickens had posted the restaurant. It was still there but was now listed as off the market. He really had decided to leave it vacant.

That made her sad again. She took a mental walk through the kitchen, touching the equipment and running her fingers across the countertops. It was a good space. A very good space. The corner closest to the dining room would be perfect as a baking area, allowing the fresh aromas of breads and cakes to waft into the customers' consciousness. There was plenty of room for a pass-through where chefs could place prepared dishes for servers to grab and go. Seamless and efficient. Regina loved efficiency. And it wasn't hard to imagine at all. Yes, indeed, a good space. Perfect for experimenting with new seafood dishes. She had always liked working with seafood, particularly crab. Too many restaurants didn't try hard enough with crab, preferring to stick to tried-and-true dishes like broiled crab cakes or crab imperial. Recipes that only scratched the surface of what could be created with that wonderful delicacy that was available within a stone's throw of that little restaurant in Bethany Beach.

So much potential.

Potential that would be lost or fade into the past as the old place remained vacant.

Unless…

REGINA ARRIVED at Damon's apartment a few minutes after six, overnight bag in hand. He was on the phone when he opened the door. He smiled and winked and waved her in, then retreated to his bedroom and closed the door.

Strange.

Regina was bursting with stuff to tell him, and the half

hour she waited was enough to make her jump out of her skin with anticipation. Where to start?

The call with Javier?

The trip to Delaware?

Her visit with the counselor?

Walt's offer?

It would have to wait. Damon was obviously distracted when he stepped back into the living room. The trip to Boston had accomplished only part of what he'd hoped.

"The grandkids and their parents are joining forces. They're coming to Boston for a family meeting this weekend, and Alice isn't sure she can hold them off."

Regina put on a show of empathy she wasn't feeling. She was tired of old Alice cutting into her time, but she knew if she brought it up Damon would bring up the fees he was collecting. Fees that would allow him to spend less time hanging around courtrooms rustling up desperate clients who were too poor to pay their legal fees. He was better than that.

So she listened. And waited for her chance to spill the news.

But Damon had his mind on other things.

He came to her as he wrapped up his account of how bad things were in Boston. He kissed her in a way that communicated his desires.

"And you know what the worst part of it was?" he asked.

She had a feeling she did. She could tell from that kiss. And the ones that followed.

"I didn't get to see my woman at all last night, and I was *needing* my woman if you get my drift."

Yep. That was what she thought this was about. Damon's hands were already running down her spine, and while it felt really good, she wanted desperately to tell him everything. She wanted to know what he thought.

She wanted to let him know what she was thinking, too.

But there was no denying him when he had *that* on his mind. So she kissed him back and allowed herself to enjoy the moments as they unfolded. There were a lot of positive things she could say about Damon Palmer. He was hardworking and willing to hustle to get ahead. He was smart and funny and wore his heart on his sleeve. He was good-looking, in shape, and had all his hair.

But at that moment, the thing she appreciated most was that he was great in bed.

friday, june 6

ONE OF THE few problems with good lovemaking—and in Regina's opinion there were very few—was that a person tended to forget things.

Like setting the alarm for the next morning.

Damon had awakened first, at seven-forty. He cussed a blue streak about a 9 a.m. court appearance he had no way of making. But Damon being Damon, he calmed down and shook it off.

"You had something you wanted to talk about last night," he said as he jumped into one of his dark gray suits. "How about lunch?"

"Okay. I don't have anything on my calendar." Ouch, it hurt to say that.

Regina showered, then checked the job sites in case something new had popped up. It hadn't. She had an email from Art Geller, though.

Hope you got my voicemail. Are you available to talk this afternoon?

She still wanted to get Damon's opinion, so she replied as much, referring to him as her attorney rather than her boyfriend, though. She ended with, *I will let you know one way or another later today*. Then, with time to burn, she did a quick search through the apartment listings for Bethany Beach.

It didn't hurt to look.

DAMON HAD a two-hour gap in his schedule, so there was time to tell him everything. They met at a tapas place near his office. They ordered, then Regina jumped in with her item-by-item list.

The trip to Delaware. He was more concerned than anything. "That's a long way to go with no one knowing where you are."

He was right. She could have been butchered to death on some back road between Wilmington and Bethany Beach. No one would have known where to look for the pieces. She promised Damon and herself that she would do better.

He wanted to know if the second visit changed her mind about anything.

"Yes and no," she said. She went so long about the kitchen space and the left-behind equipment that Damon's eyes glazed over.

"I could make it work. I'm certain of it."

"Of course, you could. I have no doubt." That was a good reply. He might get more loving later for that.

He grew much more attentive when she pulled out the envelope Walt Mickens had given her.

"He drove you all the way to Wilmington?" His radar was on full alert.

Regina considered explaining how hard it was to get

from Bethany to the bus station in Georgetown and how unreliable the bus service was. But that would make it sound like she was trying to justify taking Walt up on his offer, so she just answered that he had.

Damon seemed satisfied. He wasn't the jealous type, anyway. She wasn't either, even after a couple of past relationships where a little jealousy might have come in handy. He opened the envelope and scanned Walt's proposal for a few moments.

"This is incredible," he finally said.

"You think so?"

Damon perused it once more. "I do. He's allowing you a thirty-day opt-out. If things were to turn bad or you didn't want to be there anymore, you would only be on the hook for one month's rent."

Regina had thought it sounded good, too, but was content to let Damon show off his legal skills.

"He's willing to invest in bringing the building up to code and pay for some of the interior modifications." Damon looked up. "Some paint and decent lighting would brighten up that dining room."

"It would still be a stretch." Regina rattled off the improvements that would be needed, some basic equipment, and better tables and chairs in the dining room.

"I can help with that," Damon said.

"I appreciate that, but I don't want you to give me money. How about we work out a loan?"

He thought about it for a few moments. Regina would have been more concerned if he hadn't. He understood risk and how relationships sometimes come to quick and ugly ends. She didn't believe for a moment that they were headed in that direction, but stuff happened sometimes.

"That's a good idea, but let's not get the cart before the

horse," he said. "Are you serious about this? I have to confess that I noticed a change in you when I got back last night. Was it because of this?"

"Well, not really. It was because of Javier."

Damon's eyes narrowed. "What did he do?"

She told him about the phone call. About how Javier accused her of contacting Art Geller. He had his phone in hand before she was finished, flipping through his contacts in search of Javier's number. He stopped when Regina played him the recording she'd made. It sounded as vile and angry as the first time, but Damon's anger turned into glee.

"That should be good for another fifty thousand." He cackled as he slapped his knee. Then, more serious, he said, "Damn, Regina, you're devious."

"You're the one who told me to install the recording app."

"Yeah, but I didn't expect it to work so well." He shook his head. "Javier's attorney is going to be mad as hell when he hears this. Tell you what, Regina. Let's call that reporter together. You do the talking, but I'll make my presence known and make sure he doesn't trick you into saying something best left unsaid. Want to go back to my office and call him from there?"

"Sure, but there's one more thing I want to tell you."

Damon listened closely to her account of the visit with Sandra Del Greco, Professional Counselor. When she got to the part where she had gotten emotional on the subway, he took her hand.

"Did she give you good advice?"

She considered answering that her advice was a repeat of what she'd already been told by Walt Mickens.

I sense so much greatness in you, Regina.

But that, as competent as Sandra Del Greco was, and how awesome a listener she was, it had been Walt who had helped her the most. He barely knew her, yet he had looked into her eyes with such sincerity and said he sensed greatness.

Nope, better to leave Walt out of it.

"She said that I can accomplish anything I want."

"And what do you want?"

She reflected on the past few days. The trips to Delaware. The restaurant. The call from Javier.

Walt Mickens.

Why did her thoughts keep returning to him? What strange spell had he cast over her that had her considering pulling up stakes and leaving the city?

She sighed as she looked into Damon's compassionate eyes.

"I think I want Bethany Beach."

"Is that all?"

"And I want Javier to pay for how they treated me, but more than anything, I want to show them how wrong they were."

saturday, june 7

REGINA WAS AWAKENED by the buzz of her
cellphone.

Damon.

"Hey," she said sleepily. "Did you get back okay from
Boston?"

"Not until midnight. Sorry to wake you so early. Can
you send me that recording of Javier?"

Regina came fully awake. "Now?"

"Yep. And while you're at it, pull up the *City Beat Investigator's* website. The crap hit the fan overnight. Javier's
lawyer has left four messages—each angrier than the one
before it. He's threatening to destroy your reputation and
wipe you out financially."

"They've already ruined my reputation. And as far as
my finances, there's not much to get."

Damon laughed. "True enough. Send me the recording,
then look at the story. I'll call the lawyer and be by to pick
you up for our trip south. That's still on, right?"

Of course, it was still on. Regina had thought of little

besides Bethany Beach since they'd discussed it earlier in the week. If Walt Mickens was surprised by her call two days earlier, he didn't show it. He would be at the shop when they arrived later in the day.

"I'll be ready at ten."

"Since we're both up, we might as well get an early start," Damon said. "How about I pick you up at nine?"

That sounded even better. An extra hour of daylight to get another look at the restaurant. There was only one thing, though.

"Would you mind waiting until we're in the car to call their lawyer? I want to hear his response when you play the recording."

"That's a good idea," Damon said with a chuckle. "You can listen while I pin his ears to the wall."

Regina suspected that the recording would do more damage than anything Damon had to say, but she still wanted to be part of it. She sent the recording, then took a quick shower and packed her bag. She was already excited about the trip, but her difficulties with Javier going public added a bit more enthusiasm. Once she was ready to go, she pulled up the Investigator's website. The headline made her flinch.

"Something Stinks at Gasconade."

"Owners Show Their Worst Side After Injury to Chef."

Holy crap.

For such a soft-spoken and unassuming guy on the phone, Art Geller pulled no punches as a journalist.

He had spoken to two former Gasconade employees and two current ones. Each sang Regina's praises as a chef and person.

Great boss. Talented chef.

Really cares about her employees.

Put so much into making Gasconade successful.

She was surprised to see the name of one of the former employees because she and Regina hadn't always seen eye to eye. Her comments were still among the most positive in the article. The names of the two people still working at Gasconade were withheld, but she could tell from the quotes that one was Jacob Klein, her last hire and the employee she would poach if she had the opportunity.

Their comments about Javier, his partner Lance, and Lance's girlfriend, Blossom, were less glowing.

There are two partners. One is a bully, and the other is a freeloader.

The new manager hides in her office. I don't even think she knows my name.

Whoa.

Only two quotes were attributed to Regina. The first was her description of her injury. It was straightforward and didn't cast any aspersions on Gasconade or the partners. The second detailed her years at Gasconade and how it had become such a large part of her life. Nothing libelous. Nothing like the things she had recorded Javier saying to her.

DAMON'S PLAN TO return the call was short-circuited when Javier's lawyer called. He was already wound up by the time Damon switched the call to speaker. He allowed the guy to yell himself out.

And then he was done. They could hear his labored breathing, but Damon still didn't speak. He motioned with a finger to his lips for Regina to remain silent. No problem.

She had no intention of saying anything. Ten seconds passed. Then thirty before the other guy said, "Hello?"

Damon put his fist to his mouth to keep from laughing out loud.

"I'm still here," he said stoically.

"We need to meet and get this out in the open," the lawyer sniped. "Or I'm going to fire the first shot in court on Monday."

"Oh, trust me, dude," Damon quipped. "The first shot's already been fired."

"What do you mean?"

He pointed at Regina's phone. She already had the recording queued up. She pressed the button, and Javier's tirade burst from the speaker. After about fifteen seconds, he motioned for Regina to hit pause.

"There's plenty more where that came from," Damon said.

"I want a copy of that recording, Damon."

"Sorry. No."

"I'll get it quashed if this thing goes forward. My client was recorded without his consent."

Damon rolled his eyes as he waited for a light to change. "Obviously."

"When did that conversation take place?" It was obvious from his tone that some of the bluster had been knocked out of him.

"Ask your client, Leon. Don't expect me to do your work for you." Damon winked at Regina. "Unless you want to pay for my time."

That did it. He was gone. Not even a goodbye or see you soon. Damon threw his head back and laughed. "Gosh, that was fun."

Regina thought so, too. "But what happens next?"

"Their side goes into damage control. Gasconade was identified in the headline, and while the *City Beat Investigator* isn't the *New York Times*, a lot of people read it. Javier has to be worried it will cost them business. They'll focus inward for a few days at least." He grabbed her hand and kissed it. "Which is good for us, because we can head out of town without worrying about those losers."

REGINA'S TUMMY fluttered when they reached the Bethany Beach city limits. She had spent so much time the past couple of days thinking about the restaurant, trying to imagine it cleaned up and open for business. The kitchen was easy, but that dining room? It had eighties diner vibes going, and that wouldn't play. She had told Walt Mickens to expect them at 2:30 but arrived forty-five minutes early. The unlit neon sign on top was visible from a quarter mile away.

"Three Mile Millie's," Damon said as they approached. "Has to be the dumbest restaurant name I've ever heard." He glanced over at her. "What will you call it?"

Regina thought about it as she checked herself in the mirror and ran a hand through her hair. It didn't help. It never did. Her hair was crazy, like the pictures of Grandma Cole during the blown-out Afro days of the 1970s. The only solution was to cut it short, but Regina had resisted long enough that it had become part of her image, and as crazy as it might look sometimes, it was also what earned her the most compliments.

"Who said I was going to take it on?" she replied.

"You took the train, a bus, and two Ubers to get here last week," Damon said with a laugh.

They pulled up in front. The restaurant was as before. Dusty windows, old wooden door. The garage looked the same, too, except there were different cars out front. Felix Whitlow was busy polishing a gleaming red and white coupe.

"Well, I'll be..." Damon's eyes were locked on the car. "That's a '57 Fairlane."

Regina studied the car. "How do you know that?"

"I've told you about my buddy, Marcus, right?"

Marcus and Damon were inseparable as boys, pledging to go to law school and into practice together. Marcus didn't finish college, though, and the two lost touch in their twenties.

"That boy and his daddy spent years working on a '57 the same color as that one. It had belonged to Marcus's grandfather but hadn't run for twenty years. They were fixing it up for Marcus to have when he went off to college."

"How did it look?"

Damon had a faraway look as he gazed at the car. "A lot like that, but it never ran. Marcus's father was killed in a hit-and-run upstate. Marcus couldn't handle being around the car after that, so he sold it." Damon paused before adding, "He probably drank away whatever he got for it."

Felix waved at them, then went back to polishing. "I'm going to go have a look," Damon said, gesturing to the car.

Regina said she would find Walt. And she did. At his desk in the back of the garage. He looked up and smiled, and it felt as if they were two old friends meeting up after a short time away.

"Regina," he said warmly as he came around the desk and shook her hand. Then he glanced past her. "Where is Mr. Palmer?"

"He's admiring the car that Felix is working on."

"Ahh, the Ford. It's an absolute beauty, isn't it?"

"Damon certainly thinks so. The only thing that would make it better would be if it belonged to Beyoncé."

The hint of red in Walt's cheeks made Regina wonder if the car actually might be.

"C'mon now, Walt. If that whip is Beyoncé's, you need to tell me."

Yep, his cheeks were definitely pink. "No, no," he blurted. "Nothing like that."

The man didn't feel comfortable discussing his customers. Fair enough. Regina had served a few celebs over the years. Success in the New York restaurant scene depended on good but understated service. Don't fawn over stars. Don't call attention to their presence. If they called attention to themselves, it was one thing, but for her or her staff to do it was another thing entirely. Walt's approach was similar.

He returned to his desk and opened a drawer. "Would you like the keys to look around a bit?"

"Let's talk first. Damon has some questions." She looked through the large glass windows at the front of the shop where Damon was mid-story as Felix continued to polish. "If I can pull him away from that car."

She went to the door, pushed it open, and waited until Damon finished his story about his friend Marcus's long-ago car.

"I've always wondered what happened to it after he sold it," he mused.

Felix waved when he spotted Regina, then, to Damon, "If it's like most cars of that era, it was crashed or rusted out." He wiped at a smudge on the hood ornament. "If everyone had held onto them, there wouldn't be much business for Walt and me, now would there?"

Damon laughed. "Good point, man." He turned and walked to where Regina was waiting. "Are we ready, boo?"

"I told Walt we wanted to talk about the agreement."

He came close and lowered his voice. "Want to guess who that Fairlane belongs to?"

"Beyoncé?"

Damon snorted. "Wouldn't that be cool? Nah, it belongs to Tony Sampson. He was two years ahead of me in law school. He has his own practice in Baltimore. Must be doing pretty good for himself." He glanced back at Felix, then whispered, "Mickens's boy back there said this was the third car they've done for him." He shook his head. "I'm still chasing the dream while Tony's living it. Doesn't seem fair, does it?"

Regina wrapped her arm around his and squeezed. "Baby, play that game. You're doing fine. You have enough work to keep you busy. There's food on the table and a roof over your head."

"You sound like my daddy." He laughed. "I'm not in Tony's league, but someday maybe. Alice might bring in some business. She promised to send her friends my way."

Regina wasn't sure if more clients like Alice would be a good thing. The woman's family battles continued to escalate, and she assumed her retainer meant she could call anytime. Damon wasn't complaining, though, and when Regina sneaked a peek at his checkbook a couple days before, the numbers were impressive.

His cheerfulness dissolved as they made their way to Walt's office. He was putting on his game face. Regina had seen it before. Even though they were still in the looking phase, Damon took meetings seriously. He showed up prepared and ready to fight if necessary. It seemed almost unfair, as Walt probably expected nothing beyond a friendly conversation. For Damon, there was no such thing. That was okay, though, because it was a big step, and there would be plenty of time for friendly conversations after the paperwork was signed.

If it was signed. Regina still had worries, but then, she'd always worried when it came to big decisions. Damon was the opposite. He could close a deal and sleep like a baby.

That guardedness she had seen in Walt on their first visit returned when Damon entered the office. They shook, and when he referred to Damon as Mr. Palmer, Damon didn't cut through the formality. He pulled the envelope from his coat pocket and unfolded and smoothed the single-page proposal Walt had given Regina the week before.

"I suppose you found that to be pretty straightforward," Walt said.

"Not what I usually see in New York. One-page agreements might have worked great back when that Fairlane out front was new, Mickens, but today? Not so much."

Walt didn't flinch. He sat back and waited to hear more. Damon removed his pricy Montblanc pen and used it to point to parts of the proposal as he spoke.

"Like here. You're not specific as to what improvements you'll take care of and which are left to Regina."

Walt shrugged. "I figured we could put our heads together and determine what's needed. My expertise doesn't extend to restaurants, so I'll need help."

"Yeah, but we can't sign anything without knowing how much she's on the hook for."

"Of course not. Mr. Palmer, I've always taken an informal approach to matters of business. Some would say that it could be to my detriment, but I've found most everyone I come across to be honorable." He turned to

Regina. "If you are interested in pursuing this, we can call in a local contractor and the two of you can meet and discuss your needs."

"Paid for by who?" Damon asked.

"I'll do what is necessary to make the space functional. Flooring, walls, that kind of thing. Beyond that will be Regina's responsibility."

Damon studied Walt across the desk for several moments. Walt held his gaze. It was, Regina knew, another of those little tests of dominance that people in Damon's line of work frequently played. Walt was unfazed. He had said what he felt needed to be said. The ball was back in their court.

"Call your contractor friend, Walt," Regina said suddenly. "Perhaps he can see us this weekend?"

Damon snapped his head in her direction. "Regina? There's still more to discuss."

"And we will. But let's start with the building. If we can't make it work, there's no need to talk about the other stuff." She looked across the desk. "Walt?"

He already had his phone in hand. "I'll call him."

"What if we want a second estimate?" Damon said quickly.

"Then you should get one," Walt said as he punched in a number. The conversation between Walt and the person on the other end of the line was formal as if they weren't close friends. Walt mentioned a previous meeting, then asked about availability. While they spoke back and forth, Damon's phone rang. He checked the number, then excused himself. He was in a far corner of the garage, engaged in his call, when Walt lowered his phone.

"He rarely works on Sunday, but since you're in town, he'll come by tomorrow morning at nine. Will that work?"

"Of course, and give him my thanks."

Walt finished the call and looked toward the garage where Damon was still on his call. "What changed your mind?" he asked, his calm smile returning.

"I'm not sure. And, for the record, my mind isn't completely made up. A lot will depend upon what the contractor says. Money is a big factor." She shook her head and smiled. "A factor as in, I don't have much of it."

"I understand. And since we're being transparent, I've only met the contractor a couple times. He's new to the area. His grandfather and he are partners, and from what I've heard, they're quite good." He glanced at Damon again. "I want you to know that I'm not trying to deceive you."

"Walt, please don't get the wrong idea about Damon. He's looking out for my best interest."

Walt nodded but didn't speak.

"I've gotten walked on by a few people in recent months, and he wants to make sure it doesn't happen again."

He leaned in and placed his elbows on the desk. "I won't take advantage of you, Regina. It's not my way. Plus, how uncomfortable would it be for us to be working practically side by side and be at odds?" He motioned toward the garage where Damon was slipping his phone into his pocket. "Now, if I can just convince Mr. Palmer of that, we'll be in a good place."

Damon was distracted when he returned. He looked askance at Walt as if he wished he wasn't there, then said, "Regina, can we speak privately?"

Walt stood up and moved toward the door. "You stay here. I need to go inspect Felix's work." He closed the door as he left.

"Damon, what's wrong?"

"I need to get to Myrtle Beach by tonight."

"What happened?"

"Alice's grandson, Richard, showed up at their summer home. He insisted the property manager give him a key. Apparently, he and his wife had a falling out, and he's planning on staying for a couple weeks."

"No, Damon. I need you this weekend. Can't that wait until Monday?"

He shook his head. "I need to make my presence known, Regina. Her family needs to know that the old rules don't apply anymore."

"Send the police. He's trespassing. They'll know what to do."

"Can't do that. I need to handle this myself. Let's talk to Mickens and see if we can reschedule in a couple of weeks."

He was opening the office door when Regina stood up. "No. I'm not going."

He closed it again. "What do you mean? You want to go back to the city? Do you want me to drop you off at the airport in Salisbury?"

"No, Damon. I want to pursue what we came here for."

Damon rolled his eyes without realizing it, but Regina caught it and wondered about the thoughts behind it. Was she coming across as a petulant child? Did she need to have things her way or no way?

And if that was the case, so what? They had made the trip for one reason, and by gosh, she wanted to pursue it to the end. And if that meant two more Ubers, a bus, and a train, so be it.

"I'm staying here. I'll meet with the contractor in the morning."

"What do you know about buildings and stuff?" Damon countered.

"What do *you* know?" Regina answered quickly.

He looked at her for a few moments while he considered his next move. It wasn't like he had a lot of them. He couldn't force her to go with him. He had to either go to Myrtle Beach or stay with her.

He chose Myrtle Beach.

"I'll get things straight with Mickens," he said. "I'll make sure he watches out for you."

"Damon, I don't need watching. I'm a grown woman, you know?"

He sighed and shook his head. "I'm sorry, boo. That was out of line. But I really need to hit the road. It's five hundred miles. I can get there by eleven tonight and do what I need to do."

———

WALT COULDN'T KEEP himself from trying to catch a glimpse of Regina and Palmer as he chatted with Felix. They usually left at midday on Saturdays, but Felix had asked for a few hours of overtime to catch up on Christmas bills.

"That one's a blowhard," Felix said with a nod toward Damon Palmer.

"Perhaps," Walt said. "Not that much different from some of our clientele, though. They want you to know they've made it."

Felix measured his words as he always did when they were talking about other people. Walt never dabbled in that kind of gossip, and Felix knew it. He also knew how much he could say before Walt would bring the conversation to an abrupt end.

"In his case, I don't sense he's made it yet. There's

something...off about him. Why was he trying to impress a nobody like me?"

"You're not a nobody, Felix." Walt patted his shoulder. "You're an important part of this enterprise."

That was Felix's clue to change the subject. He moved on to Philadelphia Eagles football, a subject in which Walt had only a passing interest. He had to admit that he had sensed much the same about Damon. Control was important. Maybe it was a lawyer thing. There hadn't been many dealings with attorneys. The owner of the Fairlane was one, but you would never know it by the way he dressed and acted when he came to town. There was also Cisco Yount, who had an office across the road next to the storage place. Cisco could barely scrape two nickels together by the end of the month, but it never stopped him from bragging about one big case or another.

It had been fifteen minutes since he'd given up his office. He was starting to wonder if they were getting cold feet again, but when he turned for a quick look, Palmer was coming out.

"Mickens, I've been called away. Regina is staying." He turned to see if Regina could hear. Satisfied she couldn't, he said, "I would appreciate it if you kept an eye on her."

What a curious request. Regina Cole was perfectly capable of holding her own. There was no need to butt heads with Damon, though, so Walt nodded. "Certainly."

Regina came out, and the two of them went to Damon's car. She returned a few moments later with an overnight bag. She looked lost standing next to the building, and Walt wanted very much to, as Damon had said, keep an eye on her. He also knew that she wasn't the lost little girl she resembled at the moment. Her strength was under the surface, not visible, but always there. It was easy to tell with some people, and Regina Cole was one of them.

"I guess you're stuck with me," she said.

Walt took her bag. "Felix," he said over his shoulder. "I'm going to take Miss Cole into town."

HOW COULD Damon rush off and leave her? How could he act as if everything was fine? Those were questions Walt contemplated between snippets of uncomfortable conversation on the drive into Bethany. Regina was embarrassed. She'd said something about being a burden, then said it again after Walt assured her she wasn't. Then she defended Damon's abrupt departure. Building a new practice, having to hustle clients, blah, blah, blah. It meant nothing to Walt.

Damon Palmer was one of those men who put things ahead of relationships. It was a trait that crossed the spectrum of age, race, and wealth. Rich men played golf. Poor men hustled side gigs. Some hunted and fished. Others gambled or took getaway trips with their buddies. The results were the same. Spouses or significant others defended them at first, then sought out their own interests. Reading. Church. Television or a movie, alone or maybe with a friend. Give it long enough, though, and things changed. People became bored. Resentful. Eyes wandered. Minds considered possibilities that some acted upon. Relationships fell apart. Divorces happened. Everyone lost. And in moments of sad reflection, they wondered where it all went wrong. And sadly, they rarely concluded that it all went back to commitment.

At least Walt could comfort himself with the thought

that with him and Joanie, it was never a lack of commit-ment. That would have been preferable to reality. You could become more committed, but it was a lot harder fixing what tore them apart.

"Are you okay, Walt?"

Regina's question crashed through the veil of melan-choly that Walt had foolishly allowed to settle over himself. Melancholy was an uninvited guest many Saturday after-noons. That was why he had no qualms about staying late at the shop.

Saturdays hurt the most.

Saturdays used to be family time.

"Oh, yes. Just thinking about some work matters." Time to change the subject. "Did you and Mr. Palmer have reser-vations at a local hotel?"

She winced at the mention of Damon's name. Definitely a touch of melancholy there, too. "No, we planned to play it by ear. I thought we might try the SaltAire. Michael is such a kind man."

"He is, indeed," Walt replied, resolving to bring himself fully back to the moment. He had the spare bedroom at his place. It had been years since anyone other than his mum stayed there. The cleaning service had been in two days earlier. Not that it got messy, but it was at its best. And it would give him time to learn what Regina's vision was for the restaurant. He was excited about the possibility of it being open again. And he became excited about the possi-bility of the two of them discussing it. In his living room. With a bottle of wine. And a crackling fire in the hearth.

And those possibilities were why he needed to draw the line.

He turned onto Coastal Highway toward the SaltAire.

"I'm certain Michael will have something."

WHAT ABOUT WALT WAS DIFFERENT? He was reserved, lost in his own thoughts. And while he might claim those thoughts were related to the shop, Regina was skeptical. And damn that Damon. His decision to run off to Myrtle Beach left her in a bind. She would have to depend upon Walt for the entire weekend, and while he was amenable, and certainly had something to gain if she leased the restaurant, she still felt she was putting him out. The man had to have plans for the weekend. The local women, or men, if that was his thing, wouldn't let a smart and good-looking guy be lonely for long. He must have options. She tried to imagine what circumstances had led Walt to be where he was. A recent divorce? Broken heart?

Would she find out?

Did she want to find out?

The SaltAire's familiar façade rose into view on their left. Walt pulled his pickup under the hotel awning and shut it off. "Mind if I wander in with you to make sure Michael has a room?"

There was kindness in the way he asked, which she appreciated. There were some men she'd known over the years for whom such an offer might have been a prelude to getting into her room.

"Of course." She started to open the pickup door, then remembered his chivalry. If Walt Mickens wanted to open her door, she would happily allow him to. It felt good to be doted on, even if it was by the guy her boyfriend had dumped her on.

When they entered the lobby, Michael was helping another guest. He glanced their way, smiled, and finished what he was doing.

"Miss Cole, I'm delighted to see you back." His smile didn't wane when he acknowledged Walt, but Regina could see a momentary look of confusion there.

Walt picked up on it, too.

"Miss Cole's friend, Mr. Palmer, got called away unexpectedly, Michael. I was charged with bringing her to see if you have a room."

"Oh, of course. I'm sorry to hear he won't be joining you, Miss Cole. And yes, we can put you in the same room as before."

They stepped away from the desk while Michael made the arrangements.

"Thank you for everything, Walt."

"I'm happy to help. May I collect you at half-eight in the morning for our meeting with the contractor?"

She smiled. "You sound so British sometimes."

Walt raised his arms in one of those *what can I say* gestures.

"I'll look forward to being collected at...half-eight. And thank you again for everything."

Walt turned to leave. Regina picked up her key and was nearly out of the lobby when she heard him call her name. She returned to where he waited.

"Would you consider dinner with me? Something nicer than last time?"

She hadn't considered her plans for the afternoon and beyond, other than perhaps TV and a hot bath. Had Damon not flown the coop the evening would be a lot more interesting. She had even brought a nice dress in case they did things up in Bethany Beach.

Dinner sounded wonderful. A lot nicer than delivery pizza and an old movie or TikTok videos on her phone. And, she had to admit, Walt Mickens was enjoyable company. Intriguing, and maybe a bit mysterious, too.

"I would love to join you for dinner," she answered.

They agreed on a time for Walt to pick her up. His eyes danced as they said their goodbyes. She felt her spirits lifting, too.

"Have a good evening, Michael," she called out as she passed.

"Miss Cole, a word?"

She returned to the desk. Though the lobby was empty, Michael still lowered his voice when he said, "Walt is one of the kindest people I've ever known."

"He's certainly been very kind to me," she said, not sure where the conversation was leading. She stepped away, but Michael wasn't done.

"I know him well, Miss Cole. And while I've enjoyed meeting you, there's much I don't know about you."

Okay, this was getting weird.

Regina said nothing. This was his show.

"I heard you making plans, and I just wanted to say, please don't hurt Walt."

What the... "Michael, we're going to dinner. That's all. He's being nice because that's what he does."

She hoped her tone made it clear. *Do not get into my business.*

"I understand. Have a good evening, Miss Cole."

SHE ENTERED the lobby and spotted Walt seated near the door. He grinned as he stood to greet her, handsome in dark slacks and a leather jacket over a light blue open-collar shirt.

"Regina, you look radiant."

Wow! He's good. Did they teach that stuff in England?

His words made her feel tingly inside. Damon was quick with a compliment, but there was something in the way Walt's eyes took in every inch of her, appreciating her before speaking.

"You clean up pretty good yourself."

Seriously? Was that the best she could do? You clean up pretty good? Do better, girl. You're from New York, not some Texas dude ranch.

Walt chuckled, then offered his arm. They walked to his car.

"No station wagon?" she teased as she got into the white Toyota. He closed her door and made his way to the other side.

"The wagon went home with its owner," he answered as they drove off. "I booked a table at a place in Rehoboth Beach." He glanced at her as they pulled onto Ocean Highway. "The choice was a difficult one. It's not often that my dinner guest is an actual chef."

"You did pretty well last time," she said.

He laughed. "Burgers and beer are easy. But tonight is more upscale. I hope it meets your expectations."

"I wouldn't worry about that, Walt. Tonight is more about the company than the food, anyway."

What the hell? Where did that come from, Regina? More about the company than the food? He probably thinks you're hitting on him.

"Perhaps we can be successful on both fronts," he responded simply. A nice way to let her off the hook.

It was dark, and traffic was light on the drive to Rehoboth Beach. Walt explained how the Delaware and Maryland beaches were basically a chain of interconnected small towns, sharing little beyond the ocean itself. Rehoboth and Ocean City, Maryland, were larger and offered more nightlife, while the smaller resort towns, like Bethany, were quieter and more relaxed.

Regina enjoyed his travelogue and getting to learn about an area that might become her home. The twenty minutes it took to reach Rehoboth Beach's picturesque boardwalk passed quickly. Walt pulled into a parking space and pointed out a small outdoor amphitheater on their right.

"The Rehoboth Beach bandstand. My grandparents brought me with them to see a Barry Manilow tribute show when I was in seventh grade." He grinned as he added, "Some kids from school spotted me. I'm still living it down."

"I feel your pain." Regina laughed. "But if it makes you feel better, I kinda like Barry Manilow. The guy knows his way around a love song, doesn't he?"

"That he does."

Their walk to the restaurant took them along Rehoboth's expansive boardwalk, past a patchwork of storefronts. Other than a french fry stand and a couple of saltwater taffy shops, everything was closed for the evening. The Atlantic roared in the darkness as unseen waves crashed the shore.

A sudden breeze made Regina shiver. Her thin cover-up was proving inadequate for the nighttime dip in temperature. Walt noticed and removed his jacket. Before she could utter a protest, he had placed it over her shoulders. The dark leather was soft to the touch. Its scent was masculine but without the overpowering smell of cologne or soap. She imagined his house smelled the same.

She smiled at him. "Thank you."

They silently enjoyed the surroundings until reaching the restaurant. The establishment's name, Ivory, was displayed on a small, tasteful sign over the entrance. The place was smaller than Gasconade, and the entry was more dated. Regina suspected most seashore restaurants strived for a nautical or coastal theme, but Ivory's décor felt like a grand restaurant from the 1960s. Darker colors, thick white tablecloths, and servers in jackets and ties. Walt presented himself to the maître d' and within a few moments, they were escorted to a corner table with a view of the boardwalk.

"You come here often?"

"A few times a year. Client meetings mostly." He picked up the wine list, considered it for a moment, then handed it to Regina. "I'll put myself in your hands this evening."

The list was impressive, with a delightful combination of domestic and imported vintages, including selections from a couple of local wineries. There would be no trouble finding something good. Their server, a middle-aged man named Carl, handed them thick leather-bound menus.

"Any specials?" she asked.

"Yes, ma'am. We have a delightful shrimp and blue crab salad. There's also pan-seared salmon with spring-pea risotto and a roasted half-duck with potato hash and wild mushrooms."

"What do you recommend?"

Carl smiled. "Our crab cakes are the best you'll find. They're typically served with mashed potatoes and haricots verts, but with the latter not quite in season, I recommend the pickled beets."

Regina raised an eyebrow. "Haricots verts are out of season, but beets aren't?"

"Notice I said *pickled*. Our chef prepares them using an

old family pickling process. They're stored in our basement until served."

"Then I'll have the crab cakes, mashed potatoes, and those enticing pickled beets."

Carl's cheeks were pink with delight. "You will not be disappointed." He turned to Walt. "And you, sir?"

The tone of Walt's cheeks rivaled Carl's. "I usually order a steak and baked potato, but I'm moving in a faster crowd this evening." He laid his menu on the table. "Whatever Miss Cole recommends is what I'm having."

Regina returned her attention to the menu. "The grilled filet would be the safe choice, but how about stepping out of your comfort zone, Walt?"

He nodded and motioned for her to continue. Carl watched with delight as she studied the menu.

"How is the sauce in your chicken francaise, Carl?"

"Sumptuous. Lemon butter, white wine, and some magical secret ingredient that our chef swears he'll take to his grave."

"Perfect. Bring that for Mr. Mickens. And I'm assuming you can recommend wine, too."

It was Christmas, Easter, and the Fourth of July rolled into one for dear Carl. He reviewed the wine list and bantered back and forth with Regina until they settled on a choice. Carl floated off toward the kitchen.

"I think he's in love with you," Walt said with a wink.

"Hopefully, I gained his respect and he'll tell the chef. The chef will make sure his crew prepares everything to perfection."

"I would never have considered the chicken, but now I can't wait."

Regina pointed a finger at him. "You're okay with sharing, right?"

"With you?"

"No, silly, with the people sitting in the bar. Of course, I mean with me. I'm dying to try the sauce. Maybe I can figure out the secret ingredient."

Walt grinned like a schoolboy caught making mischief. "Well, okay. Provided you don't take more than your share."

Carl returned with the wine. He poured a small amount into a glass and handed it to Regina, aware that it was her opinion that mattered. She sipped, smiled, and handed it across to Walt who did the same.

"You like?" she asked.

He nodded his approval. Carl poured and departed.

"If I said half the things you said," Walt said, "the server would think I'm hard to please. With you, he's tripping all over himself to make a good impression."

"Foodies know foodies. And I'll bet that at some point he'll ask me what restaurants I've worked at."

"I won't touch that bet, Regina. But I'm curious, too. You're certainly more knowledgeable than anyone I know. What's your background?"

She sipped her wine and gathered her thoughts. He deserved more than the glossed-over version that left out the bad stuff, but how much more? She decided to lay out the basics and see where things went from there. How she'd developed her love for cooking as a kid, school, first jobs. He listened intently and was fully present.

Maybe too much so.

She'd just mentioned Gasconade when Carl returned with their food. While the presentation wasn't on par with what she preferred, the mixture of colors and aromas made up for it. And the portions were more than what Gasconade patrons were used to. The crab cakes were large and broiled to a light brown. Their delicate coating gave way to her fork, exposing lump crab meat with little filler.

"Tartar sauce?" Carl asked.

Regina cast a disapproving glance. "Do they need tartar sauce?"

"No, madam. But some guests prefer it." He paused uncertainly before asking the big question.

"You seem so...*knowledgeable*, madam. Are you perchance a restaurant operator yourself?"

"No." Regina glanced across the table and winked at Walt, who was hanging on every word. "But I might be soon."

"Promise me you'll let me know the name and location," Carl said, his voice lower and more intimate. "It would be an honor to dine at any establishment you oversee."

"If you move to Bethany, you'll have to fight him off with a stick," Walt kidded after Carl had departed. "Maybe you should consider hiring him away."

After making sure he was out of earshot, Regina whispered, "He's delightful, but not for the kind of place I run."

"Will it be like your previous restaurant?"

Something about the question caused Regina's stomach to churn. Was it the pain of her separation from Gasconade? The looming court battle?

The shattering of her confidence?

She mentally grasped at straws until she knew what bothered her.

Walt knew she wasn't currently employed. He'd referred to Gasconade as her previous restaurant. She had never mentioned her current situation. She looked up from her plate and found him staring at her. What was up with that?

Then she remembered. He'd asked her a question. Would a new place in Bethany be similar to Gasconade?

"Gasconade was more of an upscale farm-to-table restaurant.

A good answer. Generic. No clues given as to what had transpired there.

And then Walt dropped the bomb.

"It was tragic what happened to you there."

Regina dropped her fork. It bounced against her plate, sending a dollop of mashed potatoes skyward before hitting the floor. Carl was on the fork like a lineman on a fumble. He produced a fresh one and placed it next to her plate before stepping away.

Regina locked eyes with Walt. "How did you... Have you been looking into my past?"

"Not at all, Regina."

"Did Javier Rocha call you? If he did, Damon will—"

Walt raised his hands in front of him. "No one called me."

"Then how do you know about Gasconade?"

"Felix came across a story in the *City Beat Investigator*. They still maintain an active classified advert section, and he sometimes finds cars for sale that he can restore and resell." He leaned in closer so as not to be overheard by diners at a nearby table. "I would never purposefully dip into your past."

He sounded genuine, but Regina had learned in recent months that some people could sound sincere without being sincere. She cocked her left eye and smiled as she asked, "Even if they might lease your restaurant?"

Walt laughed. "I knew everything I needed to know about you the afternoon we met. Food is your life's calling.

It was obvious in the way you moved about the kitchen and cleaned up all that old equipment."

"You should have been taking better care of that, you know?" she teased. She reached across the table and patted his hand, drawing away his attention while she moved in with a fork in her other hand to snag a bite of his chicken francaise. She shoved it in her mouth and savored it for a few moments before returning for more. "The crab cakes are perfect, but this might be better," she said through a mouthful. "Want to trade?"

Walt made a show of sliding his plate out of reach as if protecting something important. "I thought we were sharing. You've not exactly been forthcoming with any crab cake."

They spent the next few minutes sampling from each other's plates. It was, Regina thought, not the kind of thing one did in a more exclusive restaurant like Ivory, but darn it, they were having fun. And when Walt beat her to the last bite of crab cake, she laughed and waved her fork at him menacingly. A man in an executive chef's uniform entered the dining room with a flourish and looked around before his gaze settled on Regina. He made a beeline for their table.

"Madam, my waiter overheard you state to your dinner partner that you were hopeful of figuring out what makes my sauce so unique." He motioned with his chin toward Walt's empty plate. "I'll have you know that many have tried, but none have succeeded. I will indulge you if you choose to make a guess, but I was thinking a small wager might make things interesting."

His accent and frankness screamed New Jersey. And there was something in the way he spoke, perhaps the hint of a challenge, that Regina couldn't pass up. She glanced at the name stitched on the front of his uniform. "Chef Daniel, what kind of wager are you thinking?"

"I have a sink full of dishes and a dishwasher who didn't show up tonight. Can I assume you know something about running a dishwasher?"

"Perhaps," Regina said slowly, trying to sound less confident than she felt. "And if I guess your secret ingredient?"

"Dinner's on me."

Regina glanced at Walt as she considered the proposal. He and Carl had become interested bystanders as the wager took shape. Walt shrugged. It was her decision.

"Let's go for it. But Chef Daniel, I don't want to expose your secret ingredient for everyone to hear. It could have a disastrous effect on your business."

His laugh would have been perfect for a Western movie villain. "It won't matter because you will be wrong, but if you wish to whisper it in my ear, madam, we can do it your way."

CHEF DANIEL WAS INCREDIBLY POMPOUS. Walt had, as people in the UK would say, little time for him. The grin on his face as he bent over to hear Regina's whispered guess said it all. It was a con as old as the world. A shell game without shells, a game of chance with no chance for Regina. Undoubtedly, whatever secret ingredient she whispered would be wrong.

Then again, maybe not. She winked at Walt, and he wondered if the field was as tilted in Chef Daniel's favor as he'd suspected. The drama built as she learned close to the chef and cupped a hand to his ear to keep them from hearing what she said. She resembled a slightly larger version of a little girl in the schoolyard sharing secrets with a trusted friend. Whatever she said was short, no longer than a word or two. The moment that followed was shorter still. Less than a second. Chef Daniel's grin melted away. His eyes narrowed. Walt hadn't played much poker, but he could spot another person's tell, and he'd just witnessed Chef Daniel's.

Regina nailed it.

The chef's grin returned, but it was too late. Too late to fool Walt. Too late to fool Carl.

Definitely too late to fool Regina.

"That's not it!" Chef Daniel snapped.

"It absolutely is," Regina said calmly.

"Not even close."

They were at an impasse. Regina knew she was right, but she weighed that against causing a scene in the middle of a busy restaurant. Walt wondered if she would let it go or push back. Piles of dirty dishes hung in the balance.

"What do you think it is?" A fifty-something woman asked from a nearby table. "I've been trying to figure out for years how they make their incredible sauce."

Regina smiled as she turned back to Chef Daniel. "Shall I tell her?"

He raised his hands in an *I don't care* gesture, but there was something different about his countenance. He thought before responding, and in that moment's hesitation, Walt knew Regina had won. And then she helped him save face.

"Maybe I'm wrong," she answered the woman. "I had an idea, but the more I think about it, I'm not so sure."

Chef Daniel nodded his approval, then scurried away.

Before they could discuss what had happened, Carl

returned with dessert menus. He beamed at Regina. "I heartily recommend the bananas foster. The Basque cheesecake is delicious, too."

"Oh, gosh," Regina said. "Dessert sounds good, Carl, but I'm stuffed."

"Same here," Walt echoed.

"You don't understand," Carl said. "Dessert is complimentary." He glanced toward the kitchen. "Your meals are complimentary. Danny—Chef Daniel—insists." Carl leaned in and whispered, "Take it! He never does that. The governor was in a few weeks ago, and Danny wouldn't even comp his meal."

Regina grinned at Walt. "In that case, he'll have the bananas foster, and I'll have the cheesecake."

TEMPERATURES HAD DROPPED FURTHER when they left the restaurant. Walt again placed his jacket over her shoulders. It was going to be a chilly two blocks for him, and when Regina leaned into him, he didn't resist. And when he put his arm around her shoulders, she didn't resist either. Quite the contrary. She fit nicely there. He wasn't as tall as Damon, and his arm didn't come at her from up above, but more straight across. A good fit, indeed.

"When did you know you had him?" Walt asked as they strolled along the boardwalk.

"As soon as I tasted the sauce. I've experimented with ingredients enough to recognize how they interact. It wasn't hard. Had he not made a spectacle of himself, I would have let it go completely."

"You allowed him to keep his secret. That was quite gracious."

"He's a talented chef. There's no doubt about that. But with that cocky attitude, he wouldn't last a week in the city." Regina turned her face toward the surf. A cool but refreshing mist pricked her cheeks. "A girl could get used to evening strolls along the beach." She glanced at her hand. And sometimes escaping the city is just what a girl needs, too."

They strolled silently for a few moments. Regina liked how Walt didn't feel the need to fill every moment with conversation. She was shivering despite the weight of his coat. Not him, though. His arm remained steady on her shoulders. Still a good fit. Still nice.

"I'm sorry for what I said earlier," he whispered. "About your work in New York."

She turned so she could see his profile in the dim light of the lamps lining the boardwalk. He looked straight ahead, unaware she was studying him. Why had she thought there might be some ulterior motive to his comments? Had she grown so cynical that she couldn't see an act of kindness?

"No apology needed, Walt. I was out of line in the way I responded. It's... There's been so much..." What was she trying to say? Just because she couldn't trust some men didn't mean she had to be rude to a nice guy like Walt. "Sorry for the way I responded. You didn't deserve that."

Many men would have considered that an opening to probe further. They would have pushed for more information or brought up her injury. Walt wasn't one of them.

He motioned toward the parking lot. "That's us."

He didn't remove his arm from her shoulder until they were at the car. The sigh that escaped Regina's lips was louder than she'd intended. If he noticed, he didn't mention it. They kept the conversation light on the drive back to Bethany. It was just past the city limits when Regina had a thought.

"Can we drive out and see the restaurant?"

There were no questions about why she would want to see it at night. Or complaints about having already taken up so much of his time. He didn't hesitate at all.

"Certainly."

The road leading out of town was still busy at 10 p.m. Most of the traffic was, like them, heading out of Bethany. Regina mentioned it. Walt filled in the details.

"The bars and clubs along the beach stay busy on week-ends. More locals than tourists until summer. A lot of people from Georgetown and Dover avoid the beach during the winter."

"Can that work for a restaurant out here?"

"I believe so. Locals won't throw their money around as much as the summer crowd, but they recognize value."

"Would someone from say...Georgetown recognize the value of macadamia-crusted salmon with a cucumber mint salad?"

Regina liked how he weighed his reply. She watched the scenery fly by as she waited.

"Never underestimate locals," he finally answered. "The beach crowd definitely helps new businesses get off the ground, but it's the locals who sustain them."

"Help me understand."

"Bethany and the other beach towns are mobbed with tourists from July Fourth through Labor Day. They crowd the beaches and fill up the restaurants. Even the worst of the restaurants make it in summer. Come late September though, the tourists are gone. Back to Philly or Baltimore or

Washington. For eight months, you depend upon locals. There are some places that don't even try. They board up the windows and head south for the winter. Those that stick it out and thrive year-round learn how to attract locals."

"That's my hope, too. Assuming we can make this work."

Regina could barely see the restaurant when they pulled into the parking lot. Other than a few security lights around the perimeter, the place had an almost eerie, abandoned feel about it. The night sky was foggy, and the unlit Three Mile Mille's sign loomed over the building like a ghost. Regina leaned forward for a better look.

"Does it still work?"

"Hard to say," Walt said with a shrug. "Armand had a neon sign guy from Wilmington come down and inspect it. He was hoping to get it back in working order again. The guy said he could do it, but it wouldn't be cheap."

"Would you be okay with having it removed?"

The question troubled Walt. "I suppose so. I was kind of hoping someone might consider reopening as Three Mile Millie's. There's so much history. People stop by almost every week to share stories of eating there when they were kids."

"The memories are sweet, Walt, but it wouldn't fit what I want to do with the place."

He avoided a reply as they got out and approached the front. It was incredibly desolate at night. People wanted to feel safe when they stopped for dinner. Could that be achieved? Walt unlocked and stepped in ahead of her to turn on the lights. The illumination helped, but the parking lot was still gloomy and uninviting. Exterior lighting would be a must.

Everything appeared different inside, too. The harsh fluorescent in the dining room was more intense at night, like exiting a darkened movie theater into bright sunlight.

Walt squinted as he moved to the center of the room. "It's been a while since I was in here at this time of night."

Regina returned to the door and switched off one of the three switches that controlled the lighting. Then a second. With one-third of the lighting, the place still glowed like a beacon on a hill. It was better, though. She moved to a side wall and knocked on the paneling. A hollow sound echoed through the room.

"Walt, do you have a crowbar?"

"Excuse me?"

"A crowbar. I want to see what's behind the walls?"

He went next door to his shop, returning a moment later with the requested tool. He approached the spot where Regina had knocked on the wall, considered his next step, and handed it to her. "I'm not sure I can bring myself to do it."

"But you're okay if I do?"

He nodded tentatively. Regina didn't wait for him to reconsider. She jammed the forked end of the crowbar into a seam and pushed it to the side. A chunk of cheap pine paneling fell away from the wall, revealing framing and, beyond that, a section of aged brick. Regina clapped her hands with delight. "Just what I was hoping to find!"

"How did you know?"

"Your shop has brick walls. At some point, they were painted white, but I assumed that someplace under this awful paneling, the restaurant was the same. What do you think?"

"I think it's... What do you think, Regina?"

"It's lovely. And perfect. And do you want to know

something else?" She looked at the drop ceiling. "I bet that whatever is up there is perfect, too. Will you get me a ladder?"

"I...I took it home earlier this week to do some work around the house."

Regina scrambled onto a chair and pointed to a table. "Hold it while I climb up and have a look."

He did. And she did.

She popped a ceiling tile out of the grid but was still too low to see. "Maybe if we put another table on top of this one I'll be able to—"

"Gosh no, Regina. You'll break your neck. I have a better idea. Crawl back down. I'll be right back. "

He returned with a selfie stick attached to his cellphone. "We use this for overhead shots of the cars we're working on." He extended the stick and turned on the phone's spotlight. Even extended, the device was a couple feet short.

"I'll climb back up," Regina said. Once in place, she turned on the phone's video option and extended it into the ceiling. After moving it about for a few moments, she pulled it back, disconnected the selfie stick, and reviewed the video. "Oh, my gosh, Walt, look at this!" She handed the phone down.

Walt replayed the video and gasped at the sight of row upon row of decorative ceiling tiles. "I had no idea."

"Probably original," Regina said from up above. "Any idea when the place was built?"

"Early 1930s."

She clapped again. "Definitely original. I'm liking this better and better!" Her clapping caused the table to shake.

"Regina, come down before you fall." He held out his arms, and she allowed him to place his hands around her waist.

She felt weightless in his grasp. The muscles in his lower arms and biceps bulged but didn't strain. It was incredibly sexy, and she had to reset her thoughts to drop ceilings and cheap paneling. He gently placed her on the floor and allowed his hands to linger at her waist. Their faces were a foot apart. Regina knew she needed to take a step back, but her thoughts had other ideas.

Those ideas were erased by Damon's voice breaking the silence. "When I said keep an eye on her, this ain't what I had in mind."

sunday, june 8

TENSION during the previous night's ride to the SaltAire was thick enough to cut with a knife. Damon remained quiet at first, waiting for Regina to apologize. She hadn't, though. There was nothing to apologize for. The things she'd felt as Walt held her in the air were best left inside, but nothing had happened between them.

"Don't you trust me?" she calmly asked after he'd made a comment about how it looked to walk in and find her in Walt's arms.

"Well, yeah, but..." He'd started off on a tangent about how eyewitness accounts were so important in court, but she cut him off real fast.

"This isn't court, Damon. It's us. You either trust me or you don't."

He didn't say much else. When they reached the hotel, she succumbed to his advances, and they'd made slow, silent love that left them too exhausted to argue. He woke up happy and ready to take on the day.

"You say this contractor is Mickens's friend? Can we trust him?"

"They're not friends, exactly. More like acquaintances. And Walt is paying for some of the renovations, so if the guy's bid is high, he pays too."

Damon muttered something about kickbacks and collusion but brightened as they enjoyed a sumptuous country breakfast in the SaltAire's lobby restaurant. Michael greeted them warmly from his usual spot behind the registration desk. Regina made introductions and picked up on Michael's relief that she was with a man other than Walt. What was up with that? Why did Michael feel the need to protect a man who was strong and at peace with his life?

"Nice guy," Damon said as they headed for the parking lot. "How did you find the place?"

The last thing she wanted to say was that it was Walt's suggestion. "I heard about it somewhere or other."

The ride out of Bethany was pleasant. Sunny skies and low-eighties temperatures offered a glimpse of what life might be like during the height of tourist season. A steady stream of cars passed on their way toward town. How many of them might have stopped at a roadside restaurant in the middle of no place? The prospect of finding out made Regina giddy.

But what if the contractor said the place was beyond repair? What if the job was too big? Or he didn't have time in his schedule? What would she do if the walls and ceilings were concealing layers of asbestos?

What if Walt decided it wasn't worth it?

Think positive thoughts, Regina. You've come this far.

Don't allow those doubts to creep in now.

You can do this!

"Let me handle the contractor." Damon's words pierced her doubts. It would be easy to let him, but that wasn't how Regina wanted things to play out.

"No, Damon. I'll be involved in the discussions."

"But you don't know how these people can be. I deal with this stuff every day."

"I know restaurants. And I know what I want this place to be."

It wasn't often that she came back at him with such certainty. Damon glanced at her, then did a double take. "Okay, but when it gets to the legal stuff, I'll—"

"Damon, I'm not a child!"

His eyes grew large at the sharpness in her tone. Regina might've owed him an apology, but none would be coming. Not after he'd left her high and dry to run off to Myrtle Beach. What had happened with that, anyway? There was no better time than the present to find out.

"And how did you get back to Bethany so fast?"

"I didn't think you cared," he said dismissively. Then, realizing a change in direction might be necessary, he added, "The grandson was a no-show. I was on the Eastern Shore of Virginia when Alice called. I told her to get a locksmith and have the locks changed." He leveled her with a stern gaze as he said, "Unlike you, Alice takes my advice."

He just couldn't leave it alone, but Regina would be damned if she let his butthurt attitude ruin her excitement. She gazed out the window until they pulled into the restaurant parking lot. The car Walt had picked her up in the previous evening was already there, along with a beat-up pickup truck.

"Would you look at that thing," Damon said. "Hopefully that's not the contractor. Because if that beater is the best he can do, we're in trouble."

Regina's excitement was off the charts as she scrambled out of the car. She willed herself to slow down, aware of how silly it would look if she went from parking lot to restaurant in a dead run. Damon came alongside and took her hand. He pulled open the restaurant's front door and allowed her to pass through first. Walt was standing in the center of the room next to the table he'd rescued Regina from the previous evening. A pretty thirty-something brunette and an older man with a shock of white hair were with him.

"Regina. Mr. Palmer," Walt said warmly. "Come in and meet everyone."

Damon's eyes locked on the old man before shifting to Walt. His message was clear. After the previous evening, he didn't trust Walt. And the old dude was too far over the hill to take on such an ambitious renovation. Regina squeezed his hand, willing him to keep an open mind. Then, past them, she saw a stepladder in the middle of the kitchen. A set of legs was perched on the next to the top step. The rest of him or her was in the ceiling.

"This is Charlie Staley," Walt motioned to the older man. "He's still new around here, but we cross paths occasionally."

Charlie stepped forward and shook their hands. His eyes were clear and bright, and there was a hint of mischief there, too. "Two years I've been here. How long does it take to become a local?"

"I'm still trying to figure that out," Walt quipped. "Charlie has a nice place out on Vines Creek. Good fishing, I've heard."

"It is indeed," Charlie said. "Guess I'll have to get you out there sometime, Walt." He turned his attention to Regina and Damon. "Folks, this pretty lady is my granddaughter-in-law, Kate. She's more of a local than all of us. She teaches at the local college."

"Kathryn Shea-McGinnis," she said, shaking her head

as she glanced at Charlie. "Call me Kate. And don't worry about him. He's harmless."

"Yeah, but does he know anything about restaurant renovation?" Regina winced at Damon's snark, but Kate and Charlie smiled.

"He's forgotten more than the rest of us will ever know," Kate said. "I've known him two years, and he continues to amaze me."

"It's not me you have to worry about, though," Charlie added. He motioned with his thumb to the set of legs protruding from the kitchen ceiling. "I leave the real work to my grandson, Austin."

Hearing his name, the man in the ceiling descended the ladder. He was younger than Regina expected. Early twenties maybe. Nice physique, lots of hair. She looked him over, then glanced back at Kate.

"I robbed the cradle," she said with a laugh. "It was quite the scandal. Spinster college professor falls for hunky handyman."

"I built her a fence," Austin said as he joined their circle. "She liked it so much she married me." He extended his hand to Regina. "Austin McGinnis. Grandpa and I run a construction and remodeling business. Between us, we have sixty-three years of experience."

"Sixty for me and three for him," Charlie said. "But don't be deceived by my grandson's age. We have more work than we can handle. He's talented and smarter than anyone I know."

"If you're so smart, why aren't you in college?" Damon pressed. The others didn't know him well enough to pick up on the sarcasm in his tone, but Regina heard it loud and clear. She pulled her hand from his.

"Oh, I tried college, but it wasn't for me."

"Penn," Charlie said proudly. "Austin's an Ivy League boy. He finished his degree in December."

"My parents would have killed me if I hadn't," Austin added sheepishly.

Regina resisted the urge to elbow Damon in the ribs and remind him he hadn't attended a prestigious college. Fortunately, Austin spoke up before she acted on the impulse.

"Regina, I hope you don't mind that I came early to get a good look at things."

"Of course not. What do you think?"

"There's a lot of potential."

Regina wanted to jump up and down and clap her hands. But potential was one thing. Reality, another.

"I see you've already been looking at what's behind the walls and ceiling," Austin said, nodding toward the spot where she'd pulled away the paneling. "What did you think?"

"I love the brick walls." She pulled out her phone and showed everyone the picture she'd taken of the area above the drop ceiling. "If these decorative tiles are as nice as I hope they are, we really have something."

Austin studied the photo, then retrieved several of his own. "I think they're better."

Regina gasped as she looked at the pictures on his phone. His light source was better, and the intricateness of the tile was evident despite years of accumulated dirt and grime. "It's beautiful."

"From what Walt tells me, you're pretty good with a crowbar. If you want to demo the walls and ceiling, it could save a thousand or so on the cost of the job."

The feeling was like what Regina experienced when one of her culinary creations became a hit addition to the Gasconade menu. She especially liked how Austin recognized her skill and mentioned it in front of the others. *Pretty good with a crowbar!*

"When's that supposed to happen?" Damon said, stepping forward. "We've got to get back to the city."

Austin nodded. "Of course. I can get a couple guys in here to knock out the job. Once that's done, there's a lady in Lewes who is a master at restoring old ceilings. Regina, what look are you wanting to achieve? I'm assuming an industrial vibe, but I don't want to impose my ideas."

"That's it exactly," she said happily, delighted that Austin had a grasp on things. "Bare walls, lighting that takes advantage of the space while making it look bigger than it is." She glanced at the green and white checkered floor tile. "Something better than that."

"Polished concrete?" Austin asked.

"Or painted?" Regina countered.

"Painted would be nice. And easier to maintain."

For the next half hour, they disappeared into their own world as they made their way around the dining room and kitchen. Austin offered suggestions but remained attuned to Regina's ideas. He stopped occasionally to mumble comments into the voice recorder on his phone or make notes in an app. By the time they rejoined the others, Damon had stepped outside.

"Phone call," Walt said.

Austin asked, "Shall we wait for him before continuing?"

"That's not necessary," Regina replied. "He might be awhile."

"First impressions," Austin said. "The job isn't as big as I had expected. What you want, Regina, is made easier by the bones of the building. The walls, ceiling, and concrete floors. I can draw up an estimate and send it to you and Walt later this evening."

"What's your schedule look like, Austin?" Walt asked. "I know you're busy."

"Getting the demo guys here will be an issue. Those guys get scheduled out weeks in advance. Maybe Grandpa can pull some strings, but no promises."

"I'll get on it first thing tomorrow," Charlie said.

"No."

Regina's sudden objection caught the others by surprise. Was she changing her mind? Was the job too big? The location too remote?

"What?" Austin asked.

"No to hiring out the demo. I'll do it."

The room was silent. It was a big undertaking. Hard physical labor. Dust and dirt everywhere. They knew it. Regina knew it, too.

"But," she added. "I want to open July fourth weekend."

Charlie couldn't have looked more surprised if she'd said she wanted him to part the Red Sea. Austin was shaking his head before the last words were out of Regina's mouth.

"That's impossible. You're talking..." Austin pulled an old-fashioned pocket planner from the pocket of his jeans. "Four weeks."

"I prefer to think of it as twenty-six days," Regina said casually.

Charlie raised his hand. "We ain't miracle workers, Miss Cole. Austin and me are pretty busy as it is. I'm afraid you'll need to find yourself another—"

"Charlie?" Kate stepped forward. Regina had nearly forgotten she was there. She'd allowed her husband and his grandfather to take the lead, but she suddenly reasserted herself into the conversation. "Can I have a word with the two of you?"

Charlie and Austin followed her out of the restaurant.

Regina turned to Walt. "Think there's a chance?"

"Depends upon how persuasive Kate can be. If I was a betting person, I'd—"

He paused when they returned. Charlie looked grim, but Kate and Austin were smiling.

Austin held out his hand. "Four weeks."

Regina accepted his hand and ratified the deal.

"Hmph," Charlie groused.

"Grandpa had a trip planned, but he can reschedule."

"A bus trip to the Wisconsin Dells. Jane and me have been planning it for months." He paused. "Jane's my wife and Kate's best friend." He glanced at his granddaughter-in-law. "But Kate got her on the phone and explained everything, so we're delaying the trip until September. I guess the weather will be better anyway."

Austin asked, "You're going to do the demo, right, Regina?"

"I can't wait to get started. Austin, do you have a crowbar I can borrow? Walt's is kind of small for such a big job."

Their laughter made her blush. That hadn't come out exactly as she intended, but everyone knew what she meant.

"We can do better than a crowbar," Charlie said suddenly. "I might have some time to pitch in. No charge."

"Me too," Kate said. "The college is on break this week. I would love to help." She smiled at Regina. "It will give us a chance to become friends."

"Who's becoming friends?" Damon called out as he returned from outside.

"I'm going to stay and tear out the walls and ceilings," Regina said.

Damon's eyes became stony. "That's not a good idea. You don't have any experience with that kind of thing. And your hand is—"

"I need this, Damon."

His disapproval was obvious as his eyes flitted from Regina to Walt. He wanted to push back. Regina could tell. And why did he have to mention her hand? That was out of bounds. She would tell the others when she was ready. Until then, it was none of their business. But now, with Damon opening that door, she had to say something.

"Kitchen accident at my previous job. I'm getting better, though."

The last thing she wanted was their sympathy, and as she looked from Austin to Charlie to Kate, all she saw was kindness. No one glanced at her hand. No one asked if she was taking on too much.

"So, do you want the job or not?" Austin said.

"I want the job." She glanced at Charlie and Kate. "And the help."

"How will you get around? Where will you stay?" Damon wasn't giving up yet. And he had a point. She had no car, and they'd checked out of the SaltAire.

"You can have my car," Charlie said. He motioned to the parking lot. "I've got old Calvin. That's my truck. He's been with me for most of my life. I'll have Austin run me home. We'll bring the car back for you."

"That's so kind, Charlie. But I don't have a driver's license."

"Stay with us," Kate said without so much as a sideways glance at her husband. "Our place is just an old beach

143

cottage, but there's plenty of room. And I'll be around all week to play chauffeur."

Regina wanted to hug them all.

Damon was pissed at the world. "Sounds like everything is settled, then. Regina, I've got to get back. Alice needs help with some stuff. I might as well get a jump on it."

WALT LOCKED up and watched as the others loaded into Charlie's old truck. Regina and Kate crawled in back and looked as happy as two kids, squealing with delight as Charlie playfully fishtailed before leaving the parking lot. Walt's last glimpse was of Regina's untamed hair blowing in the breeze as she laughed and held onto Kate's arm as they bounced along.

God, she was beautiful.

And now it was likely she would be spending more time in Bethany. That made Walt happy. While that hint of past hurts was still there, he could tell she was special. A woman to be reckoned with. And cared for.

It didn't appear that Damon Palmer fully grasped that need. He was more intent on controlling Regina. Perhaps there had been a time when she might see through his intention and rebel against it. But time and the unfairness of life had tempered that rebellion. It was as if Regina felt she needed Damon Palmer to help set her life back on its intended path.

She didn't.

Nor, for that matter, did she need anyone. Least of all, Walt.

That thought pained him as he walked to his car and headed home.

Because, deep down, Walt wanted her to need him. At least a little.

That was why he was willing to put his money into the restoration. He had no interest in being involved with a restaurant. There was plenty to do as it was.

But he wanted Regina to succeed. Succeed beyond anyone's wildest imagination.

And he wanted to be part of it. For her. But also for himself.

Because truth be told, he was falling in love.

wednesday, june 11

FELIX TAPPED on the office door. "Everything okay, boss?"

Walt looked up from his computer. "Of course. Why do you ask?"

"It's Wednesday afternoon, and you've been cooped up in here since Monday."

"I fell behind on paperwork. And with those two new restorations coming in next week, I felt I needed to be caught up so I could help you in the shop."

Felix raised an eyebrow. "I figured that with everything going on next door, and Regina Cole being in town, you would—"

"Work first, Felix. I can't ignore my business to help get hers off the ground."

The tenor of his voice was unmistakable. Felix backed out and gently closed the door. Walt returned his attention to the computer and stared at it for a few moments before realizing that he hadn't moved the cursor in an hour. It wasn't like he was avoiding the restaurant. He'd dropped by Monday morning, spending a half hour sipping coffee and visiting with Regina and Kate while they waited for Charlie. He showed up a few minutes after eight with a pickup full of demo tools. A refuse company dropped off a dumpster about the same time. Regina grabbed a crowbar and stood in the doorway, champing at the bit to get started. Walt didn't want to interfere, so he'd gone back to the shop. When he'd returned later to check their progress, he found the three of them laughing and carrying on like old friends. His attempts to join the conversation were welcome, but he still felt like an outsider.

Then, on Tuesday, he'd texted Regina to see if she might wish to break away for lunch. Receiving no reply, he left on his own for a quick bite at the Bethany Diner a couple miles up the road, making sure that Regina and the others wouldn't see him exiting the parking lot like some loser who couldn't find a lunch companion.

So, yeah, Felix was right. It wasn't like him to stay cooped up in his office. But darn it all, he'd expected things to be different. When Armand ran the place, it was nothing for him to pop into the shop to help himself to a cup of coffee and catch up on the local comings and goings. That door swung both ways as Walt often stepped over for a quick bite or to kibbitz with the servers. Loose and informal. Time to work, but also time to relax.

Was Regina going to be all work and no play? Perhaps that was what was needed to succeed in the restaurant business. The prospect of things being all work between them made Walt sad. He'd enjoyed their time together. He'd even considered knocking off early and going over to help, but how would that look? They certainly appeared to be having a good time, but how would it look to Regina if she thought he could so easily set aside his own work to hang out and knock down some walls? She was obviously attracted to go-getters. Damon Palmer was the epitome of that. He was also a pompous ass, but perhaps those traits went together.

It was time to stop sulking. He wasn't quite ready, though. Maybe another afternoon of stewing in his own juices would do the trick. He would allow himself to daydream for the rest of the day, then come back tomorrow mentally sharp and ready to work.

The next knock on the door was lighter. Walt kept his eyes glued on the computer screen, preparing the apology Felix deserved as he waved for him to come in.

"Hi, stranger." Her voice came like a fresh breeze, clearing the funk from a lost day.

Walt looked up and smiled but restrained himself from acting like a happy puppy. "Hello, Regina. I thought you were Felix."

She stepped in and collapsed into the chair across from his desk. "It's six-fifteen, Walt. Felix left an hour ago. And besides that, he's taller than me. And he's a man. Are we that hard to tell apart?"

Walt laughed despite every attempt to remain stoic. "Of course not. I just meant that... Well, come to think of it, the way you're covered with dirt and sawdust, it might have been an honest mistake."

It was her turn to laugh. "The dirt is the least of it. I can hardly feel my arms. Swinging a crowbar is hard work. And when I'm not working on the walls I'm on a ladder pulling down the ceiling grid. Even that doesn't compare to the terror of a mummified bobcat falling out of the ceiling."

"Good lord, Regina? Are you serious?"

She nodded. "It turns out that Three Mile Millie's sponsored a men's softball team in 1968. Millie's Bobcats. I guess someone thought it would be a good idea to stuff one and make a trophy out of it. When Millie's closed, the poor thing was stuck up in the ceiling and forgotten." Regina shuddered. "Until today."

"And how do you know all of this?"

"It's mounted on an oak plaque. An inscription on the underside explains everything. Kate and I wouldn't even go back inside until Charlie promised the coast was clear. He offered to throw it in the dumpster, but I couldn't bring myself to toss the poor thing. Kate and I named it. Bartholomew Bobcat. Maybe I'll name a menu item after him to make up for all the years he spent in the ceiling."

"Perhaps you should name the restaurant in his honor," Walt said with a wink. "I can envision the sign. 'Bartholomew Bobcat's'"

Regina gave it some thought before breaking out in the giggles. "Sounds more like a strip joint than a fine dining establishment, don't you think?" She leaned forward, wincing as she placed her arms on her knees. "Perhaps you would prefer a strip joint next door. Good for business, maybe?"

Her teasing caused his cheeks to burn. "I'm not even sure that's legal. But no, the clientele I attract is more suited to a nice restaurant."

"And speaking of business," Regina said, turning serious as her eyes bored into his, "Where have you been all week? If I didn't know better, I'd think you were trying to avoid me."

"I know you've been busy, and I'm a tad bit backlogged over here. So..."

She reached across and placed her grimy right hand over his clean left hand. "We're going to be next-door neighbors, Walt. I want a neighbor who drops in and tells me who's doing what to who around town. And I want to be able to mosey in here and unload if I'm having a bad day. Are you going to be that kind of neighbor, Walt?"

God, yes. And more if you'll allow me.

Walt coughed to push away the thoughts clouding his common sense. "Of course. As I mentioned when you first arrived, I've missed having the diner next door."

"That's good, but remember, it's not a diner anymore. That's the past. Adeline will be a destination, not just a place to eat. People will—"

"Adeline?" Walt sat up in his chair.

"That's going to be the name. It was my grandmother's name, though no one ever called her that. She was Addie to all her friends and family. Sad, isn't it? Such a lovely name, and she never got to use it. Do you like it?"

Walt smiled. "Lovely indeed, but I thought you might... I mean, the sign is already up there, and—"

"Three Mile Millie's? Seriously, Walt? There's no way I can serve cavatappi pasta or grilled Tuscan porkchop at a place called Three Mile Millie's."

Walt was preparing to counter her argument when his phone buzzed. He glanced at caller ID. "Forgive me, Regina. It's business."

"I'll step out."

"No need. Just a customer checking on progress."

REGINA LISTENED as Walt walked the caller through what remained to be done on their vehicle. His easy-going manner played well with his customer, making them seem more like old friends. He wasn't some guy being kind because that was his way. Walt was someone very special. And the way he made her feel? Her thoughts took her back to Sunday night when he'd helped her off the table. And the walk along the Rehoboth Beach boardwalk when he'd offered his jacket and arm.

Why hadn't someone snatched him up?

Had it not been for Damon, there was no doubt that she would be interested.

Damon. Oh, yeah. Him. He hadn't returned her calls, and his texts were short and devoid of sentiment. He was punishing her for staying in Bethany. What would he think if he knew how much fun she was having? How much she was enjoying her burgeoning friendship with Kate, Austin, and Charlie?

What would he think of the feelings she was having for Walt?

Stop it, Regina. Stop it right now.

He wrapped up the call. "Now where were we?"

"I have a favor to ask."

He waited for her to elaborate.

"Will you teach me to drive?"

"You already know how to drive. You drove me to Wilmington."

"I need some practice with the rules of the road. I want to take the driver's test in Delaware, but I need a refresher."

"Now?"

"I was thinking tomorrow? Right after you close?"

"Don't you have work to do in the restaurant? It seems to be taking a lot of time."

There was something in the way he asked that made things clearer. "Are you feeling that I haven't been paying you enough attention the past few days, Walt?"

He waved her off, but the pink spreading across his face and neck said plenty.

"Walt Mickens, are you jealous of the time I'm spending next door?"

"Not at all. It's just... I will be delighted to help you refresh your driving skills."

Regina bounced to her feet, came around the desk, and kissed him on the cheek. "If all men were as kind as you, the world would be a better place. Now, take me back to town so I can clean up. Tomorrow will be a big day."

thursday, june 12

THE DAY MOVED at an interminable pace, but Walt didn't mind. He had regained his bearings and was fully alive. Regina came by first thing to remind him of their driving lesson. As if he would forget!

I'll slip over later to see your progress, he'd casually mentioned.

Not yet, she'd said. *We need a little more time. I want to surprise you with how far we've come.*

Charlie and Kate had shown up ready to get to work, as they had the previous three mornings. The sounds of construction, or in this case, deconstruction, seeped through the concrete wall separating Walt's office from the restaurant. Austin stopped in before lunch with a set of blueprints tucked under his arm. He had a good feeling about Austin. And Regina? Well, there was no denying his feelings for her. Keeping them to himself was more difficult.

He spent much of the day assisting Felix as they finished the restoration of a 1940 Ford pickup. Felix noticed his improved disposition, even venturing a guess that Regina's attention might be the reason for the turnaround. Walt reminded him that she was in a relationship. Felix grinned knowingly but changed the subject out of respect for his boss. Their years together had created a bond more like family than employer and employee, and while Felix might sometimes overstep his place, Walt valued him too much to be bothered.

There was no hiding the grin that spread across his face when his phone buzzed a little after four and he saw Regina's name. Felix saw it too, and started to say something, but Walt raised a finger to stop him before stepping out of earshot. "Good afternoon."

"Are you ready to see what we've done?"

"I am. Are you ready for your driving lesson?"

"First things first. Come on over."

Walt washed up in back. He tried to appear casual as he passed through the shop, but Felix watched his every move.

"Back in a bit," he said, making sure the door closed before Felix peppered him with questions.

The lot in front of the restaurant was empty. The dumpster was overflowing. Metal ceiling grid jutted out in every direction. Busted green and white tiles mingled with shards of paneling and yellowed ceiling tiles. Dust and dirt collected on the ground, but the restaurant's front door was spotless. It had been years since it looked so clean.

SHE WAS SO excited for him to see it! Yeah, the restaurant was going to be her own creation, but she knew how much it meant to Walt, too. She had wanted to clean things up before he saw what they'd accomplished over the past few days. Kate had offered to stay and help, but Regina let her off the hook. It was something she wanted to do herself. She'd spent two hours running her hands over every surface, from the rough textures of the brick walls to the smooth windows and door handles. She'd needed that time to make it hers.

Mission accomplished.

It was far from complete. Austin's work would continue until the last moment. But what Walt was about to see, the bare floors and walls, the decoratively tiled ceiling, the space itself, was a glimpse of what would be. And when she saw the wonder in his eyes as he got his first glimpse, she knew it was worth it.

She pulled open the door with a flourish. "Hello, sir. Welcome to Adeline."

He paused to take it all in. She sensed his delight. It was several moments before he spoke.

"Regina..." He shook his head in amazement. "I had no idea such beauty was hidden just out of sight."

His words touched something in her that he hadn't intended to touch. He was talking about the restaurant. How, almost by magic, they had chipped and peeled away the years to expose the beauty that the space once possessed. But there was something else. Something in the way he looked at her as he uttered those words. Had he also been speaking about her? Was it her beauty he was noticing for the first time?

And what if it was? What happened next? How did she feel about all that? It could make things messy. She'd committed herself to Damon. And he'd committed himself to her, right?

Right?

Had Damon ever said anything like that, though? He'd told her she was beautiful, but never so sincerely and completely unexpected. Darn that Walt. He was making things difficult, and he had no idea.

He stepped into the dining room, silently considering every square foot before turning to her again. "Tell me what you see."

She did.

She moved about, feeling as light as a ballerina, as she showed him the layout of the tables and the station where customers would be greeted. She demonstrated how freshly prepared dishes would make their way from kitchen to table. Seamlessly. Gracefully. Efficiently. He understood, probably because he'd developed such a flow in his shop. There were many differences between restaurants and auto shops, but more than a few similarities, too. Movement was critical to both. Hinder it, and time and money were lost.

Regina gazed at the ceiling. "The tile expert is coming next week." She shook her head sadly. "It's going to tear me up not to see the work in progress."

"You won't be here?"

"Damon texted that there's a settlement meeting with the owners of Gasconade. They're being pilloried in the media and want it to go away."

"That's encouraging."

She smiled. "That's why I want you to prep me for the driving test. I'm taking it tomorrow. If I pass, I'll be able to come and go during the renovation."

Walt offered her his arm. "Let's get started, then."

———

THE THOUGHT of Regina's departure caused a sour feeling in Walt's stomach. What was left for her in New York? Her future was that little roadside restaurant. It was

Bethany where she would reclaim her reputation. Far from the big city. Far from Damon Palmer.

He'd considered using one of the cars being restored for her driving lesson but, in the end, decided his SUV was best. She could practice in it, then take it to the motor vehicle department for her exam.

"This is unnecessary. Your driving skills are impeccable. We'll take a drive along Coastal Highway and along a few back roads to help you get comfortable. You'll pass with flying colors."

The conversation remained light as Regina concentrated on the road. Walt directed her south toward Fenwick Island and the Maryland state line. From there, they ventured west through the communities of Selbyville and Frankford before returning to Bethany. The trip was just over an hour—plenty of time for Regina to grow comfortable behind the wheel. It was a few minutes before six when they arrived back at the shop. Regina shut off the car and turned to face him.

"You are the best teacher! I'm going to ace that test."

"You certainly are. Would you like to celebrate over dinner?"

"I'm still filthy from the restaurant. Raincheck?"

"How about I cook for you? Drop me off at home and I'll get things started. You run back to Kate's, shower, change, and come back. Seven-thirty?"

She thought on it for a few moments before flashing that lovely smile. "Perfect. You don't think I'll get a ticket for driving without a license?"

Walt laughed. "I'll text you my address. As long as you stick to the side roads, you'll be fine."

THE PLACE WASN'T like Regina expected. She'd assumed that everyone lived in beachy cottages within easy walking distance of the Atlantic surf. Walt's place was west of Coastal Highway, on a narrow, woodsy road tucked in behind a strip mall. Tall, skinny evergreens surrounded the house.

Regina parked in the narrow drive and stepped onto a wooden porch that creaked under her feet. There was no doorbell, so she knocked. A motion light came on overhead as Walt pulled open the door and unlatched the screen. He wore an untucked long-sleeved t-shirt over khaki slacks that hugged his thighs. It was a pleasant view. A well-worn pair of brown boat shoes finished the ensemble nicely.

"You didn't tell me this was a casual affair," she teased.

He eyed her from head to toe, taking in the cute calf-length dress that she loved for the way it accentuated her figure without appearing overtly sexy.

He nodded appreciatively. "I'm glad I didn't. You look lovely."

They stood in the doorway for a moment, silently appreciating one another, before Walt waved her in. "Welcome to my home. I've got steaks on the grill and baked potatoes in the oven. Nothing fancy, but I don't usually get to the store until the weekend."

"It sounds perfect. I'm famished."

"Another half hour should do it. The steaks are on low. I assume you prefer medium-rare. Would you like a quick tour?"

Walt led her through the living room to the rear of the house. "This is where I spend most of my time," he said as they entered an expansive great room and kitchen. The smell of baking potatoes made Regina's stomach growl.

"Would you like a snack?"

"No." She laughed. "But if I pass out, wave a steak under my nose. That always works. Walt, I can see why you love this space. Those floor-to-ceiling windows must provide a wonderful view during the day."

"Just more trees. The soil is such that hardwoods don't do well. Fortunately, the jack pines love it." He opened a door onto a deck and stepped out. "It's quite peaceful."

Regina followed. Temperatures were in the sixties. The starry sky gave everything a warm glow. "Can you hear the waves?"

"Too far away. But you can sometimes hear the semi-trucks downshifting on Route 26. Mostly, it's just crickets and frogs. I used to love sitting out here with my grandparents." He leaned against the porch rail and took a deep breath. Regina did the same.

"There's nothing like that scent in New York," she whispered. "What is it?"

"The sea gives it spice. The sweetness comes from the marshlands west of here. Jefferson Creek. Little Bay. Ponds that don't have names. They support an ecosystem that's hard to fathom sometimes, a combination of new life, old life, and, sadly, death."

Regina glanced at him as he spoke. His words were for her, but his eyes scanned the horizon. Treetops waved gently in the breeze. From somewhere deeper in the woods came the sound of footfalls scampering from left to right.

"Deer," Walt said, barely above a whisper. "A doe or young fawn. Sometimes, I can hear the bucks rubbing their racks against the trees."

"Are you a hunter?"

He shook his head. "Don't care for guns. It's not that I'm a tree-hugger, as Americans refer to the conservationists. I just never took it up." He turned so they were facing.

Their eyes met, and in the darkness, Regina saw things there she hadn't detected before. Longing. Desire. There was a moment when she thought he might lean in and kiss her. What would be her response? Would her desires win out? And if they did, would she be able to rein them in? But then Walt glanced over her shoulder at a gas grill. The moment was gone.

"Our dinner should be ready," Walt said.

Was there a hint of disappointment behind those words? Regina sighed and attempted to rebuild her resolve.

"I can't wait."

HE'D NEARLY KISSED HER. It was too soon and entirely inappropriate. But he'd almost done it anyway.

And what would have been her response? Might she slap him? Run for the hills? Call off everything, pack up, and leave Bethany, never to return? Walt thought it might be for the best that he not find out. She didn't need him coming between her and Damon. Not with everything else going on in her life. One thing at a time. Or maybe two. Her case against her former employer had to be stressful. Then there was the new restaurant. She'd jumped in with both feet. So much change in one person's life. The last thing she needed was having to deal with his advances.

It would be dinner and a hasty return to Kate and Austin's. Strictly business.

Landlord and tenant. Professional.

"Let me set the table," she said when they were back inside.

Walt pointed her toward the plates and silverware, then retrieved the steaks. He'd intended to prepare a salad, but the lettuce he'd purchased at Hocker's the previous week had wilted. He scanned the pantry, hopeful of finding something to finish the meal.

"Regina, I have canned baked beans, canned corn, and applesauce. Do any of those sound good?"

She came over and eyed the steaks sizzling on a metal tray. "Those ribeyes are huge. I'll be fine with the baked potato."

He pulled them from the oven and placed them next to the steaks. "Then the least I can do is add the accoutrements. Butter and sour cream? Chives?"

"But, of course," she said, doing her best to mimic his accent. "Those... *accoutrements* sound delicious."

THE STEAK WAS DELECTABLE. A nice cut, trimmed well, and grilled to perfection. The baked potato was a gooey clump of decadence. The man understood the secret to good food wasn't adding a lot of fancy ingredients. She liked that.

And she liked him. He was easy to visit with. Just like before, the conversation flowed. Walt's questions kept her talking through dinner. It was only when he got up to fetch dessert that she realized he was also a master of something else.

Avoiding saying much about himself.

"All I have is butter pecan ice cream," he said, returning to the table with a gallon tub, two bowls, and a scoop.

"Only a little for me."

He dished up a scoop for each of them, then returned to his seat. He opened his mouth as if to ask another question, but Regina beat him to the punch.

"Walt, tell me what brought you here."

"Bethany? Like I said, my grandparents summered here. They owned this place. My sister and I—"

"Not that. I mean, *here*. To this moment. You know all about me, but all I know about you is that you came here to visit your grandparents, liked it, moved here, and inherited their house. You're obviously good at business. But what's the other stuff?"

He studied her for a moment. "What other stuff, Regina?"

"The personal stuff. The stuff that makes you, you. Remember when you dropped me off at the SaltAire? The night Damon had to leave?"

"Of course."

"After you left, Michael pulled me aside. He wanted to make sure I didn't hurt you."

Walt glanced away. Had she gone too far? Was Walt Mickens one of those people who preferred their past to remain there? He coughed, trying to make eye contact, but couldn't. It was several moments before he replied. Long moments, during which Regina rethought her decision to pry into his personal life.

"There are people who feel I need protecting." He spoke slowly, his words tinged with sadness. "Long-timers like Michael. They knew me...knew us...back then."

Us?

He rose from his chair and left the room. When he returned, he placed a framed photograph in front of her. One look at the little blond-haired girl in the picture was all it took to understand that something terrible had happened. Something sorrowful and tragic enough to leave a gaping hole in the poor man's heart. She looked up from the photograph and into his eyes. His broken heart was on full display. His hands trembled. His shoulders sagged as if they carried the weight of the world as he relived a time when he'd lost someone more important than life itself.

Her name was Hannah.

THERE WOULD BE NO SLEEP. Not for a while, at least. The best Regina could do was lie in bed and stare at the gently whirring ceiling fan. Kate and Austin were in bed when Walt brought her back. She'd considered staying, just to be close to him. To make sure he was okay after sharing his stories of Hannah. It never came to that, though. Walt wanted to be alone.

It never should have happened. Children play in trees all the time. Regina certainly had, even in New York City. There'd been an elm tree in their backyard. Her father hung a rope swing from it, and Regina and her friends delighted in jumping from the swing onto the soft squishy grass. They would scale its highest reaches, to where the branches could barely support their weight. It seemed as if they were a hundred feet in the air, but Regina later understood it was more like ten.

Poor Hannah was half that distance from the ground. Low enough for Joanie, Walt's former wife, to reach out and touch her while she climbed. Low enough to fall to the ground and rise again. Frightened by the wind being knocked from their lungs, but still fine.

Except it hadn't been like that at all.

Joanie had stepped away to retrieve her phone. Close enough to carry on a conversation with her daughter. But too far to catch her when she fell.

Walt heard everything. The thump of his four-year-old

daughter striking the earth. Joanie's response, subdued at first, then more frantic when it became clear things were worse than thought. He was in his car somewhere between the shop and the playground when an ambulance blew past. He knew where it was headed. Bethany wasn't a big city. There weren't many emergencies. So, he followed. And prayed.

Walt believed in the power of prayer. Joanie, too. They'd prayed together.

And it worked. Hannah came home. Everything was fine.

Two mornings later, she didn't wake up.

Further details were left out. Walt couldn't go there. Just telling her that much had left him spent. There weren't tears. Regina suspected that he'd learned how to turn off that part of himself.

Other parts had turned off, too.

Like the part that would fight to save his marriage.

Poor Joanie, she'd taken it hard. Blamed herself for something that could happen to any parent. Walt's words were nearly inaudible, but Regina could make out that he'd blamed her, too. Silently. To himself. But somehow Joanie sensed it.

"We buried our precious daughter," he whispered. "Eighteen months later, we buried our marriage."

Four years later, he still grappled with the memories. And the hurt. And while he'd insisted that he was okay, and practically pushed Regina out the door at night's end, she sensed he was emerging from all that.

And, perhaps, she was part of his recovery.

It was something she might want to pursue further. After all, who didn't want to help someone who was hurting? Especially someone so kind? So genuine?

But first, she had to help herself. A settlement meeting with the guys from Gasconade was scheduled for the following Monday. She picked up her phone and reviewed her terse text exchange with Damon.

Damon: *Monday at 10 AM. Their lawyer's place.*

Let's ride down together.

Damon: *I'll be in Boston all weekend. Taking a shuttle back Monday morning. Meet you there.*

Are you angry at me, Damon?

Damon: *Why would I be? See you then.*

She tossed the phone onto the bed and buried her head under the blankets. Come hell or high water, she would get at least a couple hours of sleep. Tomorrow would be her last day in Bethany for a while, and she wanted to spend it at the restaurant.

And maybe steal a few minutes with Walt.

friday, june 13

WALT WAS WAITING at the curb when Regina peered out Kate and Austin's living room window. Ten minutes early. The Delaware DMV office in Georgetown didn't open until nine. It was a forty-minute trip from Bethany, but Walt had insisted they meet at seven-thirty. It turned out to be a good decision.

The previous evening was difficult, but he looked like a new man in the late-spring sunshine. Fresh-scrubbed, hair combed into place, except for those adorably pesky strands sweeping down his forehead. His face lit up as she crawled into the car next to him.

"Let's get this done," Regina gushed as she clicked her seatbelt.

"Not so fast." He reached onto the floorboard between them, picked up a thin paperback, and handed it over. "The Delaware driver's manual. There are a couple of things we didn't think of."

"Uh-oh. Like what?"

"You need to be a resident of Delaware."

"I'll tell them I'm moving down when the restaurant is done."

Walt shook his head. "You need a physical address. Have you considered where you might live?"

"I'll put down Kate's address. It's not like they'll check."

Again with the head shaking. "You need two forms of documentation. A lease. Maybe a utility bill. That kind of thing."

"Welp, that excludes me. You might as well drop me at the bus depot."

"Not so fast," Walt said, waggling a finger. "I might know of a place that's available."

"A rental property?" Regina leveled him with her best look of disapproval. "Or are you thinking I'll move in with you?"

Walt's cheeks glowed. He tried to speak, but the tenor of her voice brought him up short. "I mean... you can live at... Would you mind if we stop by the shop on our way out of town? There's something I need to... I want... Can we just stop?"

"Of course." She grinned to let him know she was teasing. "But if you think we're going to share a toothbrush holder, you have another thing coming."

There was something so innocent in the look on his face. For having been through so much, the man was without deceit. He couldn't lie if there was a gun held to his head. He probably didn't even *use* the word. Fortunately, they were minutes from the shop. Regina looked longingly at the restaurant. Walt pulled to a spot in back and removed a keychain from his pocket.

"Come with me, please."

He led the way to an exterior door. After trying several keys, he found one that opened it.

"What is this?"

"The original owners lived up here. It's dated and hasn't been used in for about five years, but perhaps it will meet your needs."

"You never told me there was an apartment back here. I didn't even know there was a second floor."

"The windows in front are concealed behind the shop signage, but there's plenty of light from the back."

The stairway was dusty but solidly constructed. Walt led the way. Regina fell in behind and ogled his butt. A door at the top of the stairs was open. Walt reached inside and clicked on an overhead light. They entered a brightly lit living room with hardwood floors and windows on three sides. File boxes filled most of one wall. Two doors led deeper into the apartment.

"Nine hundred square feet. Two bedrooms, one bath, a kitchen that needs some TLC," Walt said. "Somewhat off the beaten path, but close to work, wouldn't you say?"

"For sure." Regina laughed. "Show me more."

He led her into a small kitchen. The stove and refrigerator were from the previous century. No dishwasher. Ceramic countertops and cheap cabinets. "Previous tenants weren't gourmet chefs. There was never the need to update."

Regina eyed the area for a few moments before turning to him and smiling. "It reminds me of the kitchen in the house where I grew up. Do the stove and fridge work?"

Walt nodded. "The gas is turned off, but I keep the refrigerator plugged in. Sometimes, I store things in the freezer. It's never let me down."

"Okay..." Regina said slowly. "Let's see the rest of the place."

He led her back into the living room and into a short

hallway. A bathroom was on the left. Tub with shower, sink, toilet. Nothing fancy, but more than enough room to turn around. A door led into a bedroom barely large enough for a twin bed. The last room, at the head of the hallway, led into the master bedroom. Larger than the second bedroom, but still not a lot of room. The cream-colored walls were free of the scuffs and dings common in apartments back in New York.

"Heat comes from the same boiler that serves the restaurant and shop," Walt explained. "It's ancient, but I keep it maintained. There's no air conditioning, but a small window unit should cool things nicely."

"I could always open the windows. I'm sure there's a nice cross breeze."

"And if you're worried about safety, the downstairs entrance has two deadbolts, plus there's a separate entrance that goes directly into the shop. Crime isn't an issue out here, and I have plenty of cameras and motion sensors. Security lights come on anytime someone pulls onto the lot at night."

"Are you forgetting where I'm from? I know how to handle myself. What I need to know is, how much is rent? Because I'm interested."

"The space isn't very large. If you need more space, I'm sure you can find something—"

"It's twice the size of my place." She returned to the living room. "And the windows make everything so bright and cheery." She placed her hands on her hips and looked into his eyes. "How much?"

Walt studied a spot on the wall as he thought about it. "How about...nothing?"

"No way. I don't need charity."

"And I don't need the income. If I did, I would have

169

rented the place before. It's not like there isn't plenty of opportunity."

"I insist on paying rent."

"Okay... How about two lunches a week? And unlimited access to the coffee maker?"

"How about all the meals you can eat? And I pay the utilities."

He nodded slowly as he stuck out his hand. "Deal. Oh, and there's one more thing."

Regina waited for him to continue. He led her to a rear window. A blue Honda was parked below. "The car comes with the apartment."

"Get out of town! There's no way, Walt!"

"It belonged to the previous tenant. He fell behind on his rent and left it as collateral. It didn't run, but Felix tinkered with it. We use it as a loaner for clients who drop vehicles off for quick repairs." He pulled out a set of keys. "It's twenty years old, but it's yours."

Regina stared at the keys for several moments as a tingling spread from her arms and legs to her core. The apartment. The car. Amazing gestures of kindness from someone she barely knew. Had something like it happened in the city she would have assumed there were strings attached. Rarely were such kindnesses extended without an expectation of something in return.

When she didn't immediately respond or reach for the keys, Walt dipped his head and looked away. "Regina...I know this might all seem...too much. I need you to know that my intentions are pure."

"I appreciate that. But why? Why me, Walt?"

He took a deep breath before gazing into her eyes. "I hope I'm not being too forward, but I sense greatness in you. In the past, I've always hoped for the best from my tenants, but in you, I don't have to hope. I know you're going to make the restaurant a success. And honestly, Regina, I want to be a small part of that success. Even if it's just providing a place for it to happen."

His sincerity made her heart melt a little. There really were people out there who acted on intuition and feelings. Who led with their hearts. Who trusted. She wanted to tell him, but he spoke before she got the chance.

"I know there's been pain in your life. As you learned last evening, we have that in common. Perhaps this town and these people can do for you what they've done for me."

"What's that, Walt? What have they done?"

"Been there for me. Often without even realizing it. Supported me and encouraged me. Bethany is a special place, bustling with excitement in the summer—overflowing with tourists—but at its core, it's a small town. I want you to discover that side of it. Once they know you're here to stay, the locals will go out of their way to help you be successful." He grinned. "So, what do you think? Want the apartment?"

Regina rolled her eyes. "I mean, yeah. A place to live and a car? How can I pass up an offer like that?"

WALT COULDN'T REMEMBER the last time he felt so happy. Perhaps it was unwise to allow someone he barely knew to have such an impact on his thoughts, but Regina was not just anyone. The thought of her being close by gave him joy. She was like a rocket ship on its way to faraway places that few have experienced. There had been some fits and starts of late, but when liftoff came, and he knew it would, her ascent would be something to behold.

They returned to his office and completed the paperwork that qualified her for a Delaware driver's license. At her insistence, they took the Honda. She drove. They stopped for coffee at a gas station a few miles from the DMV. When they arrived at the motor vehicle headquarters, Walt took his coffee to a bench out front while she went inside. Forty-five minutes later, she reappeared, waving a slip of paper and grinning from ear to ear.

"Let's find lunch," she exclaimed. "It's on me."

"I know just the place. Are you driving or should I?"

She waved her shiny new driver's license. "I'll drive. You tell me where to go."

HE DIRECTED her to the Bethany Beach boardwalk, the same area she and Damon had explored on their first visit to Bethany.

"There's a little diner down the way," Walt said as they passed the bandstand and made a right.

The day was sunny and cloudless. The waves broke rhythmically against the shore as walkers and joggers moved along the beach.

"I can't wait to see it during tourist season," Regina said.

"It's getting close."

The shops along the boardwalk were open for business. A half-dozen people called Walt by name. It had, as he'd said, a small-town vibe. "Here it is," he said as they approached their destination.

Regina moaned. "Not here."

"You've eaten at Milo's?"

"Hardly," she scoffed. "After some greasy old fry cook yelled at me for looking in the window, we took a pass."

Walt chuckled. "That would be Harvey. He took you for a pushy tourist."

"The only one who was pushy was him."

Walt pulled open the door and motioned her through. "Just give it right back to him."

Harvey was at the register when they entered. "Hey, Walt." His grin disappeared when he recognized Regina. "You gonna make a mess of my windows again?"

Regina was poised to give it right back to him, but Walt stepped in. "Harvey Bodenschatz, meet Regina Cole. She's taking over the restaurant attached to my place."

Harvey studied her for a few moments. There might have been some softening around his eyes, but the guy's face was so battle-tested it was hard to tell. "Yeah, I mighta heard about that."

"I wouldn't put much stock in what you've heard, Harvey," Walt said.

"I wasn't born yesterday, Walt. And as far as I'm concerned, lady, whether you make it or not is up to you. The location is terrible for pulling in the beach crowd, so you'll need the locals to survive. That means you'll try to pull customers away from me, and I'll be damned if I'll let that happen."

Regina tensed, preparing to give Harvey what-for. But then he cracked a smile that caught her completely off guard. "Truth is, there's enough business for both of us. Now go sit yourselves down, and I'll show you how real food is made."

"I think you won him over." Walt grinned as they took their seats.

A strawberry-blonde took drink orders, left menus, and batted her eyelashes at Walt.

"Thank you, Francine," he said.

She practically swooned at his kind words.

"She has the hots for you."

Walt paused mid-sip. "Francine's nice. Not my type, though."

"She's cute. I wish I had her butt." Regina laughed at Walt's wide-eyed reaction. "I'm serious. That thing is carved from stone. I bet she does squats in her sleep."

"Do I detect a note of jealousy?"

"Hell, yes, I'm jealous."

"It's not necessary. Your... I mean, it's not necessary."

Regina laughed loud enough to draw attention from diners seated nearby. She grabbed the menu. "What's good here?"

"Everything."

Harvey came up behind her, coffee urn in hand. "My eggs are the best in town."

"Just don't order them shirred," one of the people said from the next table. "He gets royally pissed when you ask for them shirred."

"Damned tourists," Harvey barked as he topped off their mugs. "Some woman from Jersey came in last summer and demanded to have her eggs shirred."

"Shirred eggs are delicious," Regina said.

"Serve 'em at your place, then, missy. Here they come scrambled or sunny side up. If you ask nice, I might poach 'em for you."

"Fine. I'll take sunny side up. And I'll also try your scrapple."

Harvey raised an eyebrow. "Do you even know what scrapple is? Where you from, anyway?"

"I'm from New York. And, yes, I've had scrapple. I want your take on it, though."

"I got my own seasonings. I serve it crispy and extra spicy."

"Bring it on." Regina grinned. "Maybe we'll swap recipes. Your scrapple for my shirred eggs."

"It would be nice to get some shirred eggs here once in a while," Walt offered, trying hard to keep a straight face.

Harvey considered the two of them for a few moments, shrugged, and stomped off toward the kitchen.

REGINA PAID THE TAB, left a generous tip for Francine with the buns of steel, and tucked Harvey's scrapple recipe into her purse.

"I can't believe he gave it to you," Walt said as they headed to her car. "Are you going to use it?"

"No way. It's his. Harvey understands that. Plus, scrapple isn't appropriate for the menu I have planned for Adeline."

"What about shirred eggs?"

"Probably not. That's why I'm okay with teaching him how to make them. Harvey's a tough old guy, but he's still a chef at heart like me. We're always open to new things." She grinned at Walt. "Who knows? You might see shirred eggs as a weekend special at Milo's one of these days."

The drive from the boardwalk was uncharacteristically quiet. The thought of leaving had Regina at loose ends. So much had been accomplished over the past week, and being part of that progress made her feel better than she had in months. Kate had already become a friend. She and Austin were a perfect couple, despite their age difference.

He was self-assured and outgoing. She was more laid back and studious. But they made it work. Austin's grandpa Charlie was a sweetheart with a heart as big as the ocean. And even grumpy old Harvey Bodenschatz had warmed up to her.

Then there was Walt. Why was she so drawn to him? He certainly was handsome, and that accent was incredibly sexy. But it was more than that. Though he was only a few years older, he had what people called an old soul. He'd lived and seen a lot in forty years. Experienced joy and heartbreak. More heartbreak than a man his age should bear.

But he had persevered. When some would have given up, he'd focused on the future. One step at a time. Building a successful business. Making friends. Finding his place in a town where outsiders were considered with skepticism.

Yep, she would miss Walt most of all.

And Millie, of course.

That's how she'd started referring to the old girl in her thoughts. Millie. And while it didn't fit her vision of the future—Adeline—it was fine for the work in progress. Lovely Adeline would emerge from poor downtrodden Millie. A real Cinderella story.

"Regina?"

"Oh...I'm sorry, Walt. You caught me daydreaming."

"About scrapple?"

She smiled. "About the future."

"I was asking if you would mind dropping me at home." He pointed to a spot on his shirt. "A bit of strawberry jam. I have a client coming by and would prefer to meet him with a clean shirt."

She turned off Ocean Highway onto the street leading

to his house. She pulled up in front and put the car in park. "I'll wait here."

"That's unnecessary. My car is here. I'll need it later."

It wasn't how she thought they would part ways, and his abruptness caught Regina off guard. She didn't particularly want him to go, and he was in no rush.

"Any idea when you'll be back?"

"I guess it depends upon what's waiting for me in the city. There's the meeting with the attorneys, of course. And I have a couple of hand therapy appointments." She held it at eye level. "I'm not sure how much more they can do. It's still hard to grip a knife sometimes, but otherwise, it's as good as it's going to get. I just wish it didn't look so..."

There was nothing more she could say. Regina was still self-conscious of the mangled remains of her left hand. A couple of physicians had recommended counseling, but other than her session with Sandra Del Greco, where she'd talked about the future, she'd resisted. As she stared at the space where her fingers used to be, she wondered if she should reconsider.

Walt gently placed his hands over her injured one. He gazed into her eyes as he caressed it. It was a sweet gesture that warmed her tummy, but it was nothing compared to what she felt when he lowered his head and kissed it. It was only a few seconds but expressed so much.

"Thank you for lunch," he said softly.

"Thank you for...everything." Tears welled up as she spoke. She fanned her face. "I'm still in a state of disbelief that this is happening."

Their eyes locked. Regina felt herself moving ever so slightly toward him. She wasn't sure, but he might have been doing the same. But if he was, he stopped and reached for the door handle.

"I really should be going. My client is scheduled to arrive soon."

And then he was gone. Regina watched him go inside, then remained for a few moments in case he came back out to get her. To ask her to come in. Because if he had, she would have.

No question about it.

Which meant it was time to go. She still had to pick up her stuff at Kate's. If she didn't get a move on, she would arrive at the height of New York City rush hour.

Yep. Time to go. Even with a heavy heart. And a desire to stay and continue what she'd started. She wanted to be there for Millie's transformation into Adeline.

And see Walt.

IN THE END, she couldn't get out of town without one more look. And it was only ten minutes out of the way. All she needed was a reason. And then there it was. Her laptop. She'd left it at Millie's. She was happy she'd messed up.

Kate promised to have her room ready when she came back. She also recommended a discount furniture store a couple of miles outside Bethany. It was on the way to Millie's, so win-win. Regina checked her bank and credit card balances, did some math, and determined she had a little money to blow on furniture. The place was nice enough, though the salesperson was pushy. He softened up when she mentioned where she would be living. He knew Walt. Everyone knew Walt.

After more quick math, she picked out a queen-sized bed and dresser and a plain-Jane sofa and chair. The salesman wanted to show her kitchen tables, but when she told him she'd reached the end of her budget, he offered the name of a good second-hand place in Dover.

"Ask for Sonja and tell her I sent you." He pushed his business card into her hand. "She'll set up free delivery since you know me."

He might have been coming on to her, but the prices were good and she would have a place to rest her head. The salesman promised to hold the purchases until Regina had the apartment cleaned up. All that was left before hitting the road was to get one more look at dear Millie.

THE PARKING SPACES in front of the restaurant were open. Austin had texted that he was finishing a job at one of his parents' beach rentals but would return on Monday. Regina was happy to have some alone time to wander around. The scents of sawdust and tile glue had replaced the musty smell that had greeted her when she first saw the space. Sawhorses were strategically set up to maximize efficiency. Austin had a good eye for that kind of thing. He wanted a minimum of wasted movement. At some point, he had dropped off scaffolding for restoring the ceiling. The look, smell, and feel of progress were invigorating.

She pulled out her phone and started a list of tasks she would tackle when she returned. Most important was making sure the left-behind kitchen equipment was in operating order. Regina was confident that she could handle the basics—plug everything in and check to see that the range and ovens were heating at their proper temperatures. Stuff that experienced chefs did with their eyes closed. The equipment alone would save a lot of upfront money. And while Walt had assured her all was well, she had to see for herself. She resisted the urge to jump in and start. Traffic would be nuts if she hung around too long. She sighed, grabbed the laptop, and paused in the door before exiting.

"See you soon, Millie. We're going to transform you into Adeline before you know it."

She took a left and walked toward Walt's shop. A bay door was open, and Felix was pulling a car in when he spotted her and waved. She continued inside and headed for Walt's office. The door was closed, and someone was in there with him. After a few moments, he spotted her through the window that overlooked the shop. She liked how his face lit up when he saw her and hoped hers did the same. He rose from his desk and came to the door.

"I thought you would be halfway home by now."

Home. The word suddenly seemed foreign to her. The restaurant was still little more than an empty shell. The upstairs apartment was empty. Yet in many ways, she already considered Bethany Beach her new home. Everything felt so comfortable. The guest room at Austin and Kate's, the space they had already started calling *her* room. Millie. Walt's shop. She remembered a quote she'd read a few years before. The writer was forgotten, but their words were as fresh as ever.

Home is a shelter from storms—all sorts of storms.

Life had been stormy since the accident. Hospitals, surgeries, rehabilitation. False accusations and disparaging remarks about her abilities as a chef.

Self-doubt.

Depression.

And some of the darkest thoughts Regina had ever had.

None of that carried over to Bethany Beach. There, she

felt alive. She was looking ahead again, imagining a future doing what she loved. Doing what her grandma used to say she was *born for*. Spending time with people who valued her. Respected her. *Liked her*.

Home.

"Regina? Is everything okay?"

"Oh... I just remembered that... I forgot..." She blushed and held up the laptop.

"I see." Walt glanced back to his office.

"Oh, shoot, I'm sorry, Walt. I didn't mean to interrupt your..." She turned to leave. "I need to get on the road."

"Have you got a moment? I want you to meet someone."

"I don't want to interrupt."

"Nonsense. Come in."

Regina followed, silently chastising herself for getting in his way while he was doing business. He was unperturbed. When they stepped into his office, a nice-looking forty-something man stood to greet her. He was casually dressed, but it was easy to see he was someone of means. Handsome, physically fit, good haircut, manicured nails.

"Tony Sampson, this is Regina Cole."

Regina stuck out her hand, still feeling like an intruder.

His smile put her at ease. "Good to meet you, Regina."

"Tony lives in Baltimore. We're restoring the first car his grandparents ever bought."

"A 1957 Fairlane," Tony said, his face breaking into a broad smile. "Grandpa Sampson used to say he never felt more important than the day he drove it off the dealer's lot."

"How it got here is a long story," Walt added. "Tony had to do a lot of detective work to find it."

"Not me. I'm a terrible detective. But I know people who are quite good. I paid way more than I should have, but when I get in that car and think of how happy it made my grandparents..." Tony shook his head and tried to conceal the tears. "Do you have a car being restored, Regina?"

"She and I are in the midst of a different kind of restoration," Walt said. "Regina's opening the restaurant."

"That's wonderful news! I remember stopping there with my parents when I was a kid, back when it was still Three Mile Millie's." He laughed as he recalled, "My sister and I ordered the same thing every time. The Millie kid stack. Two pancakes buried under a scoop of vanilla ice cream and a mountain of whipped cream. Please tell me you're going to put the Millie kid stack on your menu. I'll be a customer for life."

"Oh darn, I hate to be the bearer of bad news, Tony, but we're going in a different direction."

"Regina is moving from New York. She operated a restaurant there."

Tony was impressed. "What part of town?"

"Brooklyn. A little place you've never heard of."

"I spend a lot of time in New York. Try me."

"Gasconade."

Tony's eyes grew wide. "Get out of here! I used to go there with friends. You owned it?"

"Executive chef. What's your favorite dish there?"

"The mushroom risotto when I was test-driving being a vegetarian." Tony laughed. "That lasted about four months. Otherwise, I loved the prime rib sliders on the lunch menu."

Hearing Tony's favorites brought a flood of warmth for a time when life was good and the future looked bright. Regina had experimented at length before introducing the risotto. It and a butternut squash ravioli resulted in a twenty percent increase in customer traffic. They chatted for a few moments about her plans for the space next door. Felix made an appearance and announced that Tony's car was ready to go. He pointed to where he'd parked it outside Walt's office window. Seeing it jarred Regina's memory. That car had been parked out front then.

"You went to NYU Law."

She'd surprised him again. "How do you know that, Regina?" He made a show of unbuttoning his puffer vest and looking at the plaid shirt underneath. "I'm not even wearing the sweatshirt."

"I know that sweatshirt," Regina said with a laugh. "I'm dating someone two years behind you. Damon Palmer."

Was it just her, or did Tony's smile drop when she mentioned Damon? Probably just from having to recall someone from a couple of classes behind him. NYU was big, right? Whatever.

The smile returned. "Damon's on his own these days, I hear."

"Yes. He recently landed a big client, though. That's why he was unable to come down." She glanced at Walt before adding, "It was Damon who encouraged me to strike out on my own."

"Well, if you'll forgive me for being so upfront, Damon is one lucky man." Tony grabbed his backpack and prepared to leave. "Walt, as always, a pleasure. When I come back in August, dinner is on me." He turned to Regina. "If you're available, I'll expect you to join us." He motioned toward the wall that separated the office from the restaurant. "Or maybe we'll be eating next door."

Regina winked as she said, "If that's the case, maybe I can whip up a special order of my mushroom risotto."

"Remember, I used to be vegetarian." Tony laughed. "These days I would prefer the prime rib sliders!"

Regina accompanied them to the parking lot where they spent a few moments admiring Tony's car. The day was getting away from her, so Regina said her goodbyes and broke away. If Walt seemed more standoffish than usual, she attributed it to being with a client. As she got in the car, she glanced back and saw him looking her way. There was a slight smile on his face as he nodded a warm farewell before turning his attention back to Tony.

"Business first, Regina," she mumbled as she pulled onto the highway.

OBSERVING a satisfied customer as he walked around his newly restored car was a high point of Walt's job. Some people didn't understand how much a part of people's lives their vehicles could be. Tony was no exception. He ran his fingers over the hood and caressed the fabric of the seats. He admired his reflection in the hubcaps. It should have been a wonderful moment for Walt, too, but his mind was elsewhere.

What about Damon Palmer had caused Tony to pause like he had? Walt pushed the envelope a bit more.

"Uh...Tony, there was something else I wanted to talk to you about."

The way Tony gazed at his car told Walt that he would prefer hitting the open road, but their friendship took precedence. "Want to talk here?"

"Perhaps we should go back inside. I promise to only keep you a few minutes."

REGINA'S NECK and shoulders tightened up as she got closer to the city. By the time she crossed the Verrazzano-Narrows Bridge, they were stiff and sore. She tried to convince herself that it was caused by a week of physical labor, but it only grew worse as she navigated block after block of narrow Brooklyn streets. Hard work hadn't caused the ache. It was stress. And the closer she got to home, the more she felt it.

She'd texted Damon four times and received no response until a terse, *In meetings. TTYL* as she turned onto the street in front of her apartment.

"Fine, asshole," she said, immediately regretting it. Damon had been distant all week. For the past couple of weeks, for that matter. When she'd pressed him on it, he'd blamed the pressures of building his practice and hustling clients. *You've always hustled clients*, she'd reminded him on the phone.

Yeah, but I always knew there would be a paycheck whether I scored new clients or not. It's different when my livelihood depends on it.

Point taken. Adeline was still a few weeks from opening, yet it already consumed her thoughts. How much more intense would it be when her livelihood depended on customers walking through the front door? She needed to be more understanding of Damon's situation.

She pulled up to a secured parking area behind her building and thanked her lucky stars she'd had the foresight to call ahead and speak to the building manager. There was only one spot available. It could be hers for $350 a month. She'd considered taking her chances on finding street parking, but the myriad laws governing where and when you could park were more than she wanted to deal with. Besides, it would only be a few weeks before she could say goodbye to her exorbitant rent and the outrageous cost of parking. There were plenty of spots in Bethany where she could park for free. For now, she would grit her teeth and pay. She punched in a code the building manager had texted and proceeded to her designated spot. It was a good thing she was alone, as the spot was so close to a chain-link fence that there was no room to open the passenger door. The area was sketchy, but a security light provided enough illumination for her to grab her stuff and make a dash for the building's rear entrance. Her phone buzzed as she unlocked her apartment. She dropped a suitcase and pulled the phone from her purse.

"Hey, Damon." She kept her voice level. He might be stressed out by work, but that was still no reason not to treat his woman with respect.

His tone was upbeat. Very much the Damon she'd fallen for. "Hey, boo. What a week! I'm in a cab back to my place. C'mon over. We'll order Thai and catch up."

"I'm walking into my apartment. You come to me? I have something to show you."

She knew how he felt about her place. It was little. Not enough windows. Loud neighbors. Typical Brooklyn. Usually, he would cajole her to come to his place with promises of good wine, a soft bed, and an eighty-inch TV. She didn't have the energy to get back out, and since he would also want sex, she needed to conserve what energy that remained. Plus, he'd been showing his ass of late. It was atonement time.

Damon seemed to understand all that. He gave the cabbie her address. "Sounds great, boo. See you in a half hour." He took on that suggestive tone he used to get her into bed. "I can't wait to see what you want to show me."

Regina could imagine him disconnecting the call,

winking at the cabbie, and saying something about one of them getting lucky that night. Boys will be boys. Would Walt say something like that? Play up an innocent comment to build street cred with a cabbie he would never see again? She couldn't imagine it happening. And why had she felt compelled to even tell him about the car? He would take one look at it and ask what she'd paid for it. She could lie and throw out a number, but Damon knew cars. If her figure was too high, he would crow about her being taken advantage of. And if she told him the truth, that it went with the apartment—the apartment that Walt was renting her for the cost of a few meals a week—what would he say about that? He was already skeptical of Walt's intentions.

Nah, best to leave it alone for the time being. If Damon asked how she'd gotten back to the city, she would cross that bridge when she got to it.

By the time he buzzed into her building, Regina had her bags unpacked, clothes put away, and dinner ordered. Enough Pad Thai and fried rice to feed ten, but it reheated nicely. She had changed into a comfy sweatshirt and soft pair of jeans when he came in, still clad in suit and tie. He gathered her into his arms and kissed her with an intensity that made her catch her breath. The old Damon was back.

"Baby, this separation thing is for the birds. How about we find you an opportunity back here in the city? I know a guy who might have a line on a space in Williamsburg. It was a burrito joint until last fall. The owners have had no luck finding someone to take it over, so they've lowered the..." He picked up on the way she was looking at him. "Or has that ship sailed?"

Regina laughed. "You wouldn't believe how much we got done this week, Damon. That ugly old paneling is gone. And the ceiling is—"

"Who do you mean, *we*? Who's helping you?"

Darn it. She should have known better than to drop that *we* reference. Too much, too quick.

"We is... Austin. You remember? The guy who..."

She nearly slipped and said, *You insulted by asking why he wasn't in college.*

"Is doing the renovation work. He was there all week with his grandfather. And Kate came to help, too. Damon, she's so sweet. I think we're going to be great friends. I stayed at their house, and we had a ball."

"Of course," he said, nodding slowly. "Austin and his older wife and his much older grandfather." He paused a few beats. "And...anyone else?"

"Nope. That's it. Just the four of us. We worked from first light right through the day." She wrapped her arms around herself and smiled. "My muscles haven't hurt this bad in forever." She reached out for his hand. "Now, let's eat."

Delicious Thai food and the sight of Regina in a pair of jeans that accentuated all the right things kept Damon smiling through dinner. He even helped clean up, bringing plates from the table to the sink where he reached around Regina with both arms to place them in the soaking water. She dried her hands on a towel and leaned back against his chest.

"You said something about a surprise," he cooed as he slid his hands along her hips.

Regina had hoped he would forget but still had a story to fall back on. "Yes, I have pictures of what we got done. They're on my phone in the living room."

Damon was in no hurry to see pictures of an old restaurant. He nuzzled her neck and was turning her to face him when the doorbell rang. Regina broke away to answer. She recognized the visitor, a man in his fifties wearing a Yankees windbreaker and cap.

"Hi, Stanley."

"Hiya, Miss Cole. Sorry to bother you after hours. I was downstairs unplugging the Stonemans's john when I remembered I hadn't left you a key."

Damon had joined her at the door. She didn't bother with introductions. "Key?"

"Yeah, for the backyard. To park your car. Sometimes, the code box doesn't work, and you need to unlock it with this." He handed over a rusty metal key. Regina's hands were shaking as she took it. She tucked it in her sweatshirt, hopeful that Damon hadn't noticed.

Wishful thinking. Damon noticed everything.

"Yes, thank you, Stanley."

She closed the door and prepared to face the music. Damon appeared confused.

"Key? Why would you need a key to the parking area out back unless... Is it for me to use?" He smiled broadly. "It would be great to have a place to leave the Caddy when I'm here."

It was the moment of truth. Relationships were built on trust. But she'd also heard her mother say that the occasional little white lie calms storms. Regina didn't like storms. Nor did she like not being forthcoming with the man she was involved with.

"I have a car." She deliberated telling him everything. That would head off an interrogation. "And an apartment. They were a package deal. It turns out that there's an upstairs apartment behind the restaurant." She smiled broadly and raised her arms. "Who would have guessed?"

Judging by the look on Damon's face, forthcoming

didn't work. "An apartment...and a car...upstairs from the restaurant?"

"Actually, it's upstairs from the garage. It hasn't been rented in a few years, but it's big and spacious and close to work, so how could I—"

"How much?"

"You'll appreciate my negotiating skills, Damon. I bartered for free meals."

"You're not paying rent? How much for the car?"

Regina's mouth went dry. Damon's barrage of questions was bad enough, but the look in his eyes reminded her of a defense attorney grilling a guilty suspect. There was a time when she would have told someone who spoke to her that way to go to hell. What had happened? Why was she so...weak? She took a deep breath and spit it out. "The car is old. It belonged to a former tenant. Walt kept it maintained in case the guy came back. But he never did, so he gave it to me."

He got up from the sofa and paced about the tiny kitchen. "Don't you see what's going on, Regina?"

She knew what he was alluding to, and she didn't like it one bit. "Walt is kind. Nothing more, nothing less."

"He wants to get in your pants, Regina."

Damon glanced away as he spoke, leaving him no time to react when Regina jumped to her feet and slapped him across the left cheek.

"Shit! Regina, what the—"

"Don't you talk that way about me, Damon!"

"I was talking about him, not you. I trust you, Regina. It's Mickens that—"

"Leave."

"Don't you see what's going on? He's putting the moves on you. He sees a woman who is alone. Her boyfriend is four hours away. He puts her up in his fancy apartment and gives her a car. Eventually, he's going to—"

"Get out. Right now. Don't make me call the cops." Regina's pulse raced as she pointed toward the door. The anger drained from his face as he realized he'd gone too far.

"Look, baby. I didn't mean that you and Mickens were actually—"

"Damon, leave now." The anger was gone, but she was no less resolute. They remained there for what seemed like many minutes but was only a few seconds before Damon left. There was no door slamming or final words. Only a quiet exit.

REGINA'S PHONE dinged a text announcement. It was ten-thirty. Damon left two hours earlier. She expected it was him texting to apologize.

Did you make it home safely?

Walt. Seeing his name made Regina smile. A hot bubble bath hadn't accomplished that. Neither had a bowl of Ben and Jerry's Cherry Garcia. And she certainly wouldn't have smiled if the text were from Damon.

Yes! The car did great. Thank you again!

His reply came straight away. *You're welcome. Have a relaxing weekend.*

She laid the phone on the side of the bed where Damon would have been had he not been so stupid. They hadn't had many arguments, but the silent treatment was his modus operandi. He'd figured out what Regina's childhood friends knew early on. She didn't like conflict, and she would almost always take the steps to get past it.

"Not this time," she mumbled as she turned off the

bedside lamp. A few moments later, the phone dinged again.

Are you okay?

Walt again. Did he have a sixth sense that she was having a bad night? She considered her response before letting fly, *Damon wasn't very kind this evening.*

She read and re-read the text, anticipating Walt's reply. He wouldn't ask what Damon had done or said. His concern would be for her. Did she need anything? Could he help? And he would mean it. Even if it meant dropping anything and coming to her rescue, he would do it. That was the kind of man he was.

She would not drag him into her mess. Everything would be better tomorrow. And perhaps, Damon had a point. Regina had questioned why he ran off every time his new client, Alice, called. Was that any different?

Yeah, she decided, it was. But that wasn't Walt's problem. She deleted the text and typed a new one.

I'm good. Thanks for asking.

saturday, june 14

REGINA HADN'T EXPECTED sleep to come so easily after the blow-up with Damon. She'd slept long and hard as her body, mind, and muscles recharged after the exhilaratingly hectic week in Bethany. It was after nine when she woke up. Her first thoughts were of the diner, and how much better it looked. Her thoughts then drifted to Walt and his many kindnesses. And how good-looking he was. Other thoughts moved in erotic directions she knew were wrong, but what did a girl have if not the occasional fantasy?

She reached for her phone and checked to see if Damon had texted or called. Nothing. That was his way. He was stronger than her and could wait until she extended the olive branch.

"Not this time, mister."

She'd done nothing wrong. Some might view her acceptance of Walt's kindness as a betrayal of her relationship with Damon, but his benevolence came without strings. Sure, there might be an underlying spark between them, but the fact remained that they hadn't acted upon it. And they wouldn't. She wasn't that kind of girl, and Walt had no interest in sneaking around. Not with all he'd endured in his personal life.

If Damon wanted things to be right, it was up to him to make them that way. Regina tossed her phone on the bed and headed to the shower. There was a tautness in her calves and thighs as she padded to the bathroom. As a chef, she spent most of her day on her feet, but the work she'd done at the restaurant that week was a different kind of physical exertion. One she'd found downright enjoyable. She turned the water on extra hot and luxuriated under the skin-prickling stream until the water grew tepid. Any plans she might have had with Damon were on hold, and the Saturday stretched out in front of her like a blank canvas that she planned to paint any darn way she wanted. Perhaps a stop at the Brooklyn farmer's market where she'd made so many connections during her time at Gasconade. She'd avoided the place in recent months, not wanting any of her friends to see how trampled down she was.

It was a different day. And she was slowly but surely becoming the old Regina.

WHEN SHE RETURNED to her apartment building that afternoon, she was loaded down with bags overflowing with everything from asparagus to mushrooms and parsnips to spinach. Vendors she'd grown close to during her time at Gasconade were overjoyed to see her back in the game. They were quick to recommend farmers' markets in Wilmington and Dover, as well as an auction market in the tiny community of Laurel, a few miles from Bethany.

It had been a good day.

She was fumbling through her purse in search of her key when she heard him behind her. She glanced over her shoulder but could barely see him, nearly concealed behind the biggest flower arrangement she'd ever seen.

"Damon?"

He peered out from behind the shower of flowers. "I've already come by twice. When I made my second appearance, one of your neighbors asked if someone had died."

"Well, let's get inside so they can stop worrying." She was still unhappy with the way he'd acted the night before, but the flowers—gaudy as they were—were a sweet *mea culpa*. Still, if he didn't straighten up pretty quick, she would... Well, she didn't know exactly what she would do and hoped she didn't need to find out. Damon had to sort through his jealousy on his own time.

He carefully placed the arrangement on the tiny coffee table in front of the sofa. Its immenseness cut off the view from the kitchen to the living room. He came to her, his head bowed in contrition.

"I royally screwed up yesterday. I should have never made that comment about Mickens wanting to... I'm so sorry."

Regina waited for whatever would follow. Whether she accepted his apology was still to be determined.

"It was such a shock. The apartment. The car..."

Careful, mister. You're about to screw up by justifying your actions.

"But..." he continued, measuring each word. "None of that matters. We're in a committed relationship. I can't be assuming that you'll run off with some small-town mechanic."

Spiteful, perhaps, but at least he was taking responsibility for his actions. Regina could live with that. She smiled. "Apology accepted." She kissed his cheek. "But you're on a short leash, buddy. With everything left to do to get Adeline ready, I don't need to deal with a jealous boyfriend."

He grinned. "Well, Regina, my dear. That won't be a problem."

"Good. I'm glad to hear that because—"

"I'm going with you."

Wait a minute. Had she heard right?

"You're coming along? But...what about work?"

"With Alice paying the bills, I cut back the rest of my client list. I kept the ones I can handle remotely and fired the rest. I'll help at the restaurant during the day and do Alice's work at night. And now that you've got that nice apartment I can use that as my base of operation. You said it has two bedrooms, right? I figure one can be for us, and I'll use the other as an office. All I'll need is a desk and a Wi-Fi connection."

"Damon, I can't believe that you're— I mean, you're giving up so much. And it's all so fast. Are you sure this is what you want to do?"

"I'll keep my place here while I finish the cases I have pending, then I'll give thirty days and let it go. You should do the same." He pulled her close. "Bethany is going to be our home, baby. Let's jump in with both feet." He kissed her deeply, and while it didn't feel quite the same as before, it was nice. He was nice. And with the mysterious Alice, he was in a better place financially. They could make a nice living in Bethany with her at Adeline and him servicing Alice's legal needs while he built up a clientele. Perhaps Alice had friends who needed an attorney to fight off their dead spouses' spoiled kids.

Yeah, it could work.

But why was she so uneasy? She should be overjoyed that things were working out. She was so close to having it all. Her own restaurant, her man, and a new life in a resort town where other people went to get away, to play, to relax.

"You've gotten quiet on me." He kissed her forehead. "What's going on in that pretty head of yours?"

"You surprised me. I'm having to sort everything out."

"First impressions?"

She smiled. "First impressions are good. Kinda hard to believe it's coming together."

"It's coming together like it's supposed to, boo." He pulled his phone from his back pocket. "I need to finish some paperwork and pack for the trip, but how about we celebrate first? It's been a while since we've been to that soul food place you like so much?"

Ooh, he was pushing all the right buttons. Soul food was the kryptonite that could melt her heart. "The place in Prospect Heights?"

"That's the one, baby. I remember. Blackened catfish, right?"

Regina laughed. "With mac and cheese and stewed tomatoes. Oh, my goodness, that sounds perfect right now."

She made the first move this time. A kiss that hinted that more would follow. Damon picked up the signals and wasted no time leading the way. It was time to enjoy a late-afternoon sampling of the best of NYC because things in Bethany were about to get real interesting.

monday, june 16

WALT ARRIVED at the shop earlier than usual and tried to wrap his mind around work matters rather than Regina's return from New York City. Though she'd assured him she was okay when they'd texted, he'd sensed there was something amiss. Would she want to talk about it? More to the point, would she be receptive to hearing what Tony Sampson had shared with him about Damon? Perhaps she already knew the man for what he really was, but if she didn't? Was it Walt's place to enlighten her? Those were questions he couldn't answer, and besides, he had to be certain of his own motives. Was he watching out for Regina's best interests or was his desire to tell her the truth about her boyfriend a ploy to get him out of the way?

Austin and Charlie arrived a few minutes before eight. The Watson twins, Jason and Jared, pulled in right behind them. The boys were in their early twenties and had a history with the police, small stuff mostly, back when they were still kids, but enough to make finding full-time employment difficult in a town that never forgot. Walt had heard that they were doing part-time construction work and hoped that Austin's influence might help them remain on the straight and narrow. He stepped outside as the four men were unloading tools and supplies.

"Place is open," he called out. Austin gave him a thumbs-up and led the way inside. Ten minutes later, the hum and grind of power equipment filled the air. Walt was back at his desk when Felix arrived. He poured himself a cup of coffee and took a seat.

"Did you see who's next door?"

"If you're referring to the Watson boys, Felix, I did."

"You're okay with that?"

"I trust Austin and Charlie. If they think the boys can do the work, I support them. Besides, it's not like they're violent felons. They've never hurt anyone, have they?"

Felix shrugged. "Petty crimes mostly. Stripping copper from empty houses. I guess they've paid their dues, but they still worry me, boss. Maybe Austin doesn't know."

Walt sipped his coffee and debated saying more. If anyone could appreciate the Watson twins getting a second chance, it was Felix. Walt didn't want to remind him he'd been convicted of car theft in his twenties, a charge that put Felix behind bars for seven months. People changed. Felix was as good an example as anyone.

But it proved unnecessary. After they'd sipped their coffee and contemplated the circumstances, Felix coughed, scratched the back of his neck, and got to his feet. "I guess I should go over and wish 'em well," he mumbled.

"Good idea, Felix. Encourage them."

Felix turned back at the door. "Where's Regina? I expected her to be here by now."

"Perhaps she was delayed in New York."

"You haven't talked to her?" Felix gave him a curious look. He'd figured out there might be more between his boss and the new lady next door than just business.

"Honestly, Felix, I have too much to do, and Regina would say the same." He pointed toward the garage. "After you go next door, I need you to get started on that Packard."

Felix waved his hand and hurried out. He was a wonderful employee but sometimes needed to be reminded of his place. Walt glanced at the clock. It was eight-forty and still no Regina. He went to his office window to see if he might have missed her. He was mulling over when to share the information Tony Sampson had gleaned when she pulled into the lot. She parked at the far end of the lot, out of his line of sight. Walt pushed open the office window to steal a peek.

She wasn't alone.

Damon Palmer was with her. They were dressed in jeans and flannel shirts and looked ready to work. Regina led the way. She didn't notice Walt at the window. Damon did. Their eyes locked. Damon stared him down for a few seconds before continuing inside. The encounter left Walt weak in the knees. Palmer's appearance unsettled him. He returned to his desk to consider what might happen next.

REGINA PARKED AS FAR AWAY from Walt's end of the building as possible. Her hope was that Damon and Walt wouldn't cross paths until she figured out how to tell Walt of the change in plans.

The restaurant's doors were open, and power equipment hummed inside. The pleasing smell of sawdust greeted her as they exited the car. Damon had wanted them to come back in his Cadillac. But Regina didn't want Walt to think she didn't appreciate all he'd done for her, so she'd insisted they bring the Honda. Damon groused at first about the older car's bumpy ride, but overall, he was in an ebullient mood.

"Whatever they need me to do, I'll do," he'd promised.

Regina hoped so. The last thing she needed was Damon trying to take charge. Austin and Charlie wouldn't take that well.

Two guys were scrubbing the exposed brick walls in the dining room. A completed three-foot section gleamed like new. They stopped and stared when they spotted her and Damon. The curious looks on their faces made them look like twins. Then, Regina realized, they were.

"Hello," she said. "Is Austin here?"

"In the back," they said in unison before getting back to work.

Austin came out with Charlie close behind. Their smiles disappeared when they saw Damon.

"Sorry we're late," Regina said. She'd wanted to be there two hours earlier, but Damon insisted on breakfast first. Fortunately, they could take advantage of the SaltAire's complimentary breakfast. They would stay there for a few days while they prepared the apartment.

Austin introduced the new guys. Jared and Jason. Brothers. Identical right down to the tattoos on their skinny biceps.

Damon stepped around Regina and took center stage. "I'm ready to get to work."

Austin was okay with it, but Charlie looked skeptical.

"Ever swing a hammer?"

"Only to hang a picture." Damon looked around. "But I can get materials or clean up. Just let me know what you need." He made a show of putting his arm around Regina. "I'm here to help my woman."

"Great," Austin said, giving him a thumbs-up. "We have three weeks to turn this place into a working restaurant. Grandpa and I are getting the office set up so Regina has a place to work." He looked at Regina and smiled. "We'll be done by Wednesday. Do you have office furniture?"

"I hadn't even thought of it."

"No problem. A couple sawhorses, a sheet of plywood, and a paint bucket will work until you do. By the way, Kate says hey. She wants to know if you and..." He paused. "Mr. Palmer want to go out with us tonight. There's a place out in the country called Elijah's. Decent food, good music."

"We'd be delighted," Damon said, smiling broadly.

Charlie still wasn't warming up to Damon's sudden appearance. "You can help the boys clean the walls. It's dirty work, so if you're worried about getting your hands dirty—"

"Not at all. Point me in the direction of the supplies and a ladder and I'll get started."

———

REGINA NEEDED to say something to Walt, but she kept missing him. The first time she stopped in, Felix said he was in town picking up supplies. The second time, he was on the phone with a client.

"Tell him I'd like to see him when he has time," she told Felix. "I'm going upstairs to the apartment to make some calls."

"Sure enough, Regina. I'll let him know."

The morning hours passed in a flurry of phone calls. The local farmers recommended by her friends were delighted to meet her needs for fresh vegetables. One gave her the name and number of a neighbor who raised grass-fed beef. Another recommended a lady who made her own jams and jellies. Lower Delaware was a bonanza of meat, poultry, and vegetable growers eager to help. A call to the food service wholesaler she'd used at Gasconade provided contact information for the rep who serviced her area.

"They're our competitor up here," the wholesaler explained. "But we haven't expanded to Delaware yet, so he's your only choice."

"Yeah, you're in my territory," the rep, a guy named Stokes, said gruffly after Regina told him who she was and where Adeline was located. "But my schedule is pretty full. You should try somebody else."

"I was told that you're my only option."

"Like I said, I only have so much time. And my number of accounts is already twenty percent higher than it's supposed to be."

Regina took a slow, quiet, breath. She was familiar enough with the industry to know that guys like Stokes worked on commission. Turning down clients meant leaving money on the table. "I'm not a newbie at this, Mr. Stokes. I know restaurant management backward and frontward. It won't even be necessary for you to stop by. IF you give me access to your website, and I'll fill out my own orders."

That would have been too good a deal to pass up, but Stokes was still prickly. "You're not on our regular route, either. Your place is what? Ten miles out of Bethany Beach?"

"Three. Less than ten minutes from the other places you serve."

"Ten minutes in winter, maybe, but you ain't seen how it gets after July Fourth. It would take our guy an hour to get his truck out there. And another to get back. It's too much."

Regina was ready to press her point, but Stokes said he had to go. It was eleven-thirty. Almost lunchtime. Why had Walt not gotten back to her? Had he seen Damon? And if he had, what was he thinking? She headed downstairs to find out, slowing in front of the shop before thinking better of it. She'd made the effort. The ball was in his court. She continued to the restaurant. The Watson twins were still hard at it. They'd made substantial progress. Most of the north wall was complete. Regina stopped to admire their work before noticing the unoccupied ladder on the opposite wall.

"Keep up the good work, fellas."

The twins responded with identical nods of their identical heads as they continued working. Regina went in the back and found Austin and Charlie installing glass in the wall separating the office from the rest of the kitchen.

"We figured you would want to keep an eye on what's going on," Charlie said.

"Great idea, but when Adeline is open, I'll be out front with my staff. Where's Damon?"

"He started getting antsy," Austin said, "so we sent him to pick up supplies."

Regina rolled her eyes. "Thank you, guys, for finding things for him to do. He really wants to be a part of this."

Charlie started to say something but held his tongue.

"Are you getting hungry?" Regina asked. "I was thinking about getting lunch for everyone."

"We bring our own," Charlie said tersely.

Austin cast a sideways glance at his grandfather. "Ignore him. He gets cantankerous like this sometimes. And besides, Jane packed him a lunch of leftover pot roast and potatoes. I brought peanut butter and jelly, and I'm betting the twins forgot lunch completely."

He pulled out his wallet, but Regina waved him off. "This one's on me. I was thinking about calling Milo's and having Harvey put together a takeaway order. What do you want?"

Charlie's dour face brightened at the mention of Milo's. "Chicken-fried steak for me," Charlie said.

Austin opted for a chicken salad croissant. He went back out front with her to get the twins' orders. Damon was just returning.

"It's been years since I drove a stick, but I don't think I stripped the gears too bad." He tossed the keys to Austin. "That's quite a truck you got there."

"That's Calvin," Austin said, his pride obvious. "Named for Calvin Turner, the guy who Grandpa got it from in trade. A 1963 International. A half-million miles on the clock. You didn't need to worry about using the clutch. Calvin knows what to do either way."

"I'm ordering takeout from Milo's," Regina said. "What do you want?"

"What's good?" Damon looked at Austin.

"Everything. Grandpa loves the chicken-fried steak."

"Bring me that, too." He pulled a receipt from his shirt pocket and handed it over. "That guy at the lumberyard charges way too much. I told him he was going to be short one customer if he didn't lower his prices."

Austin grimaced. It was so like Damon to think he was up to bartering with a local about things he knew nothing about. Regina confirmed the food orders and headed out. She glanced toward the shop, debating if she should ask Walt if he and Felix wanted something, but his car was gone.

"MORE COFFEE, WALT?"

Francine filled the cup before Walt answered. He smiled appreciatively, then recalled how Regina had teased him about what she perceived as Francine's interest in him and her admiration of the server's backside.

I wish I had her butt.

You have so much more going for you, he thought as he took a bite of his turkey club. But why had Palmer come back with her? What did she even see in him? His arrogance was off the charts. His stare-down that morning proved it. He'd snagged one of the kindest and most beautiful women Walt had ever seen, and he was fully aware of what he had. Walt had run into Charlie earlier in the day.

The old guy already had his fill of Palmer. *Like a five-year-old butting his nose into everything, but not doing anything constructive*, he'd growled.

Walt checked the time and took the last bite of his sandwich when Harvey came bustling past. "Tell her to hold her horses," he shouted as he wiped his hands on his soiled apron. "The chicken-fried steak is just coming out of the fryer."

Walt glanced at the front counter and nearly choked on his sandwich. It was Regina. She didn't appear impatient, but that didn't matter to Harvey. He yelled at everyone. Her clothes were fresh and clean which meant she'd not been helping with the renovation. Her hair was as wild and free as usual, going off in every direction in a way that framed her lovely mocha face. Walt took a breath and gazed at her.

"She's the lady who was with you last week, isn't she?" Francine had come to clear away his plate.

Walt nodded.

"You like her, don't you?" There was a hint of disappointment in Francine's question.

Walt shook his head half-heartedly. "She's my new tenant, that's all. City girl. Boyfriend's a lawyer."

"I didn't ask about her life story," Francine said as she headed off. "And if you really don't like her, maybe you should tell your face."

———

HARVEY CAME from the back with two bags. "I threw in some crackers and ketchup and stuff. The chicken-fried steak marked with an *X* is Charlie's. Jane made me promise not to put any salt on his food." He sighed, looked toward heaven, and grumbled, "Everybody wants it their way. This ain't Burger King. I'm telling you." He placed them on the counter. "How's it going at Three Mile Millie's?"

Regina pulled out her credit card and handed it over. "It's Adeline, and so far, so good. Except for one thing."

She filled Harvey in on her call with the food supplier. His face contorted with interest, then anger. His eyes were ablaze by the time she finished.

"That lazy son-of-a-bricklayer thinks we need him more than he needs us." He paused and what might have been a smile crossed his face. "And maybe he's right. His delivery trucks are the only ones that come out this way. But still..." He banged a fist on the counter, then motioned for Regina to follow him to the back. The kitchen was full of the sounds and smells of lunch rush. Two short-order cooks manned the grill. A woman who had to be at least seventy-five pushed dishes and cups through a decades-old Hobart dishwasher. Francine, the server with a butt that could crack walnuts, was putting together an order. She glanced at Regina, then looked toward the dining room, probably remembering her from the previous week.

"Get in here," Harvey said as he shut the door behind her. He grabbed his phone and punched in a number. "Stokes, you lazy pile of crap! Did you tell the woman opening up the place on the old highway that you couldn't help her?"

Regina's gut clenched. Harvey listened for a few seconds. Regina couldn't hear the other side of the conversation, but she knew that Harvey cut him off mid-sentence. "Yeah, you're right, Stokes. You're her only option, but if you expect to keep my business and the others around here, you'll call and tell her you're ready to work with her. I heard that the rep from Galasso Foods has been in the area this spring. It sounds like they're close to extending their territory out this way. And if me and the others have a choice of where to order from, you better believe we're jumping ship if you're not treating us fair."

He slammed down the phone without waiting for a response. The color left his face, and he actually smiled. "I'd bet you'll hear from Mr. Stokes real soon."

"He didn't know about the guy from Galasso?"

Harvey made a farting sound with his tongue. "There ain't no guy from Galasso. Stokes is as bad at reading a bluff as he is doing his job. Now get that food out to Charlie and the twins. And make sure to give Charlie the one that's his. The last thing I need is Jane bawling me out for giving her old man a heart attack."

SOMETHING HAD SET HARVEY OFF, but when he and Regina emerged from the kitchen, they appeared fine. Walt turned in his seat so he wouldn't be so obvious when they hurried past. A line had formed in front, and his table was needed. To accentuate the point, Francine brought him another coffee, this one in a foam cup.

"Time to hit the road, sweetie. You know how Harvey gets when people hog the tables."

"Sure, Francine. Hey, any idea what was going on with Harvey and Regina?"

She shrugged and hurried off. "What do you care, dearie?" she called over her shoulder. "She's *just* your tenant."

AUSTIN, Charlie, and the Watson twins enjoyed their box lunches outside. Charlie and one of the boys sat on the tailgate of Charlie's pickup. Austin relaxed in a camp chair he kept in his car. The other Watson twin, after wolfing down his meal in two minutes, was snoring loudly from a spot of lush green grass on the edge of the parking lot.

"Is he okay?" Charlie asked his brother.

"That boy could sleep in a briar patch. He'll be ready when it's time to go back to work."

Damon had taken his lunch up to Regina's apartment to eat while he made some calls. She considered following him but preferred hanging out with the guys. Austin was thoughtful and intelligent. His questions about her plans for Adeline demonstrated a worldliness that came from growing up in an affluent home. But he was so down-to-earth and fit in well in small-town life.

Charlie was crusty, but funny, too. She figured the twins to be in their twenties. Neither was married nor had a significant other. They liked stock car racing and video games. And beer. The one sleeping in the grass had talked ad nauseam about how much they'd had to drink over the weekend. Charlie finally told him to shut up. Two minutes later, he was asleep.

"How's Damon doing?" Regina asked softly as she reached for Austin's empty lunch box.

"He's doing okay. It's not the kind of work he's used to, but we're happy to have him."

"I hope you're still saying that by Friday."

Austin laughed. "Regina, I've worked with all kinds. And Mr. Palmer's heart is in the right place. He really wants this for you." He took a sip of water and raised his face toward the sun. His eyes locked in on the roof.

"Have you found someone to replace it?"

She followed his gaze to the roof where the Three Mile Millie's sign cast a shadow, hiding the sun from a patch of asphalt a few yards away.

"Walt mentioned someone in Wilmington who specializes in signs. I should look them up."

She gathered the empty boxes and tossed them in the dumpster Walt had placed between his place and hers. Charlie roused the sleeping Watson boy, and they returned to work.

"I'll check on Damon," she told Austin. Her path took her past Walt's shop. She nearly collided with him as he came around the corner.

"Oh..." he said, startled by her sudden appearance. "Good afternoon, Regina." His smile was forced. "I was headed to..." He pointed toward the dumpster. He was carrying a trash bag. It was an awkward encounter. The first of many if one of them didn't clear the air.

"Walt, are you going to be around? I need to talk to you."

"Well...I was planning to... I thought that after I threw this away, I would... Yes, I'll be here."

"I'll be back in a few minutes." She continued around the building to the stairs.

The door was open to allow a cross breeze. She climbed the stairs and stepped inside and found Damon fast asleep on the carpeted living room floor, curled on his side with a clenched fist under his chin. He more resembled a seven-year-old boy than a New York City attorney. Not wanting to wake him, she moved past into the smaller of the two bedrooms and closed the door behind her while she searched for the sign guy's number. It was a good conversation. They talked for a half hour, during which she emailed him the plan for her new sign.

"What do you want to do about the one already up there?"

"Can you take it away."

"Of course, but are you sure, Miss Cole? Old neon signs have some value. You might be able to find someone to haul it away for—"

"I have three weeks until opening day. I don't have time to find a sign enthusiast to take care of this. Do you want the job or not?"

He did. And promised he would get right on it. "I'll remove the old sign this week."

When Regina returned to the living room, Damon was sitting up, rubbing his neck, and moaning.

She bent over and kissed his forehead. "Physical labor isn't for sissies," she teased.

He nodded. "I thought upper body days at the gym were hard. Cleaning those brick walls is kicking my ass, and there's still a half day to go."

"You know you don't have to do this," she said, sitting down next to him.

He kissed her. His lips paused on hers, and she knew he was thinking that things might go further. What was it about guys? They could be exhausted one minute and ready to get it on the next. She put out all the stop signs, and with the possibility of afternoon delight ebbing away, Damon rose to his feet with the speed and grace of a ninety-year-old.

"What do you know about half-wit and dim-wit?"

"If you're referring to the Watson boys, not much. Just a couple guys who work for Austin."

"There's more. I'm sure of it. But either they're too dumb or too smart to talk much." He stretched his arms over his head to loosen up. "There's something about them that's...off. And I'm going to find out what it is."

"Damon, don't."

He raised his hand. "I'll be cool about it. But what if they have some dark past? Maybe they're axe murders or—"

"It's Bethany Beach, Damon. They're a couple of locals Austin hires part-time." She kissed him. "Now get back to work. You need to pull your share of the load."

He eyed her skeptically before a broad grin filled his face. "These tired bones are going to need a full-body massage tonight. Make sure you're ready."

His laughter filled the stairwell. And then he was gone.

WALT GLANCED up from his ever-present stack of invoices. He smiled and motioned her in.

"Are you avoiding me?" she teased as she took a seat.

He pointed to the pile of paper spread before him. "It's the end of June, and I'm still working on April's numbers." He pushed them aside. "How are you, Regina? Things going well next door?"

"Things are fine next door. Aren't you going to ask why Damon is here?"

Walt's breath caught. He was sure she heard it. Why were Americans so direct? "I assumed that with you and he being...that he'll be here from time to time."

Her smile was sweet and made him think back to when he'd hoped there was more to that smile than just friendship. That was all it was, though. They would never be more than friends. That was assuming he could keep his personal feelings in check when he was around her. Which, in a few short weeks, would be every day. Pretending he didn't have feelings for her might be one of the hardest things he'd ever done. He'd brought it upon himself, though, letting his heart get ahead of his brain. There was no turning back, though. The buzzing of a table saw and the banging of hammers was a constant reminder of that.

Her steady gaze caused him to look away. He didn't notice her arm snaking across the table and her hand on top of his until it was already there. He drew back, then tried to play it off by making a joke about too much coffee.

"Speaking of lunch, where were you? I came by but your car was gone."

"I decided to go..." He knew that if he said he'd dined at

Milo's she would figure out he was there at the same time she was. "Home. I had some leftovers."

She continued watching him, making Walt wonder if she could see through his half-truths.

"So," he asked, attempting to steer the conversation to safer topics, "what are your plans for the week?"

She pulled a notepad from her purse. "My to-do list covers seven pages. The sign guy is coming to take down Three Mile Millie. There are licenses to get and orders to place. I still need to test the kitchen equipment. I found some YouTube videos about how to do that. Pray that I don't electrocute myself."

His smile was genuine. Not pasted on like before. "Don't electrocute yourself. Why don't you have Spence Hollins do that for you?"

"Who?"

Walt pulled out a slip of paper and jotted a number. "The secret to getting by in a small town like Bethany is to have a guy for everything."

"Everything?" Regina's leering expression brought a burn to his cheeks. "You mean, like..." She batted her eyes.

"You already have a sign guy, right?"

She did.

"And a construction guy."

"I have four construction guys. Austin and Charlie, plus the Watson boys. I'm not sure I'll ever learn to tell them apart."

"Jason is the sensitive one," Walt said.

"I'll remember that. Anyway, back to what you said, I have four construction guys. Five, counting..." She paused before saying Damon's name. "So, you're saying I need another guy?"

"Spence Hollins is many guys. A generalist. He knows

the basics of electrical wiring and appliance repair. He fixes TVs and radios."

"People still fix radios?"

"Antique radios. From the thirties and forties, the big ones that sit on the floor. He can paint a little and plaster a little. He even knows how to sew."

"Quite the renaissance man."

"He's also a fisherman and crabber. He wholesales watermelons in the summer, and I've heard he has a hidden still in the Delaware countryside where he makes his own spirits."

"Wow!"

"The reason I bring him up is that he's familiar with the equipment. The previous owners called on Spence when it got too expensive to pay for service calls from the dealers in the city. Call him and see if he's available."

"Do you think he has time? I mean, with fishing and sewing and radios, he sounds incredibly busy."

Walt took a breath and let it out slowly. "Spence never has trouble finding work. His problem is keeping it. He has a tendency to get on the wrong side of people. Personally, he and I have done well. And I think you will, too. If he becomes obstinate, give it right back. Don't be intimidated."

"Sounds like some of the repair guys I dealt with in New York." Regina picked up the slip of paper. "Thank you, Walt."

"You're most welcome."

Regina waved farewell, stepped out, then poked her head back in. "Kate and Austin invited Damon and me to go to someplace out in the country tonight."

"Elijah's?"

"That's it! Why don't you come?"

Was she serious? Why would he want to be stuck at a table in some smoky corner while the four of them danced the night away? "Thanks, but—"

"Bring Francine."

"Francine? From Milo's?"

"She'll go. I asked her when I dropped by at lunchtime." Regina paused and winked. "When you were...at home."

Before he could say anything, she was gone.

AUSTIN WAS WAITING outside when Regina returned. He appeared troubled as he motioned for her to follow him around the corner of the building.

"Something happened."

Regina's heart sank. Austin wasn't a worrier, so it must be something big. Something structural? Had they uncovered issues with the roof or foundation that couldn't be overcome in time for opening day? *Please, nothing like that.* She couldn't bring herself to ask, so she waited for whatever terrible news would follow.

"Jared left."

She had to think for a moment before remembering that Jared was one of the Watson twins.

"Is he okay? I mean, he'll be back, right?"

Austin shrugged and cast a nervous glance toward the restaurant. "I don't know. We might lose Jason, too. Grandpa is in back with him, trying to convince him to stay, but I don't have much hope."

"Can you pay them more? Or find someone else? I can come up with more money if that's what we need."

"Money doesn't matter with those guys. They like

feeling that they belong. Grandpa is good at that." Austin paused. "But Mr. Palmer? Not so much."

Oh, God. What had Damon done now? She remembered their conversation at lunch and his concerns about the twins' past.

"Mr. Palmer accused Jared of being a criminal."

"Is he?"

"He was, but it's been years. But when he and Jason turned twenty-one, the courts sealed their juvenile records. They've worked on and off for me since Grandpa and I started out, and there's never been a problem. They're trying to put their past behind them, and Regina, in a town the size of Bethany Beach, that's not easy."

A cold numbness enveloped Regina. Damon was somehow responsible for losing a worker so close to opening.

"Regina, I need Mr. Palmer to leave. If he stays here, I'll have no chance of keeping the twins. And without them, Grandpa and I can't get done in time for your opening." He rubbed the back of his neck and took a deep breath. "Grandpa's so mad. I'm not even sure he'll stay."

Everything was falling apart. And not in some little one-brick-at-a-time way. This was a total collapse. Everything she'd put into bringing the place back to life was on the line. And it was because of Damon.

"Where is Damon?"

"Still cleaning walls. He called Jared out in front of Jason, Grandpa, and me, then told us we needed to do something about it. We went in the back and left him working. Jared kept on going out the back door. He ran off into the woods and is probably hitchhiking home."

Austin felt bad. She could see it in his eyes. But he was

also a businessman. No help meant no work. And that meant no money. The ball was in her court.

She patted his arm. "I'll handle it." Then trudged inside.

Damon was on an extension ladder, scrubbing a patch of brick with a wire brush. He grinned and pointed at the spot. "Hey, boo, I've been working on this for damn near twenty minutes, but it's finally looking better."

"Damon, we need to talk."

"Sure. What's up? Did something..." His grin disappeared when he looked toward the kitchen. "Did you hear that one of those backwoods boys is a carjacker?"

"Let's go outside."

"Regina, I couldn't hardly believe it myself. But when I confronted him, he—"

"Outside, Damon. Please!"

She didn't wait for his response. She returned to the spot where she'd left Austin. Thankfully, he was back inside. The last thing she wanted was a confrontation between them. Damon was a few seconds behind her, but that was enough for him to come loaded for bear.

"Did Austin say something to you? Or was it the old man? I thought they were in back with the twins."

"Jared left, Damon."

"Which one is Jared?"

"The one you called out."

"Good. He needed to get out of here. He took a seventy-six-year-old woman's car at knifepoint. Some nice old grandma who was in Bethany for the weekend with her family."

"He was a kid, Damon."

"Fifteen ain't a kid, Regina. He knew what he was doing. He was high on meth. I saw the trial transcript."

"How did you get that? Wasn't it sealed?"

Damon rolled his eyes. "Are you forgetting who I am, boo? I know people. A couple of calls and I got my hands on the kid's record."

The way he looked at her as he spoke made it clear that Damon thought he was doing the right thing. He was proud of his sleuthing skills.

"Damon, without the twins, I won't be able to open on the fourth."

"The other one's still here. Me and him can knock this job out. I'll come in early and stay late. Work weekends. Whatever it takes."

"You need to go back to New York." There. She'd said it.

Damon looked crestfallen. Then he looked pissed. "There's no way in hell I'm going back. I did what I did for you, Regina. We don't need some carjacking meth head stealing whatever he can get his hands on."

"If you stay, we lose both twins."

"Screw 'em, then!"

"And Charlie."

The fight went out of him when he realized what was at stake. He attempted to speak, but nothing more than a few sputtered expletives came out. His clenched fists laid bare the anger he was losing the battle against controlling.

"I'll give you a ride back to—"

"The hell you will, Regina! I'm not in the wrong here, but I'm the one paying the price." He yanked his phone from his back pocket and pounded on the keys for a few moments before looking up again. "Uber's coming to get me. I'll wait across the road."

"Damon, let's not be like—"

"It's not the time, Regina. We'll talk later."

"Are you going back to the hotel?"

"I don't know yet."

He stalked away and crossed the busy highway to the storage facility directly across from the restaurant. He studied his phone and made a point of not looking at her. After a couple minutes of waiting and hoping he might acknowledge her, Regina returned to the restaurant. She was about to step inside when she spotted Walt watching from an open garage bay. Their eyes met for a second before Regina continued inside.

REGINA AND AUSTIN'S cars were still in the lot when Walt locked up the shop for the night. Four hours had passed since Damon Palmer's angry exit. Walt didn't know what had happened. The usual buzzing, whirring, and hammering sounds had ceased since lunch. The Watson twins were nowhere to be seen. Charlie had gunned his old truck out of the parking lot a little before four.

Walt debated a visit next door but decided against it. If Regina wanted to confide in him, she'd had her chance. He said a quick prayer that everything would turn out okay before departing himself. He had no plans for the evening, despite a call from Francine at Milo's offering to go with him to Elijah's for the evening's festivities that Regina had mentioned earlier. Judging by what little he'd seen that afternoon, the festivities would be canceled.

"YES, Grandpa. We're headed out to see him right now." Austin licked his lips and pulled the phone a few inches from his ear as Charlie ranted on the other end. *Sorry*, he mouthed to Regina. They had moved from the restaurant to the front seat of Austin's car. After four long hours of trying to assuage anger and soothe hurt feelings, they still weren't done. Austin was a trouper, though. He caught her eye and winked as Charlie continued to bluster. "You're good with that, Grandpa?" he said, cutting in when Charlie was catching his breath. "Okay, then. We'd better get going."

He tossed the phone on the seat. "Thank goodness for Jane," he said, referring to Charlie's wife. "She knows how to get him to come to his senses."

"In this case, he's partially right," Regina offered meekly.

"Oh, he's more than partially right. Mr. Palmer went too far."

It was as pointed a remark as Austin had made all day, and while it might have been uttered at a moment when he was weary from the turmoil, he was right. Still, Regina felt a perverse need to stand up for Damon. She bit her tongue, though.

Seeing her pained expression, Austin apologized. "It will all blow over," he said hopefully. "But we still need to square things with Jared."

THE MOON CAST a surreal glow over the Atlantic as Austin pulled into the SaltAire parking lot. The happy sounds of a party on the beach a hundred yards away reached Regina's ears but brought her no merriment. It had been a hell of a day.

"Want me to wait in case he left?"

"We rented the room through tomorrow, so that's not necessary." Regina turned to face Austin. "You did good work today," she said, meaning every word. "I didn't think we had a chance with Jared."

"He only wants to be respected," Austin replied. "I couldn't have done it without you, though."

They sat silently for a moment before Regina pushed open the door. "Guess I'll see you tomorrow."

"Bright and early. And try to get some sleep. There's so much to do. We'll get past this."

She could barely pick up her feet as she trudged into the lobby and approached the desk. Michael did a double-take.

"Miss Cole?"

"I forgot my key. Is there a chance you can give me another?"

"I'm sorry, ma'am, but Mr. Palmer said you wouldn't be needing the room. He canceled the evening's reservation." He lowered his voice as he added, "My wife packed your belongings. I have your bag in back. I'll get it."

That was the first time all day when she felt she might start bawling.

Big girl pants, Regina.

"Do you have another..."

Michael was shaking his head before she finished. "All booked up. I'm sorry."

While he retrieved her suitcase, Regina shut her eyes to fight off the headache coming at her from all directions. At least she had the apartment. There was no furniture, but she could roll up one of her jackets to use as a pillow. That and a hot shower would make her feel as good as new. Feeling that she'd reclaimed at least a thread of hopefulness, she smiled at Michael, thanked him, and turned to leave.

And realized her screwup.

Her car was at the restaurant.

She could walk, but it was dark. And there were woods between the hotel and there. And animals. All kinds of animals.

Don't be stupid, Regina. No one was ever mauled by a deer. Were they?

Uber was the only option. It was ten-thirty when she walked out of the SaltAire. An Uber would take a few minutes to arrive, and the salty sea air stung her cheeks. She was searching for her phone when a car pulled up.

Walt rolled down the window and smiled softly. "Get in."

tuesday, june 17

REGINA AWAKENED with a start as a seagull cried angrily outside. She shielded her eyes against the sunlight streaming through two open windows at the foot of the feather-soft bed. The gull squawked again, closer this time, reminding her that Walt's home was less than a half mile from the seashore and, given the saltwater marsh flats out back, attracted its share of wildfowl.

She sat up and squinted against the brightness. A half-dozen black-eyed Susans in a vase crowned a tray placed on a dresser inside the bedroom door. She loved how the flowers grew wild along the back and smiled appreciatively at Walt's thoughtfulness. A carafe of coffee and a selection of pastries accompanied the flowers. Regina threw her legs over the side of the bed, grabbed a Danish and some coffee, opened the bedroom door, and padded into the hall. The place was quiet. A seventies-era wall clock like the one her grandmother used to have hung on the wall at the end of the hallway. Nine-thirty. She should have been at the restaurant two hours ago, but for once, she didn't care. She returned to the guest room, shrugged off her clothes, and went in search of a hot shower. It felt strangely erotic, walking naked through Walt's house. What would she have done had he turned up? She had no towel to cover herself and little inclination to use one. *Whew, those thoughts.* The main bathroom was furnished with guest towels and a variety of soaps, lotions, and shampoos. Someone had trained that boy right. He knew what a girl needed to make herself presentable. She turned on the shower, waited until the water was steaming, and climbed in.

Bliss!

She soaped up and shampooed her hair, then luxuriated in the warmth and allowed her thoughts to return to the previous day. Things were going so well, then boom! She'd been so angry at Damon at times. When she'd shared with Walt what all had happened, he'd surprised her by taking Damon's side to some degree.

He was watching out for you, Walt said. *Perhaps he could have handled it better, but he did what he might have done in the city where you don't know people as well as we do here.*

He was right. Damon was being protective of her. And while his way might be more of a nuclear option, and had nearly cost her a grand opening on July Fourth, he'd meant it for good. And she'd sent him on his way. He had every right to be angry at her.

Damn it all, why couldn't he be more easy-going? More like Walt?

She dried off and wrapped a towel around her head and another herself. The bathroom mirror was steamed up, so she opened the door and headed back to the guest room.

"Hello."

Regina nearly jumped out of her skin. She spun around

and came face-to-face with a pretty brunette about her age. "Who are you?"

"Perhaps I should ask you the same thing."

"I'm a friend of Walt's. I had no place to go last night, so he let me stay here."

The woman nodded. She seemed comfortable in the surroundings. It was obvious it wasn't her first time there.

"And you?" Regina pressed. "How do you know Walt?"

"I'm his wife."

WALT CHECKED his watch for the tenth time in the last hour. Ten o'clock and still no sign of Regina. When he'd dropped off the tray, she'd been snoring away under the covers. The only thing visible was the shock of hair that cascaded over the pillow like a silky brown fountain. He tried to envision what it might be like to wake up next to her every morning. Damon Palmer was a lucky man. Yes, he'd gone too far by bringing up Jared Watson's past, but he did it for the right reasons. If Regina were his girl, Walt would take whatever steps were necessary to protect her.

The sad part was, Regina didn't know everything there was to know about Damon. Walt had learned enough to worry she was headed for trouble but still couldn't decide if it was his place to say anything. What if the information that Tony Sampson had gleaned was incorrect? What if Damon's intentions were pure? Walt could only hope that things worked themselves out before someone got hurt.

Even if that someone was him.

Fortunately, all was good at the restaurant. With Damon out of the picture, the Watson boys were back at work, and Charlie Staley was whistling instead of grumbling. Austin had confided that handling Charlie was becoming harder than handling the twins. "Jane is spoiling him at home, and he's expecting the same from me. I keep encouraging them to see more of the world. Maybe take a cruise." Austin made sure the coast was clear before adding, "I found a seven-month cruise that goes from New Jersey to Europe and Africa. I sent brochures to their house, but so far, nothing."

He was only half serious, though. Charlie might be crotchety, but the love between them was undeniable, reminding Walt of the feelings he had for his own grandparents.

He checked the time once more, then returned to his office. There were phone calls to make, contracts to send out, and that pesky stack of invoices remained right where he'd left it. Perhaps that would be the day he made it to the bottom.

If he could just take his mind off the beautiful woman in his guest room.

HER NAME WAS JOANIE. And while she wasn't Walt's wife presently, she used to be.

She wasn't what Regina had expected. Walt had remained guarded about his marriage, clouded as it was by Hannah's death. Joanie was pretty in a wholesome, small-town way. She wore her hair in the latest style, dressed in a way that accentuated her pretty figure and seemed happy and well-adjusted. She assured Regina from the start that she hadn't broken and entered. Then, after Regina got dressed, they sat at the kitchen table and drank coffee.

"Mark and I live in St. Michaels, about ninety minutes

away. We rent a place in Rehoboth each June. Walt allows me to keep my beach chairs and umbrellas in the shed out back. I guess I should've called first."

"Oh, it's not like that. Walt and I aren't—"

"It's okay, Regina. I know. I noticed you were sleeping in the guest room. And even though I don't live here anymore, I still hear things. You're the new proprietor of Three Mile Millie's."

"The new name is Adeline. I'm waiting for the sign to arrive."

They chatted for a few minutes until their cups were empty. Regina detected a melancholy beneath Joanie's cheerful visage. It was to be expected after all she'd endured, but Regina wondered if poor Joanie struggled with the past. While Regina gathered her things and stuck them in her suitcase, Joanie took their cups to the kitchen, rinsed them, and placed them on the counter to dry.

"I'm going out back and get our chairs and umbrella," Joanie said as they stood at the front door. "I'm guessing that's your car out front."

Regina peered out. It was her car. Walt must've had Felix drop it by that morning. After an awkward moment, Regina extended her hand. "It is nice to meet you, Joanie. Please come visit me when Adeline is open for business."

"I promise that Mark and I will be there." She smiled, then glanced away before adding, "And Regina, thank you."

"For what?"

The words came with some difficulty. Regina could see it in Joanie's eyes as she labored over them. "For...helping Walt heal. I've prayed for years that someone would come along to help him move past...everything with Hannah... and me." Her lip quivered, but she quickly got it under control.

"Respectfully, Joanie, Walt's healing was his own. I'm just someone who happened to show up."

"No, dear. You're more than that." She took Regina's hands in hers. "You're an answered prayer. Please take care of him."

WALT WAS a few minutes from calling to check on her when Regina wheeled into the parking lot a little after eleven. She pulled up in front of the shop and made a beeline for his office.

"I feel great!" she exclaimed. "Please tell me that the Watson twins showed up."

"They've been going strong since first light. I peeked in a little earlier, and it's starting to look like a real restaurant. Oh, by the way, Spence Hollins arrived about an hour ago."

"Oh, dear, I brought lunch for everyone as my way of apologizing for how things went off the rails yesterday. I brought lunches for you and Felix, too. I hadn't counted on Mr. Hollins."

"No worries. Felix left for Northern Virginia a few minutes ago to pick up a car."

Regina glanced around the shop. "So, it's just you and me?"

"It is, indeed."

She threw her arms around him. "The flowers are lovely, the pastries are gone, and the carafe is empty. Thank you so much."

"Wow, you must've been famished."

"Well," she said, drawing back and looking up at him. "I had help with the pastries and coffee, but I kept the flowers for myself."

"Help?"

"Yes, let me tell you all about it."

LUNCH WAS A BIG HIT. Burgers and fries from a fast food place she'd passed on the way out of Bethany and a cooler of water, soda, and beer. Walt, Austin, Charlie, and the Watson boys dug in with gusto. Spence Hollins was older than Regina had expected, late sixties with a full but neatly trimmed beard and longish gray hair tucked under a cap. He was reluctant at first to join them, but after seeing the mound of food she'd placed in the bed of Charlie's truck, he came around. Everyone except Walt gravitated toward the beer. The Watson boys knocked back two each, making Regina wonder if their ladder climbing might be impaired for the rest of the day. It wouldn't matter if it was. Everyone was so happy that a few lost hours wouldn't matter.

Full, happy, and in the case of the twins, slightly tipsy, the men returned to work after a half hour. Walt headed back to his shop, and Regina followed Spence Hollins to the kitchen. "How do things look, Mr. Hollins?"

"Just Spence," he said as he bent over and peered into an oven. "Overall, the equipment is pretty good. The gas is connected, and the ovens are heating." He motioned for her to follow him to the walk-in cooler. "I hear you got some experience with one of these," he said, pulling open the door.

"Yeah, Spence. One of these bastards got me bad."

"That won't happen here." He stepped inside. "I found a couple of cracks, but they sealed up real nice. You don't have to worry about this old girl. I took care of her from the time she was installed. If she gives you trouble, call me and I'll come right out."

Regina felt herself falling for the rough-edged old man in the bib overalls. Then she glimpsed a tattoo that stretched from his right arm to his elbow. "Spence, is that..." She leaned in closer. "Do you have a tattoo of a topless woman?"

Spence ducked his head and nodded. "Yeah, that's what happens when you're drunk and far from home."

"Military tattoo?" Regina asked with a wink.

"Army. Should've spent the money on something useful."

"Tattoos are back in style."

"Not this kind, dearie. Now, let's talk about that dishwasher. She's a real piece of work."

OTHER THAN A FEW PHONE CALLS, the afternoon was quiet. Walt whittled away at invoices, then straightened up the workbench and toolboxes. Felix was a whiz with machinery, but not so good at remembering to return things to where they belonged. In his earlier years, Walt harped on him about his lack of order, but as he'd aged and matured and the business took off, he realized that the shop and its tools were more Felix's domain than his. He didn't harp anymore, but he would occasionally straighten things up, if only to assuage his need for order. He was tinkering with one of the lifts when Austin came in.

"What are you working on, Walt?"

"Mostly tinkering."

"You've got some real beauties in here."

"Are you a car guy, Austin?"

"Not so much. I've always preferred building things. I love Grandpa's truck, Calvin, though."

Walt glanced toward the parking lot. "The old International? Felix and I could make it look brand new for you. The body looks solid."

"Maybe down the road, but right now, I prefer Calvin like he is. A solid truck with the dents and scrapes that go with being a work truck."

"We call that a patina. And I agree. Calvin certainly has his own unique character. Is there something I can do for you, Austin?"

"Kate and I are going out to Elijah's later. Want to go with us?"

Walt lowered the lift and wiped his hands with a shop rag. "Elijah's can be fun, but I think I'll pass."

"I told Kate you'd say that, but she said to ask you anyway. By the way, Regina hasn't been in, has she?"

"Haven't seen her since lunch. I suspect that she's working upstairs. She said something about arranging for delivery of some furniture."

"I'll look for her up there. Kate wants me to invite her, too."

"Oh? Really? You're asking Regina?"

"She's earned a night out. She certainly has her hands full, doesn't she? I look around and think, this is actually going to be a working restaurant in a little more than two weeks." Austin chuckled. "It scares me sometimes."

Walt laid the rag aside. "Are you worried you won't get done?"

"Oh, we'll get done." He lowered his voice. "Provided Mr. Palmer doesn't come back and mess things up with the twins. We'll pull all-nighters if we have to. The last thing I want is to disappoint Regina. I bet you feel the same way."

Walt nodded but maintained a poker face.

"That's why you need to go to Elijah's with us. If she doesn't have anyone to dance with, Kate won't want to leave her alone at the table, which means we don't get to take advantage of that hip-hop band that's out there this month."

"Hip-hop? I wouldn't have any idea how to dance to that."

Austin laughed. "Neither does two-thirds of the crowd at Elijah's. You want to go or not?" He winked as he added, "You might as well. I heard that Regina's staying at your place. There's no need to sit at home and wait for her to show up."

"We're only friends, you know," Walt said as they walked outside. The weather was glorious. Sunny skies and temperatures in the low eighties. Walt had been considering one last stroll along the shore before tourism season arrived, but the chance to spend an evening out with Regina was too much to pass up. "Count me in."

His phone buzzed in his jeans pocket. He pulled it out and smiled when he saw caller ID. "Good afternoon, Barrister."

Tony Sampson laughed at the British reference to his occupation. "Always gotta be reminding me how high and mighty you Brits are, don't you, Walt?"

"It's called respect, Tony. What do I owe the pleasure of your call?"

The mirth disappeared from his voice. "I'm following up on what we talked about last Friday."

Walt's gut felt hollow. He'd pulled Tony back in to share his concerns about Damon. About how something seemed...*off* about the man. Tony promised to look into it but also cautioned Walt about allowing his feelings to get ahead of him. Somehow, he'd sensed that Walt's feelings for Regina went beyond a simple business relationship.

"Yeah, I'm sorry if I stepped out of line by asking. It's just that I—"

"Walt, you did the right thing. I'm coming on Thursday for a long weekend. May I come by?"

"Certainly. Should I ask Regina to join us?"

"Let's talk first."

HAD she not been with friends, Regina might have worried she was being spirited away to some remote backwater where they would leave her for dead. The roads from Bethany Beach grew increasingly narrower and less traveled as they rode with the setting sun in their faces. Austin and Kate sat in the front seat of Austin's flashy red Mustang. Walt and Regina were wedged in back, their knees touching on those moments when they could stay in their seats. Dips, bends, and potholes kept them airborne for much of the ride, but Regina didn't care. It was nice to have an evening out with friends. And if Elijah's was good enough for Kate, it was fine by her, too.

"Don't expect anything fancy," Kate warned. "Mostly locals. Fishermen, farmers, and factory workers."

"But the food's good and the beer's cold," Austin added. "And the band is amazing."

"If you like hip-hop," Kate said, with a hint of exasperation.

Regina looked at Walt. "I take it you've been?"

Walt nodded. "They described it perfectly."

A few minutes later, Austin pulled into a gravel parking lot fronting a wood-frame building that looked more like a shed than a bar. Christmas lights were strung from end to end, and the exterior walls were covered by beer and tobacco ads. A small lighted sign hanging next to the door was the only indication they'd arrived at the right place.

Elijah's.

Walt crawled out and extended his hand. "You ready?"

Regina used his hand to steady herself as she exited from the tiny rear seat. Two guys leaning against a pickup and spitting tobacco into red cups checked her out, then nodded a polite hello. Regina kept her hold on Walt's hand as they headed inside. The air was filled with the heavenly aromas of fresh seafood. The place was packed, but Austin spotted a table in a corner near a small dance floor. He led the way. The lighting was dim, but a neon Pabst Blue Ribbon sign over their table made it easier to see.

"This is where we sat the first time Austin brought me here," Kate noted. "I'd lived here for years and had no idea it existed. Now I can't get enough of it."

"What's their specialty?"

"Oysters and beer," Austin said. "I like them fried. Kate gets them smoked. There's also fried clams and shrimp. I've heard they have burgers, but I've never seen one."

Austin went to the bar to place their orders as four guys and a woman set up equipment on the stage a few feet away.

Regina slid her chair closer to Walt. "You don't seem like the hip-hop type," she teased.

"It's not bad. The bands rotate in and out. Most weeks it's just a jukebox."

"I'm glad you came along," she whispered. "Austin said you almost didn't."

"Once I heard you were coming, I..." He paused. "It'll be fun. Did you arrange to have your furniture delivered?"

"It's coming tomorrow."

"And did your kitchen equipment pass muster with Spence?"

"Everything except the dishwasher. Spence said it's a mess and needs someone to keep an eye on it."

"Goodness, I had no idea. What will you do?"

She grinned. "I hired Spence as my dishwasher! He's between jobs, so I threw it out there and he said yes."

Walt's face lit up. "That's amazing! I've never known Spence to have an actual job. He's always been the local jack-of-all-trades around here."

"Well...he was a little reluctant at first, but..."

Austin laughingly cut Regina off. "I watched the whole thing. Spence has a crush on her."

Regina waved him off. "That's not what I was going to say. I think Spence views me as a damsel in distress. Kind of like the daughter he never had."

The food arrived, and they began eating and swapping portions. The band kicked things off with an Eminem hit from two decades ago. A few couples made their way toward the dance floor, but most were digging into dinner. The atmosphere was friendly and loose. No pretense. No one-upmanship. Just happy people enjoying good food and conversation. Amazing how a shack in the middle of nowhere had mastered the dining experience better than many five-star restaurants in Manhattan. She glanced at Walt as he popped a fried shrimp into his mouth. He winked at her, then reached his fork across to snag a clam from her plate.

"Hey!"

He gave her his best, *who, me?* expression as he downed the clam.

"Better than fish and chips at a London pub?" she asked.

"It's been so long since I ate anywhere in the UK that it's hard to say. The biggest difference is how much spicier foods are here."

SHE WAS LOVELY. The heat emanating from every direction darkened her cheeks and made her skin glisten. A bead of sweat trickled down her neck and disappeared into the scoop of her simple white blouse. She didn't know it was there, or how erotic it looked. Walt had to force himself to return his gaze to his dinner plate. The band wrapped up a couple of songs Walt didn't recognize. Hip-hop had never been his thing. The band's lead singer, a tall, rangy chap in a Tupac t-shirt announced they would slow things down. They hadn't made it through the first few notes before people streamed toward the dance floor. Austin grabbed Kate's hand and led the way.

"Do you know this song?" Walt asked Regina. She smiled and said she did.

"Boyz II Men. A huge hit when I was a little girl. We weren't allowed to listen to it at home. My father forbade it. Fortunately, my friends' parents weren't so strict."

Walt was about to ask why her father didn't approve, but he picked up on the lyrics and understood. Pretty mild, but maybe not for a little girl. "It's quite lovely, though."

They watched as the others moved and swayed to the slow beat. The band liked having so many people dancing, so they stretched it out. Walt shifted in his chair so he could watch Regina's reaction. She was smiling, her eyes dreamily following the movement of the dancers. She probably wanted to be out there with them, but Walt had been too timid to ask.

She caught his gaze and winked. "I went to my first high school dance in ninth grade. Somehow, the deejay snuck this one in between a bunch of Britney Spears and Michael Jackson hits."

"How can you remember something so specific?"

"Because Jayden Andover asked me to dance to this song."

"Jayden Andover, huh." Walt chuckled as he tried to envision a much-younger Regina slow-dancing with an awkward freshman boy.

"The most handsome boy in school," she continued. "Tall. Great hair. Never had a single pimple, let alone a case of acne." She smiled. "By the time we made it onto the dance floor, the song was almost over, but I'll never forget it."

Walt wanted to ask if she wanted to dance. To relive that first dance from years before. He cleared his throat and was about to plunge in when the song morphed into something faster and louder. Austin, Kate, and many others hurried back to their tables.

"That was fun!" Kate said, wiping a bead of sweat from her forehead. "Does anyone besides me need another drink?" She took orders and headed to the bar.

Austin spotted someone he knew from town and left to say hello.

"Am I keeping you from making the rounds?" Regina asked Walt.

He glanced around. There were a few familiar faces, including two former clients. No one he would rather be with than her, though. "I'm fine. I prefer to sit and enjoy the surroundings." He nodded at her empty plate. "Are you going to add smoked clams to your menu?"

"They're delicious, for sure. Speaking of that, I'm conducting interviews later this week. Austin said my office would be ready."

"Locals?"

"Nope. Spence is my only local so far. One of my former employees, a wonderful chef named Jacob Klein, and two of his friends are interested."

"And they know it's in Bethany?"

"Of course. The beach is pretty appealing to pasty-white New Yorkers. And they're young people with few ties. They can come down and try it for the summer. If it fits, who knows? If not, I'll find replacements. It's all part of operating your own business. You know that as well as anyone."

"I've been pretty lucky. Felix has been with me forever. I'm not sure what I would do if he left."

She patted his hand. "You would figure it out." She glanced toward the stage as the band was wrapping up their version of a Kanye song she'd never cared for. "I hope they play more slow songs later."

The lead singer announced a fifteen-minute break. Walt decided he needed a break, too.

"Be right back," he said as he motioned to the men's room. Others had the same idea, and the line was twenty-deep by the time he got there. Off to the side, he spotted the band's frontman ordering a beer at the end of the counter. He stepped out of line and slid in next to him.

"Sorry to bother you, but can I ask a favor?"

The guy eyed him skeptically. "Sorry, man. We're on break."

Walt pulled out his wallet and slid some bills in front of him. That got his attention.

THE BAND'S playlist blended together as the night progressed. Ninety minutes after arriving, with dinner long done, Regina felt the onset of a headache. There was so much left to do at the restaurant. She was ready to head back and get a good night's sleep. She'd spent the previous night at Walt's but didn't want to burden him again. During a restroom run with Kate, she'd asked if her room was still available. It was. She checked her watch several times, hopeful that someone would get the hint, but it didn't work, so she gamely tried to keep up with the conversation at their table. Despite being the newest of the three in Bethany Beach, Austin knew everyone. Even more than Walt. It shouldn't have been surprising, given how outgoing he was. Walt was more laid back, unconcerned with enlarging his circle of friends. And Kate? She was perfectly content to hang close to Austin and go with the flow. Nice, but not Regina's way of doing things. Still, she was sweet and incredibly intelligent, and despite different interests in everything from music to fashion, Regina felt a friendship blooming. And since they were becoming fast friends, she decided it was time to beg off for the night.

"Hey, guys, I'm sorry to be a party pooper, but—"

The music stopped, and Elijah's grew quiet. Up to that point, the band had done a masterful job of blending one song into the next, creating a never-ending playlist not unlike the New York clubs she'd frequented in the past. The silence caught Elijah's rowdy and slightly inebriated customers off guard. They gawked at one another for a moment, then looked at the band to see what was up.

"Don't worry," the leader said softly into his microphone. "We ain't going on another break quite yet. We are doing something we almost never do, though."

He paused and allowed the anticipation to build. "We had a request that was too good to pass up." He patted his pocket, and the crowd laughed. His message was clear. The band was willing to break out of their setlist, but only for a price. "Somewhere out there is a dude who wants to ask his lady to dance. He missed his chance when we played her song earlier."

Heads turned as people tried to figure out who among them had anted up to hear a specific song. Regina looked at Kate and shrugged. Kate motioned at Walt. His cheeks were on fire.

And then, everything became clear. The lead singer motioned to the others, and the band reprised the Boyz II Men number. Walt had requested it just for her, but when she looked at him, he appeared to be suffering from stage fright. The lead singer noticed it too. He held back on the lyrics as the band played and replayed the song's opening. "Let's make it easier for the mystery person," he said softly. "All you guys and girls who want to hold your special person close and sway to this slow jam, get on out here now."

The floodgate opened, and the floor was packed. Yet Walt remained frozen in place. Regina looked at Kate for guidance as Austin grabbed her hand and led her off to dance.

Ask him, Kate mouthed before disappearing into the mass of sweaty bodies.

"Hey, Walt..."

It was a second or two before he realized she was speaking to him.

"Let's dance," she said.

Wordlessly, he got to his feet. Regina led him to a spot on the edge of the packed dance floor. The lead singer watched their every move. Without skipping a word of the lyrics, he motioned for them to come to a spot near the stage that had somehow remained open. Regina took the lead again, and before the band reached the chorus, they were where they were supposed to be.

She leaned in close and whispered, "Are you going to hold me, or do I have to dance by myself?"

And then, as if a light came on, he was fully there. He smiled and opened his arms. She went into them and moaned softly as they closed around her.

"Can you believe someone paid the band to play this one?" she teased.

The red returned to his face. "Uh...I have a confession to make, Regina. It was me."

She snorted against his shoulder and tried to keep from laughing out loud. The man she'd considered so suave and refined was struggling to make his move. But then, had he even considered her in that way? Was he really interested in getting closer? After all, there was Damon. But dancing with Damon never felt as nice as how she felt in Walt's arms. They were in sync. He wasn't trying to go one way while she went another. It was nothing like...

"Jayden Andover?" Walt uttered his name softly.

"What about him?"

"I'm sure this doesn't compare."

"Jayden Andover turned out to be a jerk."

"But you said...great hair and all that."

"I'll give him that, but he was still a jerk. By junior year, he was stoned every day." She pushed herself closer. "This is much nicer. Now stop talking. I want to enjoy my favorite song. And being with you."

Wow! Had she really said that? Talk about throwing your-self at someone. Most guys would be planning their next move. Perhaps a hand sliding down her back or guy parts grinding against girl parts. Damon, for all his good traits, was as subdued as a freight train. But Walt? Little changed. He held her close but didn't come on too strong. It made him all the sexier. A little restraint on the dance floor had to equate to restraint in...other places.

God, she was sweating. Walt didn't seem to notice, so she hung on and allowed herself to get caught up in the moment. Did he have any idea how close he was to getting pretty much anything he wanted? All he needed to do was invite her back to his place for the night. But as the song ended and they fell in with the other couples returning to their seats, she knew he wouldn't make that invitation.

And it was because of Damon. He was still in the picture, looming large over any further advances. Walt wasn't twenty years old. He'd matured to where his urges didn't dictate his decisions. With him, she felt good and safe and a lot of other things she couldn't yet understand.

Perhaps it was time to set things straight with Damon.

Austin suggested they head out. "I'm in the middle of this big project," he teased. "The woman I work for would be disappointed if I don't show up at first light."

She and Walt crawled in the back of Austin's car. Walt had been uncharacteristically quiet since their dance. She reached for his hand and liked how it felt. It was the hand of a working man, and her breath caught as she imagined how it would feel if they were...

And then he eased his hand away, and her heart sank.

Why? He had to know how much she wanted him. He had to feel what was going on.

Yet when Austin pulled into Walt's driveway, he made no attempt to invite her in. He said good night and patted her knee before getting out. That was it. No invitation to stay. No kiss. Nothing. Just a pat on the knee.

Geesh, what was wrong with her?

She didn't need to ask that question. She already knew.

She owed Damon a phone call.

friday, june 20

THEY WERE fifteen minutes into the interview, and things were going better than Regina had expected. Jacob was still the same thoughtful and funny guy she'd hired at Gasconade, and while she'd hoped to hear sordid details of how things were going there, Jacob was professional and future-focused. His friends, Conor and Andrea, had plenty to contribute as well. In fact, the idea of a group interview was theirs. It was something Regina would never have considered otherwise, but she was glad she had.

When someone knocked on Regina's office door, everyone had to shift their chairs to give her room to pass. She expected Austin with some paint samples, but it was Spence Hollins. He held up a rusty piece of metal for her inspection.

"What in the world is that?"

His explanation lost her. Something about a connector from the stove to the main gas line that had been exposed to moisture. Spence's eyes shifted to Regina's left, where Jacob watched closely.

"That's trouble," Jacob said.

Conor and Andrea joined the huddle as Jacob took the chunk of metal from Spence and turned it over in his hands. Spence was grizzled and short on words. All country in the way he walked, talked, and dressed. What would he make of Jacob—an openly gay male? Did that kind of thing fly in small-town America? Regina had heard the horror stories. And what about Conor and his orange hair? Or Andrea's nose piercing? Were the differences too much?

Nah.

"I have a buddy who runs a metal fabrication shop," Jacob said as he handed the piece back. "If you get me the specs, he'll turn a new piece out overnight and send it down."

It was as good a time as any to make introductions.

"Spence, assuming these three agree to come here, I want you to meet our newest employees."

"About damned time," Spence grumbled. He eyed them skeptically. "We got two weeks to get this place shipshape. Are y'all up to it?"

"Hell, yes!" Andrea said, thrusting out her hand. "I'm Andrea. I'll run the front end." She motioned with her thumb at Conor. "That's Conor. He doesn't talk a lot, but I love him anyway. Say hi, Conor."

"Hey. I guess I'll be doing whatever the rest of you guys tell me to do."

"And," Regina said, nodding toward Jacob, "Jacob is in charge of the kitchen. He'll work with me on menu planning and food preparation."

"Head chef?" Spence asked.

"We haven't gotten into titles yet," Regina said. "What do you think, Jacob?"

"Just call me Jacob. Everything else will fall into place.

How about you, Spence? What's your specialty? Baker? Line cook?"

"Dishwashers. I can fix 'em and I can run 'em. Where are you kids staying?"

"That's still to be determined. Conor was looking at apartments on the way down. We were hoping to be close to the beach, but unless Regina is paying six-figure salaries, that's not going to happen."

"I can't help you get on the beach, but I got a double-wide on Miller Creek that's got nobody living in it. It's yours if you want it."

This caught Andrea's attention. "A double-wide? Like a trailer?"

Spence nodded.

"Are you kidding?"

Spence shook his head, then told them how much the rent was. "I'll tie up my old boat at the dock. You can use it if you ever get a day off. It's a nice little ride through the marshland. Lots of wildlife. About an hour to the Route 1 causeway. You can walk to the beach from there."

The New Yorkers were as giddy as kids at Christmas. Spence went back to work. Jacob and the others filled out employment paperwork, then, brimming with excitement, dashed off to New York to gather their stuff.

"If it's okay with you, Regina, I'll post job openings for servers and line cooks," Jacob said as they headed out. "We need to hurry if we're going to get them trained and ready by the fourth of July weekend."

Regina gave him the okay, then followed them out, making a quick detour to the kitchen to thank Spence for his kindness.

"Ain't no big thing," he said without looking up from

the back of the stove. "My place is nearby, so I can keep an eye on 'em."

The old guy was quite the teddy bear underneath. His acceptance of the three out-of-towners made her feel good about the decision to bring him on. Spence was proving to be the glue that would keep things together through the dog days of summer.

Regina caught up to the others in the parking lot. They said their goodbyes and piled into Andrea's ancient Toyota. As they pulled away, Regina spotted Walt watching through the shop window. Someone was with him, but in the sun's glare, she couldn't see who.

He had been distant on the ride home from Elijah's three nights before and had kept his distance since. She'd contemplated asking him about it, but preparations for opening continued to press at her so she'd put it off, as she'd put off talking to Damon. Why were relationships so darned complicated? She waved toward the shop as she returned to the restaurant but couldn't see if Walt responded.

THEY WATCHED in silence as Regina joined the three strangers at their car.

"Any idea who they are?" Tony Sampson asked. "The car has New York plates. Maybe they're associates of Damon's."

"Not likely," Walt replied. "Regina mentioned something about a former colleague coming to town. That's my guess."

Regina hugged them. It was obvious by how one of the

men pulled her into an embrace that he and Regina were close. He said something as he crawled into the old car that made her laugh. She waved as they drove off, then turned back toward the restaurant. She looked toward the shop and squinted into the sun. Walt waved. She waved back but kept going. Everything about her, from her regal bearing to her delicate features, was captivatingly beautiful. She didn't deserve what was happening to her. The owners of the restaurant had already made a victim out of her once. It was now up to Walt and Tony to make sure she wasn't victimized again.

"Is it time to say something?" Tony asked.

Walt hesitated.

Tony turned to face him. "It's the right thing to do, Walt. You know that, right?"

"Yes, it's just that..." He sighed. "I wish it didn't have to be like this. Tony, was it wrong for me to bring my concerns to you?"

"You did what you thought was best. You have a vested interest in the restaurant's success, and you saw something that unsettled you. It's not as if you two are romantically involved." Tony paused. His eyes followed Walt's to the spot where Regina had disappeared from view. "Or are you?"

Walt's response came haltingly. Tony, a veteran trial attorney, could tell there were feelings there. "No, it's not like that. We've gone out for dinner a couple times, but it's... Yeah, I suppose it's time to speak to her. I'll ask her to come to the shop."

THE PHONE CALL from Walt was short and cryptic.

"Can you come to my office? There's something we need to chat about."

What was going on? And who was he with? A black SUV was parked out front. Her short walk to the shop was delayed by the arrival of a white pickup truck pulling a trailer. She thought they were headed for Walt's end of the building, but the driver steered toward the restaurant. That was when she saw the *Gladding Signs and Displays* name on the side. The driver, a middle-aged man with piercing green eyes and salt-and-pepper hair, stepped out. "Miss Cole?"

"Yes. Hello, Mr. Gladding. I take it you're here for the sign?"

"I sure am." He motioned to his passenger. "This is my son, Pete. He and I will disconnect and take it down. I want to get a look at the wiring that's in place. That'll help us figure out how to install the new sign."

"I'm on my way to a meeting." Regina glanced toward the shop. "But I suppose I can postpone it."

"We brought everything we needed. You go about your work. We'll take the sign down and be gone before you know it."

Regina glanced up at the huge unlit sign that hung over the place like a sentinel. She tried for a moment to imagine how the place would look without it before deciding that the new, more understated sign she'd commissioned would be a big improvement. She smiled as she waved at the forlorn relic. "Bye, Millie. It's been good knowing ya, but I can't say you'll be missed. Have at it, Mr. Gladding. If you need anything, I'll be next door."

The air in the shop was several degrees cooler than outside. Regina paused to glimpse her reflection in the window of a car situated close by. Her hair was wilder than usual. She grabbed a paper shop cloth from a nearby box and wiped the sweat from her brow. She rejected the urge to smell her armpits and considered running back to her office for a quick spritz of cologne.

Curiosity won out, though. That and the fact that Walt had been noticeably distant since Tuesday. Something was up, and she was determined to find out what it was. She threw back her shoulders and headed for his office. The door was closed, so she knocked, then pushed it open and stepped inside. Walt was in his usual spot. The lawyer, Tony Sampson, occupied one of the two visitor chairs.

"Hello, Mr. Sampson. What brings you back to Bethany?"

Tony nodded and smiled. "Hey, Regina. What can I say? I love the beach."

He turned to face Walt, who appeared visibly uncomfortable. His mouth was twisted in an expression that bordered on agony. Something was definitely wrong. Regina's mind raced. It had to be something of a legal nature, since Tony was, after all, a lawyer.

But what?

Was Walt about to renege on their agreement? Unlikely, given how much work they'd put in.

Was it a money thing? Perhaps business wasn't as good as she'd assumed. Walt never worried about those kinds of things but looks could be deceiving. And she'd seen how he neglected the stacks of bills on his credenza. Could it be that Walt Mickens was in financial trouble? And if he was, what did that mean for her?

She considered taking the chair next to Tony but wasn't sure she wanted to be sitting for whatever came next. So she waited as Walt struggled to say whatever he had to say. And when the words came, they poured out in a torrent.

"Regina, there's no easy way to say this, so I'll get right

to it. When Tony was here last week, I asked to speak to him privately."

Walt paused long enough to take a breath. "I was worried about you. No, that's not right. I was worried about Mr. Palmer. He seemed so...brash and dominating. And I didn't want to see you hurt, so I brought it up to Tony."

WALT FELT as if he might wretch. He saw the concern when she came into the office, noticing how it heightened when she saw Tony. And with each word he'd spoken, her concern amped up.

I was worried about you.

I was worried about Mr. Palmer.

Brash...dominating.

Then, it all changed when he'd said, *I brought it up to Tony.*

The worry left her face. The concern was gone. Regina was royally pissed.

"You spoke to Tony? About me?"

Nothing was going as anticipated. She remained standing, which, despite her average stature, made her seem fifteen feet tall. He'd mentally rehearsed that part several times over the last hour. And in each rehearsal, she was grateful for the information Tony had gleaned. She asked for their advice on the next steps, then acted on it. And hopefully, in a few months, everything would be over and done with. No more Damon Palmer. Regina would be the hit of Bethany. The local papers would sing the praises of Adeline and its incredibly talented genius owner. The place would overflow with customers.

Regina would be happy. Happy with Adeline. Happy with Bethany.

And all that other stuff. The accident—the terrible way she'd been treated—would become distant memories that faded further away each day.

Walt wanted that for her. He yearned for Regina to find happiness in life.

And happiness with him.

But it quickly became apparent that he'd made a critical mistake. One that might cost him more than anything.

And Regina was about to tell him what it was.

―――――

"YOU TALKED TO TONY *ABOUT ME*?"

Regina tried to control her tone, but it wasn't happening. Not today. Not after what Walt had done. Momentarily shell-shocked, he looked to Tony for support. "Look, Regina," Tony began. "Walt came to me because—"

"Walt *came to you*. To talk *about me*."

"Yes, Regina. He was—"

"Tony, forgive me for being so direct but shut the hell up. This is between me and Walt."

Things were getting scary. Tony raised his hands in defeat. Regina focused her attention on Walt.

"You know my story. You know the hell I went through. I told you everything. And then you shared it with someone who I not only don't know but is a former classmate of Damon's?"

Tony stepped in again. "We weren't classmates, actually. Damon was a couple years behind—" He froze midsentence at the sight of Regina's finger in his face.

Still on her feet, she positioned herself so her back was toward Tony.

"My experiences in New York stripped away so much. I lost my self-assurance. I lost my stature as a chef. I wondered if I would ever find my place again." She took a breath to push away the emotions. "As you and I got acquainted, I felt I'd found a kindred soul. Someone else who had experienced pain and loss. Someone who understood. So, I let my guard down. Walt Mickens, I trusted you."

HER WORDS STRUCK LIKE DAGGERS. Each piercing deeper than the one before. Walt didn't try to defend himself. He knew he'd messed up. Caring for her was one thing, a good thing. Wanting to help was an honorable gesture.

But talking to Tony? Before speaking to her first?

That was the mistake.

There was much Regina didn't know. So much she needed to know. About Damon. About the things he was doing behind the scenes. But as she berated him, Walt knew that the opportunity to share all that was gone. He'd blown it by betraying her confidence. She was an adult. Strong. Not some weak damsel who needed protecting. He'd overstepped and was about to pay the price. After several moments, she paused, spent but still angry. Tony unwisely seized upon that pause to try to make his case, but he wouldn't get the chance.

Before the words were out of his mouth, Regina was gone.

THE TRAIN RIDE BACK to New York provided plenty of time to think. Kate had been kind enough to cancel her Friday plans to run Regina to the train station. She'd considered taking the car but wanted to leave with nothing that kept her tied to Walt or Bethany Beach.

God love her, Kate had proven herself the best kind of friend. She didn't push for details about what had happened. She could see that Regina was distraught but allowed her to share as she could. By the time they reached the train station, Regina had let most of it out. She'd shared personal information with Walt, and he'd shared it with someone from Damon's past. There was no judgment on Kate's part, other than saying at one point that, while she didn't know Walt well, she didn't see him as someone who wanted to hurt a friend.

Regina felt the vibration of her phone inside her purse. She reached for it and saw she had seven missed messages. Five from Walt, two from Damon. "Kate, will you do me one more favor? Two actually?"

"Anything."

"The car I came to your house in belongs to Walt. Will you please take it back to him?"

"Of course. Austin and I will do that tonight. What else?"

"Tell him to stop calling me. I need time to think things through."

"But what about the restaurant?"

They pulled into the train station as Regina considered her response. For the past several weeks, she'd focused on little except that delightful little roadside diner. It had consumed her thoughts, day and night, except for those

255

moments when those thoughts drifted to other things. Specifically, her feelings toward Walt Mickens.

So much for that. If she returned to Bethany, and the way she felt at the moment, that was far from certain, it would be a business relationship from that point on. No secret thoughts of how it might be to... Yeah. None of that.

"Kate, I'm not sure about my future. Please give Austin my apologies, but there's so much I was counting on that I'm not so sure about now."

As the train raced toward the city, Regina replayed the day's events over and over. Why had Walt done what he'd done? And of all people, why Tony Sampson? Someone from Damon's past, Her thoughts were interrupted by the buzz of her phone. It was Damon.

She took a deep breath and tried to sound cheery as she answered. He would be happy to know she was on her way back, but would also wonder why. How much should she tell him? How would he react when he learned what Walt had done? Or that she'd shared so much of her past with a man who was supposed to be nothing more than her landlord?

"Hey, Damon!" Could he tell her cheerfulness was manufactured?

"Hey, baby, are you sitting down?"

"Uh...yeah. I am."

"We have a settlement offer from those knuckleheads at Gasconade."

"And?"

"And...it's good. I think you'll be pleased."

"I'm headed back to New York...for the weekend. Maybe we can get together and discuss it?"

"I'm in Myrtle Beach."

Regina's stomach fluttered. With everything going on,

she'd barely given a thought to Damon's comings and goings. "Let me guess, Alice?"

"Yeah. The grandkids made another run at taking over the summer house. We're down here seeing if anything is missing. Look, boo..." Regina heard what sounded like footsteps. When he spoke again, it was barely above a whisper. "I'm thinking I can be done with this and done with Alice pretty soon, but for now, I'm stuck down here."

Stuck...yeah.

"We have what I think will be a final settlement meeting with the Gasconade boys next Thursday."

"I'll be there."

"Regina, like I said, it's solid. If the numbers look as good on paper as they sound on the phone, you'll be thrilled."

"How much is it?"

"I would rather not say until I see it in writing."

"Damon, I want to know."

"Look, boo, I don't want to get your hopes up. And I need to run. Alice needs me. Let's talk Thursday."

And he was gone. Uncertain of what the future held on pretty much every front, Regina spent the last forty minutes of the train ride sorting through what had led her to that point. Just a few hours before, there was so much excitement and anticipation of what was to come. She'd felt better about her future than at any time since the accident. All she wanted now was to get back to the apartment and sleep. Maybe things would look better in the morning. But first, she had to get home. The train arrived a few minutes late, further taxing her nerves. She checked the subway schedule before opting for a cab that would get her to Brooklyn a half hour faster. Getting around was so much easier in Bethany. It was a few minutes before ten when she arrived at her apartment. She was searching for the key when someone called to her from behind.

"Miss Cole?"

Panhandler? No. They didn't know her name? Even the regulars. Regina stood to her full height and turned to face the speaker. She was surprised to see a petite woman dressed professionally, right down to her heels.

"Miss Cole, my name is Olivia Holm. I'm an attorney in Manhattan." She fished a card from her purse and held it out.

Regina ignored it. "Not interested." She stuck the key in the door and pushed it open.

"We need to talk, Miss Cole. Tony Sampson contacted me."

"If you work with him, then I know we have nothing to talk about. Now go away."

"I don't work with Tony, Miss Cole. I'm in private practice. We need to talk about Damon Palmer."

Regina paused in the doorway. "Is Damon okay?"

"Well, physically, yes, but Miss Cole, there's something you need to know."

"If there's anything I need to know about Damon, I'll hear it from him. Good night, Miss Holm."

Regina stepped inside and moved to close the door behind her. Olivia Holm's last words brought her up short, so she stopped.

"He'll never tell you what I know. And if you close this door, there's no way I can save you."

Regina stepped back outside and allowed the door to shut behind her. She had a feeling she knew what this was about and wasn't certain she could handle hearing it.

"It's Alice, isn't it? The new client. He's involved in a relationship with her. I suspected as much."

There was concern on the young lawyer's face. Olivia Holm looked at her in the way that women do when they don't want to be the bearer of bad news. "We should go inside, Miss Cole."

"Damon's screwing around with the old lady, isn't he?"

"No, ma'am, he's not."

A sense of relief coursed through Regina's body. It lasted only as long as it took for Olivia Holm to finish what she'd started to say.

"It's worse than that."

monday, june 23

REGINA'S MESSAGE, delivered by Kate when she returned the car the previous Friday, hit harder than the most crushing physical blow.

Stop trying to call me.

Regina was hurt by his conversation with Tony Sampson. He'd tried to explain why he'd spoken to Tony, about how he worried that there was more to Damon Palmer than anyone knew. Then he asked Kate for advice. What should he do?

"Wait," she responded. "Allow her to sort through things. She's been through so much."

"But what about the restaurant? It's only a few days until opening."

That decision, Kate left to him. It turned out to be an easy one. He contacted Austin and told him to keep pushing toward getting the place ready for the Fourth of July weekend. The restaurant might be the most powerful incentive to get Regina back to Bethany. If she returned, he would begin mending the tear in their friendship. The tear his thoughtlessness had caused.

So, he waited. Though it darn near killed him, he didn't call. He went about his day like a zombie, so detached that even Felix mentioned it. Austin and the twins worked away next door, but Walt couldn't bring himself to check in. Seeing the place without Regina was more than he could take. He mostly stayed in his office.

And waited.

thursday, june 26

DAMON: *Boo, we start in thirty minutes. You good?*

On my way.

Damon: *How close?*

Close.

Damon: *I knew I should have had you come to my place last night when you got back to town. What time was it, anyway?*

Late.

Regina held up her phone so Olivia could read the text exchange. "He still believes I've been in Bethany Beach all week."

It was hard for Regina to reconcile the Damon she'd fallen for with the man waiting for her to sign off on the agreement he claimed to have spent hours finalizing. So much had changed. He wasn't the Damon she used to know, but then, she wasn't the same Regina either. She glanced across the backseat of the cab to see if Olivia was showing any signs of nervousness. Far from it. She gazed out the window as they made their way past throngs of people moving like ants along the sidewalks. It wasn't until recently that Regina had noticed how dingy things were in the city. Even in Manhattan's financial district, everything had a gray pallor.

"Not enough sunlight," she murmured.

Olivia turned and looked at her knowingly. "You've got beach blood," she said softly as they pulled to a stop in front of the building from where Gasconade's owners, Javier and Lance, operated their mini-empire.

An old-fashioned analog clock affixed to a bank several doors up showed the time was ten-past-nine. They were running late. Damon had texted three times in the last five minutes, each more desperate than the one before it.

Regina, this is a bad look.

After all the time I spent getting you this deal, you're close to messing it up.

Javier is royally pissed. If you're not here in the next couple minutes, he might take the offer off the table.

They rode the elevator to the fourteenth floor and walked side by side to the glass entrance to Amberly Slade Investments. Memories of Regina's previous meeting when they'd tried to settle things with the help of a mediator came flooding back.

Olivia sensed her discomfort and squeezed her hand. "I'm with you."

She glanced down at the diminutive attorney and smiled. Any doubts she'd had about Olivia's ability to handle herself were long gone. She was tough and ready to go to war, albeit a quiet war on her side. They entered the office and brushed past a receptionist.

"Second door on the left," Regina whispered.

Olivia didn't bother to knock. The setup was as before. Stony-faced Javier and placid Lance flanked their rotund and balding in-house lawyer. Damon was seated alone across from them. There was a momentary look of relief on his face when he saw Regina.

"There you are," he said, smiling as he approached.

Olivia stepped between them and raised her hand. "Olivia Holm." She spoke so softly that the men had to lean in to hear. "I'm Miss Cole's attorney."

Time stood still. Damon froze in his tracks. Javier rose to speak but couldn't come up with anything. His mouth hung open like a fish out of water. His lawyer looked puzzled. Lance scrolled social media and didn't seem concerned.

"What the hell is this?" Damon demanded.

"Miss Cole has hired me as her attorney. You, Mr. Palmer, no longer represent her."

"That's ridiculous!" Damon looked over Olivia's head and spoke directly to Regina. "I don't know what line of BS this woman fed you, boo, but you need to tell her I'm your lawyer."

Olivia held out an envelope that Damon snatched from her hand. "Here's your official notice. Signed and notarized. My office number and address are included. Send your final bill there. We'll review it and decide whether it should be paid."

Damon wadded up the envelope and tossed it on the floor. "If you don't get away from my client, I'll have security remove you!"

"Uh, Damon..." Lance looked up from his phone. "We don't have security."

It looked as if Damon's head might explode before returning his attention to Regina. "Let's step outside and figure out what's going on. I know you didn't intend to fire me. Somehow, this bitch got in your head and made promises she can't deliver. Let's take a few minutes to get back on the same page."

"No, Damon. Olivia is my attorney."

"You're no longer needed here, Mr. Palmer." Olivia's wispy voice and diminutive stature came across like a child in an adult world. There was no doubt, however, that she had everyone's attention. "You're free to leave. Or...perhaps you would prefer to move to the other side of the table, given how you're joining Amberly Slade as general counsel later this summer."

The other side's lawyer pounded his fist on the table and jumped to his feet. "Look, Miss Holm, I don't know what kind of scheme you've cooked up, but our firm has no interest in procuring Mr. Palmer's services."

He glanced to his left, then to his right, the only person in the room unaware that his tenure with Amberly Slade was over. Regina almost felt sorry for him. The usually cocky and self-assured Javier refused to make eye contact. Lance stared at his phone.

"Mr. Rocha?" The attorney sounded as if he was pleading.

"It's not true," Javier said, unconvincingly. The lawyer took Javier's ambivalence as hope he had a chance at keeping his job. Sweat formed on his forehead and neck as he took a seat and prepared for a battle he had no chance of winning.

Seeing he wasn't getting the support he needed from Javier, Damon snapped his briefcase shut and started for the door.

Olivia barely made eye contact as she said, "On second thought, Mr. Palmer, perhaps it might be best if you stay."

Damon's obscene response would have brought gasps of shock or disapproval in most business gatherings, but in the shell-shocked conference room, it didn't merit a second glance. "I'm going to the state bar and let them know how you got between me and Regina. There are rules against that, you know."

"Yes, sir, there are indeed. Just as there are conflict of interest rules. And rules about being romantically involved with a client."

Damon's laugh had a sinister edge to it. "Regina obviously lied to you about us. We were together several weeks before I started representing her!"

Olivia cleared her throat before speaking, but she was still difficult to hear. "I'm not talking about Regina."

Damon stepped into Olivia's space, fists clenched at his side. Inches apart and toe to toe, he was a foot taller and seventy-five pounds heavier. Intimidation ebbed from him like a dark, ugly force. Testosterone hung over the room like cheap cologne as the others watched with unveiled interest. Sharks in the water, delighted to witness one of their own take down its prey.

"Howard Pappas will testify to your romantic relationship with his mother, Alice." There was no fear in Olivia's tone. It was as if she was chatting with a neighbor in the supermarket.

Damon's laugh was hollow and confirmed what Regina already knew. He'd been lying to her all along.

"Howard Pappas is a greedy nobody who wants his stepmother out of the way so he can steal his father's inheritance."

And then, with three softly uttered words from Olivia Holm, the prey became the stalker. "He has pictures."

Damon's chin jutted out defiantly as he glared down his nose at Olivia, but Regina saw the truth in his eyes.

Javier must have as well. He whistled softly, got to his

feet, and motioned for his partner and their attorney to follow him out. "Damon, you too."

Regina and Olivia had the room to themselves. Regina recalled her attorney's admonition not to speak too freely on the other side's turf because of the possibility of listening devices. "Should we go someplace where we can talk?"

Olivia smiled for the first time since they'd arrived. A slight change in expression, but Regina had learned to distinguish it as a break in her game face. "It's not necessary. Even if they are bugging the room, there's nothing I have to say that will hurt your case."

"Even that part about Alice?" Regina tried to mask the hurt she was feeling inside, but Olivia was pretty intuitive.

"I'm sorry you had to hear it for the first time like that, Regina. I only learned about it yesterday. Damon was right about Alice's stepson. He's a money-grabbing nutcase. But the private eye he hired to tail them is pretty sharp." She reached for Regina's hand. "Are you going to be okay?"

"The lies hurt more than anything else. My...feelings for Damon had faded, but this..."

The door opened, and Javier returned alone. He took a seat and asked Regina and Olivia to do likewise. He tapped a white Montblanc pen against his open palm. "What will it take to make this go away?"

"Considerably more than your original offer."

"I'll increase it by twenty percent. Not a dime more. And that's only if you sign the agreement today." He lazily jotted the number on a legal pad, underlined it several times, and slid it across the table.

Olivia didn't bother to look at it. "You told the vice president of Cinch Corporation not to hire Miss Cole for one of their Manhattan start-ups."

"I don't know what you're talking about."

"Sure you do. The individual who interviewed her will testify to that." Olivia consulted her own notepad. "On a betting spree at Aqueduct a few months ago, you told your friend, the Cinch VP, not to hire her because she was, and I quote, 'mentally messed up.' You also said that her disfigured hand would 'turn off customers.'"

Javier cracked a smile that he didn't try to hide. He looked at Regina. "What can I say? The truth hurts."

Olivia continued, "I can also share with you what we've been told by Miss Blossom Layne regarding your treatment of Miss Cole. Care to hear it?"

This made Javier laugh. He waved his hand as if swatting a fly. "She's still pissed that Lance dumped her. She would say anything."

"I'm pretty sure I can convince a jury to believe her. It shouldn't be hard to win a discrimination suit against your company, Mr. Rocha. Let's review..." She flipped to the next page of her legal pad. It was blank, but Javier didn't know that. "Disability discrimination, conspiring with Miss Cole's attorney, libel, negligence." She nodded at the figure on Javier's notepad. "Make your last best offer, Mr. Rocha. And if we can't reach an agreement by the time your fancy wall clock strikes ten, we'll file in civil court."

Regina peeked over her shoulder. It was nine-fifty-eight.

Javier's smile was gone. He looked at Olivia with something bordering on admiration. "This case isn't worth as much as you think it is," he said, softer than before.

"Fifteen years of legal decisions that say otherwise, but if you want to risk this mess in front of a jury..."

Javier sighed and pulled back the notepad. He crossed through the original number and scrawled another. One minute until ten. He held it up for them to see. "For God's sake, woman. Are you always this much of a tight ass?"

Olivia acted as if she hadn't heard. She gathered her things and headed for the door. Regina hurriedly got to her feet to follow. They didn't make it. Javier tossed out another figure—this one a third higher than the previous one.

Olivia turned and addressed him. "Add one hundred thousand to cover my fees."

"Your fees aren't anywhere close to that," Javier snipped.

"True, but you also owe me for the remark about my ass. We want a cashier's check for the full amount. Today."

REGINA HAD PLANNED on heading back to her apartment for the night, but Olivia convinced her to stay in a hotel. *I don't think Damon will make contact, but just in case.* She recommended a couple of Manhattan's most iconic and expensive hotels, but in the end, Regina opted for a Hampton Inn in Newark. She might have recently come into a lot of money, but she was still the same practical person she'd always been.

After a quick dinner at a nearby salad shop, she settled in and thought back over the past few months. So much had happened. So much had changed. The worst of it—the accident and the legal fallout—was now behind her. But what lay ahead, the rest of her life and how she chose to live it, was still unsettled.

But it didn't have to be.

There was one thing of which she was certain. New York was no longer home. Being back the past few days had reinforced that. She treasured Bethany's slower pace and room to spread her arms without infringing on someone else's space. People took time to make sure you were okay. They cared. Sure, people cared in the city, too, but would they go out of their way like Austin and Kate? Would they invest themselves in her like Spence? Or even gruff old Harvey at Milo's Diner? Perhaps she could someday take in a stranger like Kate had done for her or help a competitor like Harvey had helped her.

Her thoughts drifted to Millie's. How was the renovation coming? It had only been a few days, but she was dying to know how Austin and the twins were doing. Was the kitchen done? Had the tables arrived for the dining room?

And Walt? Her anger toward him had diminished even before Olivia encouraged her to go easy on him. *He was worried about you*, Olivia had gently reminded her. She was right. Walt hadn't spoken to Tony because he was a gossip. He didn't intend to break her trust. He did it because he cared. Had he come to her with his concerns, Regina wasn't sure she could have dealt with them, blinded as she was by Damon's charisma. Even when the signs were there, the out-of-town trips, the calls that he stepped away to take, she had trusted him. Had it not been for Walt, she might still be hanging on.

She turned up the air conditioning, crawled under the covers, and pulled them up to her neck in preparation for a good night's sleep. The next day would begin a new chapter. The next chapter. It was time to go back. To set things straight. To apologize.

And to make her dream come true.

friday, june 27

AS REGINA DROVE SOUTH, she was glad she'd waited until morning instead of leaving right after the previous day's meeting. She was fresh and ready to get going, more excited than ever. The list of things needing to get done was extensive. There had been times when she'd considered pushing back the opening, but she hated the idea of doing that. That was a sign of poor planning, and if there was one thing Regina Cole was not, it was a poor planner.

She cruised the New Jersey turnpike at five miles over the speed limit and occasionally peered at the to-do list on the seat next to her. The final inspection was scheduled for two days before the opening. She'd heard horror stories about how exacting those could be. The only person who told her not to worry was Austin's grandfather, Charlie. *Once they know that Austin and me did the work, you'll be fine*, he'd promised with a twinkle in his eyes.

The task that worried her most was finding last-minute employees. Everything else took a backseat. Cleaning the parking lot, mail forwarding, and delivery schedules for food and staples. Phone service. So much to do. Thank goodness for the internet. The makeshift website she'd designed looked pretty good. The first evening's reservation list was seventy percent full. A little disappointing, but there was still time for it to fill out. She wanted to keep a few open seats for last-minute guests. The website made clear what was expected for evening dining. Dressy attire. No jeans, no shorts. That might hurt business a little, but people who understood the vibe she was aiming for would appreciate it. There were still some who, even after a few days or weeks at the beach, wanted to dress up for a fun evening out. Adeline's at night would provide that.

As she combed the list, her phone buzzed. "Good morning, Ms. Cole. We're getting ready to put your new sign together, and I wanted to make sure there were no changes."

The mental image of the building without Three Mile Millie's looming over it brought a rush of thoughts. Adeline's had been her aim since she'd started dreaming of owning her own restaurant. But there had been other thoughts more recently. And an affinity for Millie's that she'd never expected. Those thoughts had left her conflicted, but that would go away once the new sign was in place, right?

The rep continued, "Everything is shaping up nicely. The dimensions we discussed are perfect. And I think the sign captures everything you shared regarding the atmosphere you're looking to convey. You're going to be delighted."

Regina had no doubt he was right. The new sign would be perfect. It would communicate to customers exactly what Adeline's was supposed to be. And yet, she was still conflicted.

"I have a question."

"Yes, ma'am? Now's the time to ask."

"The old sign? The one you removed? What condition is it in? And what will happen to it?"

"It's not bad. There was some work done on it a few years back, but I'm not sure the people knew what they were doing. If it's okay with you, I'll fix what I can and use it for parts. Unless you have another plan."

Regina took a deep breath. "As a matter of fact, I do."

"WALT, I'm going to knock off early."

Walt looked up from his computer screen as Felix stepped into his office. "Everything okay?"

"Landon has a little league game in Georgetown at four. I want to get there in time to get a seat."

"Of course, Felix. I completely forgot that was today. Have a good weekend, my friend."

Felix eyed him for a moment before asking, "You okay, boss?"

"Yes. Just...occupied, I suppose. Now run along. You don't want to miss your grandson's game."

Felix waved farewell and took off. Everyone seemed to know why Walt was at loose ends. Harvey was bold enough to ask him about it when he'd stopped at Milo's for lunch the previous day.

"Have you heard from Regina?"

He hadn't. And likely never would. He'd overstepped his place in her life by getting in touch with Tony. He'd promised himself several times that should he find someone to take over the diner, he would not get so involved. Landlord and tenant. That would be the beginning and end of it. Collect rent checks and keep a safe distance. Austin and Kate remained certain Regina would return, but they hadn't been there to witness the level of her disappointment.

She wasn't coming back.

But he still checked his phone. When it would ring, he'd grabbed it eagerly, but it was never her. Tony had called three times, but Walt allowed those calls to go to voicemail. The messages were all the same. *Call me. I want to update you on what's going on.* He wasn't sure he wanted to know. Because if it wasn't good, that would take away all hope. Not knowing was better.

He returned to the paperwork he'd been staring at all day but was no closer to completing. Two o'clock became three. He heard vehicles exiting the parking lot. Probably Austin and his crew calling it a day. Bethany was a beach town, after all. And it was almost summer. A great time to get an early start on the last weekend before tourist season. A last chance for locals to enjoy their beach before it became everyone's. Walt would have done the same thing had he not been in such a funk.

And hurting.

The silence added to the melancholy. At a quarter to four, he turned off his computer and prepared to leave for the weekend. He was locking up when a car pulled up in front. Out-of-state plates. Probably someone wanting to see about a restoration job. Talk about lousy timing. He went to the window, hopeful they would reverse course and get back on the road. They remained where they were for several minutes, however, before the driver's door swung open.

And there she was.

HIS WAS the only car in the lot. Millie's was deserted and, from the outside, looked as it had when she'd left. Her heart sank as hopes of a grand opening slipped away. She gathered her thoughts before taking a breath and getting out of the rental car. The walk toward the shop seemed quite long yet quite short. How would he greet her? Would he forgive her for jumping to conclusions?

Her stomach clenched in every way imaginable as she pulled open the door. Things were as they always were with rows of cars in various stages of restoration. She looked toward his office and saw him standing at the door. Their eyes met. She made her way toward him. He did the same. They met in the middle, awkwardly. Nothing was said. The blue Honda that came with the apartment was parked to her left. She stared at it as she tried to figure out what to say. He, too, was at a loss for words, but then, he'd had no idea she was coming. No time to prepare for that moment. It was up to her to break the ice.

"I recognize that one," she said with a nod toward the Honda. "It used to be mine."

"Yes," he replied softly.

"Not many apartments come with a free car. I'll never find as good a deal again."

"Perhaps you will."

She gazed into his eyes, searching for whatever feelings might come to the surface.

He measured his words as he added, "I have a place available. And it comes with a car."

She felt her fears fading away, but after all that had happened, she wanted to be sure she wasn't confusing his signals. "If you think we're going to be sharing a toothbrush holder, you have another thing coming."

He laughed, remembering the line she'd used before. His laughter pushed her fears further away.

But then, nothing. The silence grew longer and more troubling. She had to say what she'd come to say. And she had to do it now.

"Walt, I'm sorry that—"

"Regina, please forgive me for—"

"Speaking to Tony was a terrible mistake."

"You did it because you care for me. The way I treated you was—"

"I want you to come back to Bethany."

"I want to come back to Bethany."

"For good?"

"For good."

When she couldn't take the distance between them for another second, she threw herself against him. He pulled her into an embrace she hoped would last and last. Neither spoke. Neither had to. Healing and forgiveness had their own ways of communicating.

Regina couldn't be sure how much time passed before she murmured against his shoulder, "I'll never be ready for next weekend."

"Don't be so sure," he replied as he continued holding her. "Let's go next door and look."

thursday, july 3

IT WAS a few minutes after ten when Regina gathered everyone in the moonlit parking lot. Despite the hour, traffic was bumper-to-bumper as tourists headed for their hotels, cottages, and rented homes.

July fourth weekend had arrived.

Regina looked on as her staff chatted and joked among themselves. Most were strangers to one another a few days earlier. They represented every background and lifestyle. Jacob, Andrea, and Conor were street-wise New Yorkers, equal parts excited about the future and hopeful of adapting to Bethany's slower pace. Spence Hollins was pushing seventy, grizzled, and wise in the way of longtime locals. The four would serve as Regina's right and left hands, and based on what she'd seen over the past few days, they were up to the job. The others in that dark parking lot were less of a certainty. The Watson twins, Jared and Jason, would share dishwashing responsibilities until Regina found permanent help. They were clueless when it came to restaurant work, but under Spence's tutelage, they had proven quick studies.

Andrea's servers were a mishmash of loans, temps, and castoffs from other local establishments. Since Milo's closed after the lunch crowd cleared out, Harvey Bodenschatz had been kind enough to recommend three of his girls for the evening shift. They'd laughed nervously when they got their first look at the crisp black smocks and matching slacks Regina provided her waitstaff but quickly came to understand and appreciate the new restaurant was special. They were as excited as anyone.

It was the kitchen crew that most concerned Regina. Conor spent the entire week searching for line cooks. The three he'd found didn't look the part, but they came with decent references and had proven receptive to instruction. The practice meal they'd prepared earlier that evening received hearty approval from the two dozen guests who had assembled for what Regina called a test run. Among them were Bethany Beach's mayor, members of the town council, and three media types who promised good reviews. There was also a state senator and her husband. They all enjoyed their meals and had cleared out two hours earlier, and now, with everything inside spit-shined and ready for the next day, all eyes turned to the old building's exterior.

The light shade of blue that Austin and the twins had applied gave the place a sedate, yet inviting appearance that Regina felt would pull people in. The parking lot was meticulously cleared of years of accumulated sand and debris. Parking spaces were striped, and entrance and exit points were clearly visible. The old girl looked as good as she could.

Except for one thing.

She'd put off lighting the exterior signage, not wanting people to assume they were open for business. Instead, she'd chosen to wait until that moment. She wanted to share it with her staff—her people—and a few close friends. Of course, only having been in town for a short time, she only had a few close friends. Kate and Austin stuck around after dinner. Austin had even ducked into the back to check some last-minute details. His grandfather, Charlie, skipped dinner, choosing instead to touch up door trim in the back. It was an area that customers would never see, but that was Charlie's way. He wouldn't be happy until everything was perfect.

Walt had arrived a few minutes before the test run dinner was served. Things between him and Regina weren't quite back to where they were before, and she suspected that he still harbored guilt over what had happened. Regina would never forget the look on his face when, during her brief speech at dinner, she'd singled him out for a special thank you.

None of this would have been possible had it not been for one of the kindest people I've ever met, she'd said as she asked him to come forward.

He'd struggled to keep his composure as he opened the gift she'd created for him. The details of the miniature replica of the restaurant and garage were exact in every way, right down to the signage.

And as everyone gathered in the parking lot, it was Walt who Regina sought out when the most special moment came. She spotted him lurking at the edge of the gathering and called him forward. "Walt, you've not only given me an opportunity to open my own restaurant, you've given me back a piece of my life that I feared might be lost forever."

During the short round of soft applause that followed, Austin handed Regina a makeshift light switch he'd crafted for the moment.

She thanked him and held it out to Walt. "No one has

cared more for this old place than you. Through the years it remained unoccupied, you never lost hope it would again be an operating restaurant. Because of that, I would be honored, Walt Mickens, for you to flip the switch and turn on the sign that will greet guests. The sign that will welcome them to a place that I hope will become as special to me as it has been to you."

Walt looked at the switch, then at Regina. "Are you sure?" he whispered.

"Very sure."

He reluctantly took the switch. All eyes turned to the roof of the old, yet proud establishment as they joined Regina in a countdown.

Five.

Four.

Three.

Two.

One.

There was an audible click as Walt did his thing, then a few seconds passed that made Regina worry it wasn't going to work. But then it did. In all its glory, the sign came to life for the first time in many years.

Three Mile Millie's

monday, july 7

THE BREAKFAST and lunch crowds wore Regina out, but she pushed through to evening and found a second wind when elegantly dressed diners raved about the menu items. It would be impossible to maintain such a brutal schedule, but fortunately, she only had to make it to Labor Day. And while she loved the fanciness, she was happy the dinner shift would come to an end once tourists returned home for the off-season.

The weekend receipts told an interesting story. While the prices of the evening menu were higher, the increased volume of the morning and midday shifts easily eclipsed the amount of business done at dinner. Regina smiled with the knowledge that she could survive in Bethany Beach as a year-round establishment. She calculated a few lines of numbers, then decided that could wait until tomorrow. She closed the books, pushed aside the calculator, and was about to turn out the light when she heard the front door open and close, followed by soft footsteps.

Only one other person had a key, and she smiled when Walt stuck his head in. "How are you?"

She sat back, stretched, and smiled. "Considering I've worked four eighteen-hour days, pretty good."

"What a great first weekend."

"Yes," she said. "Thanks for coming by at lunchtime. I have to admit that I was surprised to see you back for dinner."

"That was Tony's idea. He insisted on trying the Adeline menu. I'm glad he invited me."

It was quiet for a few moments. She was weary from a long day and happy to be in his presence.

"It's been quite a run, hasn't it?" he asked as he took a seat.

"It sure has. And I couldn't have done it without you."

His face reddened at the compliment.

"I've got something for you," she said.

"You already gave me the miniature replica. I must have looked at it a thousand times. Such a thoughtful gift."

"Well, that was sentimental. This is business." She reached into her desk, pulled out an envelope, and handed it to him. He opened it, glanced at the contents, then did a double take. The check left him in a momentary state of shock.

"What?"

"It's payment for Millie's. I want to buy it."

"But this is... You don't... Regina? How can you be so sure so quickly? You need more time."

"I've had all the time I need. Everything that's happened over the last two months has helped me realize that Bethany is home. It's where I want to be. You've said from the beginning that I have what it takes to make this place successful. If I'm invested here..." She pointed to the check. "And that ensures that I'm invested because we both know how hard it would be to sell the place if I change my mind."

They laughed.

"If I own Millie's, I'll always know where home is."

He seemed conflicted about accepting the check but finally tucked it into his pocket. He considered her for a few moments. "I promised myself that if you came back I would be more thoughtful in choosing my words."

"Walt, you did nothing wrong. I was the one who screwed up."

He shrugged. "I shouldn't have let my emotions muddy things up like I did. I made myself a promise to maintain more of a businesslike approach in our dealings."

"I'm not even sure what that means."

"It means..." He sighed. "You have a lot on your plate. The last thing you need is for me to... I mean, I like you very much, but..."

"Are you saying you don't want there to be anything between us?"

"That's what I thought. But as I sit here it feels rather shortsighted. And not what I want at all."

Regina leaned in so they were eye to eye. She smiled. "Are you saying you kinda like me, Walt Mickens?"

"Well..." He shrugged again.

Regina stood and went around to his side of the desk. She sat in the chair next to him and placed her hands on his. "I'm going to be busier than I ever was at Gasconade."

Walt nodded.

"Breakfast is a completely new thing for me. And being Three Mile Millie's for breakfast and lunch, then shifting to the Adeline menu for dinner, it's going to kick my butt."

He smiled gamely. "I can help out in the evenings."

She leaned in and kissed his forehead. "That's sweet of

you, but I need to do this on my own. And it's going to take every spare minute I have. But when tourist season winds down after Labor Day, and if you still like me, then, maybe we can..."

His eyes lit up. He clasped her hands tighter. "Does that mean that, even after everything that happened, you...?"

"I kinda like you too, Walt. And I see this becoming more than a professional relationship."

He spoke softly as he replied, "Me, too."

Regina gave his hands one last squeeze, then got to her feet. "But right now, what I need more than anything is sleep. Walk out with me?"

"Of course."

They made their way to the parking lot. Walt's car was parked in front of the shop. Her's was on the other end of the building. The neon sign above them lighted the area like a beacon. They gazed at it for a few moments, and when he put his arm around her waist, she moved close. Just like the first time, walking along the boardwalk at Rehoboth Beach, it still felt right.

And Regina had no doubt it always would.

bonus epilogue

The best love stories don't end on the final page. Return with us to Bethany Beach on Labor Day, two months later, to catch up with Regina and Walt. Has Three Mile Millie's first summer been everything Regina hoped it would be? Have there been sparks between she and Walt? You'll love this exclusive update!

Copy the link below or scan the QR code to get the bonus epilogue.

https://BookHip.com/QCZXFWV

afterword

People sometimes ask if there is any truth behind the events, places, and people in our writing. In a word, yes! It would be impossible to write without including a bit of ourselves and our lives and experiences.

Bethany Beach is the setting for *Table for Two*. It's a wonderful community on the Delaware coast. Unlike **Rehoboth Beach** to the north and **Ocean City, Maryland** to the south, Bethany is smaller and more laid-back. Some streets in this book are real. We made others up. **Milo's**, where **Harvey Bodenschatz** yells at you if you order shirred eggs, is purely fictional. The same for the SaltAire Hotel.

There are lots of other places mentioned, too. We don't have enough space to go through all of them, so you'll just have to visit the Delaware beaches and find out for yourself.

Everything comes back to Regina and Walt. We fell in love with them while they fell in love with each other. We hope you did, too.

Warm wishes,

Robin and Paul

also by robin paul

Garland Grove Holiday Romance Series

Christmas Presence (2021)

Christmas Carl (2022)

Blues Christmas (2023)

Christmas Comeback (2024)

Standalone Holiday Romances

Christmas Class Reunion - Inspired the Hallmark Channel Original Movie (2022)

Clear Christmas - A Later in Life Holiday Romance (2023)

Write Christmas - A Kansas City Christmas Romance (2023)

Bethany Beach Summer Romance Series

Drifting Together (2022)

Table for Two (2025)

Go to www.robinpaulromance.com or scan the QR code on the next page to learn more.